Catcher
Interference

HAVEN HADLEY

Catcher Interference
Copyright ©2021 Haven Hadley

Cover Design by Haven Hadley
Photography by ©6:12 Photography by Eric McKinney
Editing by Barren Acres Editing
Proofreading by Landers Editorial Services

This is a work of fiction. Names, characters, places and incidents are either the product of the author's imagination or used fictitiously, and any resemblance to actual persons, living or dead, business establishments, events or locales is entirely coincidental.

All rights reserved. This book contains material protected under International and Federal Copyright Laws and Treaties. Any unauthorized reprint or use of this material is prohibited. No part of this book may be reproduced or transmitted in any form or by any means, electronic or mechanical, including photocopying, recording, or by any information storage and retrieval system without express written permission from the author/publisher.

Chapter 1

Marcus

The alarm on my phone was loud enough to wake the dead. A groan left my lips when I forced myself to sit up. I cracked one eye open and almost immediately regretted it. Why did I think going out drinking the night before I was supposed to help Callen move Spencer into his house was a good idea?

While it would have been easier to allow the movers to handle everything, I couldn't blame them for wanting to avoid the extra eyes after all the media coverage they got when Callen came out. Then, with the World Series win on top of it, the press could get out of control. They both deserved to not have everyone in their business when they took this next step.

I threw my legs over the side of the bed, ignoring the slight pounding in the back of my head. Nothing a hot shower and some Advil wouldn't clear up. Like every morning, my knees cracked as I stood up. The downfall of being a catcher in professional baseball. The aches and pains for the first few weeks after the season were always a little worse than in the beginning.

A few weeks ago, I thought I'd be right as rain. Not exactly what the paper sitting on my dresser said. I'd done a bang-up job of ignoring it for the last few days. The same as I did this morning walking into the bathroom.

After a quick shower, I tossed on a pair of jeans and a black Henley. The guys wanted to get an early start, so I hopped into my car and drove over to Spencer's to help load the truck to take back to Callen's. Instead of ringing the bell, I pushed the door open, announcing my presence.

"I'm here. I know you've been waiting for me to get started." I shut the door behind me.

Maybe I was spending too much time out partying with Dominic. For a while, it was about the fun, living it up in the city. Now it was starting to feel like a cover-up for what I really wanted—a relationship and someone to go home to. So was the show I seemed to put on for everyone else lately.

"Holy fuck, Marcus, aren't you still hungover?" Callen came around the corner from another room of the house. "Your dumbass was all over the gossip blogs last night."

"No. Ibuprofen is my friend. And why do you look at that shit?"

He reached out for my hand and pulled me into a hug when I took his. "Thanks for coming to help, man. I just can't trust anyone right now. Wanted to make sure they had no idea we were moving today."

I slapped him on the back a few times. "I can't blame you. You never know what you're gonna get."

Callen stepped back and turned toward the room he'd come from. I took a step to follow and winced, my knee feeling tight.

"You should let Spencer check that out for you." I looked up and saw Callen had stopped. His eyes on me.

I shrugged it off. It didn't seem right to ask Spencer to look at my knee when we were supposed to be moving, but maybe it was time to make an appointment at his office. "It's fine. Still just a little stiff after all the games we played in October."

Callen clasped me on the shoulder. "It's been a few weeks. You still shouldn't be that stiff. Talk to him, he'll help. He's great at what he does."

"I know, but we're moving him into your place today. I'm not gonna bug him on his day off."

"Bug who?" I glanced up and saw Spencer walking into the room, a box in his hands.

Callen took the box from Spencer. "Bug you. Marcus's knees are still bothering him and I told him to talk to you."

I waved my hand dismissively. "It's fine. Nothing a little exercise won't help. Let's get you all moved."

Spencer looked between the two of us. "Are you sure? I don't mind taking a quick look."

I shook my head. "I'm sure. I'll make an appointment at your office sometime next week."

Spencer glanced back at Callen, who kept his gaze on me. "You better. You have one option year left after this. No need to give Tim any reason to not give you another long-term deal."

"I know and I promise to make the appointment. Now let's get moving."

Callen lifted a brow and I waited for him to start up another argument with me, but he just nodded as he walked toward the back of the house with me following closely behind. I stepped into the large den area where boxes upon boxes were stacked.

"Look what the cat finally dragged in." Dominic peeked his head around one of the boxes.

I flipped him off. "No need to drag this sexy anywhere." I gestured down my body. There were two ways to handle Dominic: ignore him, which didn't always work, or give him back his own shit. "Besides, it's too early for you to be a fucker already."

He came over and wrapped an arm around my neck, trying to give me a noogie, but I managed to twist out of his grasp. "Nice try," I said as I spun away, not wanting to give him a second chance.

I stopped dead when I came face-to-face with a man who wasn't on the team but someone everyone knew, nonetheless.

Kasper fucking Wilder stood in the middle of Spencer's living room in a pair of jeans and a sweatshirt. In every article, picture, and interview I'd ever seen him in, I never saw him in anything less than a full suit and tie. The jeans made him seem much more casual and that was before he reached out a hand and introduced himself.

"Kasper." There was a sparkle of amusement in his eyes as he waited for me to do the same.

But for some reason, there was nothing there. Not a single word or thought on the tip of my tongue.

"Cat got your tongue?" Dominic taunted from the other side of the room. "You act like you've never met anyone rich and famous before. Don't forget you're rich and famous, too." He chuckled. "Well, maybe not as much as Callen."

"Shut up, Dom." Callen elbowed him in the gut on the way by.

"He never stops, does he?" Brett, Callen's brother, asked. "Hey, Marcus."

I tipped my chin up to Brett and turned back to reach for Kasper's hand. "Marcus Warnes. Don't mind the resident team idiot over there. He forgets his manners at home quite regularly."

Kasper's grip tightened on mine.

"Oh, good, I'm glad you met Kasper," Spencer said, coming into the room. "I'm happy everyone could make it today since Evan sent me a text and told me he couldn't."

Kasper turned and narrowed his eyes. "What do you mean Evan's not coming?"

Spencer shrugged. "He said something came up. He was out with Brystol yesterday. I'd be willing to bet she convinced him to go shopping."

Kasper laughed, though it was a little strained. "Probably."

When he turned back to face me, he startled and glanced down to where he was still holding my hand. "Sorry about that. I wasn't paying attention."

"No problem. How about we get these boxes moved?"

Kasper grabbed one from the top. "Follow me. The truck is on the side of the house."

I picked up another box and followed him out. Seeing Kasper Wilder in casual clothes, helping my friends move, was unexpected. Yes, besides Spencer, we were all professional athletes and exposed to the limelight, but I knew how down-to-earth my team members were. Even behind all of those dollar signs in our paychecks, we were still a bunch of twentysomethings playing a game for a living.

Kasper Wilder was in a league of his own.

For the next few hours, we moved boxes. First, out of Spencer's house, then, into Callen's. It seemed like we'd never get to the end of the truck. I wanted to cheer when we unloaded the last box and only had the furniture left.

"God, I could use a beer right about now." I bent down to grab the bottom of a chair with Kasper on the other side doing the same.

"That sounds fantastic. What do you say to beers on me at O'Malley's when we're done?"

"Yeah, sure. Sounds good."

Somehow, I'd ended up with Kasper almost the entire day. Every time I had to carry something that would require two people, Kasper was there to help. Not that I minded. He was easy to talk to and it kept me from listening to Dominic, who'd apparently had too much caffeine for his own good that morning.

"Great. Let's get these last few things off the truck."

It took us less than an hour to get the rest of the furniture unloaded. By then, I swore my stomach was trying to eat itself from lack of food. Thankfully, the pizza order arrived not long after we finished. The guys who were still there sat around eating and ribbing Callen for everything they could think of. Once the food was gone, I knew Callen and Spencer would want to get started on unpacking, something they didn't need me for.

Callen clasped me on the shoulder as we stood in his foyer. "Thanks, man. I really appreciate the help."

"No problem."

"Out, bitches." Dominic backed out the door, raising the peace symbol with both hands.

Everyone else had bailed here and there throughout the day, which left me, Callen, Spencer, and Kasper standing in the foyer.

"Ready to grab that beer?" Kasper asked, pulling his keys from his pocket.

Callen looked at me and Kasper then back again. What the hell was that about?

"Yeah, beer sounds great since Callen only fed me."

Callen scoffed, "Like you didn't have enough alcohol last night."

"Yeah, yeah. Now you sound like my mom."

A smirk pulled at the corners of his lips. "Someone needs to do it."

"Oh, now that you're all settled down, you're the mature one?"

"Maybe."

I laughed and turned to follow Kasper out the door. "Remind me of that the next time you throw a fit when you go down looking."

I shut the door behind me before Callen had a chance to respond. Kasper was already waiting beside a gorgeous Aston Martin.

"That is one sweet fucking car."

He ran his hand across the top like he was caressing a woman's soft skin. No, not a woman. Why would Kasper caress a woman? He didn't like women.

I gave myself a mental shake. Kasper Wilder did not play for the same team as I did. Which wasn't a big deal, but for some stupid reason my head was making it weird. A weirdness I never felt being around Callen.

"Ready?" He unlocked the car.

"Yeah. Um... sure." I started toward his car and stopped. "I... uh... I'll meet you there." What the fuck was wrong with me? I continued to stand there acting like a jackass. "This way I don't have to come back to Callen's to get my car when we're done."

He nodded. "Good idea." And before I took one step toward my Mercedes Maybach SUV, he was behind the wheel and pulling out of the driveway.

"Fuck," I mumbled under my breath.

I wanted to smack myself in the head for being such an idiot. The guy invited me for beer, not into his bed, so why was I fumbling over my words and acting like a fool? God, I probably offended the poor guy, making him think I didn't want to be near him because he's gay.

I had to get my shit together on the drive over to O'Malley's. I climbed behind the wheel of my car and took off in the direction of the downtown pub.

The sidewalks were pretty empty in this part of town. Thankfully, I didn't have to park too far from the restaurant considering it was a Saturday afternoon. Either the warmer than normal temperatures or the allure of Black Friday shopping had kept the crowds low. When I turned the corner, Kasper stood out front, a frown marring his face.

Shit, I really did piss him off. He probably didn't want to tell me off in front of Spencer and Callen's place and cause a scene.

I took a cautious step into his line of sight. "Is everything okay?"

Kasper's gaze snapped to mine. We were both the same height. Neither could look down on the other. "No. Something came up and I need a rain check."

I shrugged it off. "No worries. Shit happens. I'll head inside and grab something anyway." Wouldn't be the first time I'd been to the pub alone. "I hope everything ends up okay."

I reached for the door, but Kasper stopped me. "What's your number?"

"My number?"

He chuckled, but it didn't reach his eyes. "Yes, your phone number. I always pay my tabs, which means I owe you."

"Don't be—" I started, but he raised his hand to stop me. Seemed like this was an argument I had no chance of winning.

He programmed it into his phone as I rattled off my number. Then he took off at a jog, promising to call. I shook my head and tugged on the big wooden door of O'Malley's. Could today get any weirder?

After a couple of beers, I left O'Malley's. The comfort of my couch was calling my name. I found myself sitting in front of the TV watching college football when my phone buzzed on the table. I picked it up to see an unknown number on the screen. Almost ignoring it, curiosity got the better of me.

Unknown: It's Kasper. Sorry to run out on you. How about box seats Monday night to a Jetties game to make up for it?

Kasper

I was drained. Physically and emotionally spent. Being with Evan and watching him suffer at the thought of the man he loved cheating on him, it was too reminiscent of what I went through with my ex. Only, Vander didn't actually cheat and Hunter did. With more than one person. At the same time. I had nothing against multiple partners, but I drew the line when I was in a monogamous relationship and my partner cheated.

Pushing those thoughts aside, I stood in front of the full-length mirror in my bathroom to make sure I was every bit as put together as any team owner was. My navy suit was tailored to fit me. The legs tapered to my ankles. I wasn't a small man but I also wasn't as big as some of the players on the Jetties.

My white dress shirt was pressed and perfect, without a single wrinkle. I left the top few buttons undone. I didn't love ties but I wore them when I needed to. Tonight, I had no plans to woo any new investors, so there was no need to go all-out.

There was an annoying, persistent thought in my mind, reminding me that being the owner of the Jetties wasn't the only reason I was dressing up. Nope, not going there. I swore off dating athletes a while ago. Not only was Marcus Warnes a ballplayer, but he was pin straight. I wasn't about to tackle two things I told myself I never would again.

No, Hunter wasn't straight when I set my eyes on him. That was the guy I dated in secret before him. He swore to me he'd come out soon, only soon never happened. I broke it off and Hunter was there to console me right into his bed.

"Get your head in the game, Wilder," I muttered to myself. Even though I wasn't getting ready to take the ice, I was still part of the team. I would show up, smile, and stay professional.

I slipped on my Patek Philippe watch and went through the penthouse grabbing my wallet, phone, and keys. There were a lot of wealthy men and women I knew who had drivers and never touched a steering wheel themselves. However, I loved driving. My black Aston Martin DB11 was well loved and well driven. It wasn't made to sit unused somewhere.

Taking the elevator down to the garage, I took the few steps to my car and slipped into the buttery leather seat. When the engine was purring, I pulled out of my spot, through the garage, and into the night air of downtown Espen.

The drive wasn't long, even with the traffic rolling through the city during the tail end of rush hour. I kept an office at the arena as well as at home. I wasn't someone who was at work, only sitting at a desk for twelve hours a day. I had more than one business. I worked on the fly. I did what I needed to from wherever I was. And I employed a team of people to afford me such luxury.

As soon as I pulled into my spot at the Jetties' arena, my assistant, Pascal, was there waiting for me. He was tall, leanly muscled, and had hair as dark as my car. His clothing was as top-of-the-line as mine was, and he wore it well. Pascal was the first person anyone met before they got to me, and he took his job seriously.

He started talking the second I had the door open. "Katie is working on the next PR campaign with Devon. He's being a good sport and even let Katie do a tease of it on social media. The fans are going wild seeing him, and King read through some of the messages they got and is responding to them."

Devon D'Agostino was a center for the Jetties and a fan favorite. Kingston Walker was the left wing. Together, with Hayes Garner, our right wing, they were an impressive first line on the ice and they were close friends off of it.

Katie wanted Devon out there more publicly. He was ruthless on the ice but off of it, he was shy and reserved. He hesitantly agreed to doing more PR. Now it was a matter of getting him comfortable with it. Katie thought the addition of King would help him relax and it sounded like it was working.

Pascal kept going. "Brick called. He's pissed you missed your meeting with him earlier today." I opened my mouth to talk, but Pascal kept going. "I know, I know. I told him you had an emergency meeting that couldn't be pushed."

As the CFO of my aviation company, Brick was someone I relied on heavily to help run my business. He was also a pain in my ass and knew it. We grew up together and went to the same college, even roomed together. We kissed once to see if there was anything there. There wasn't. We went together like oil and water, but I loved him like a brother.

"And Marcus Warnes is in your suite. He just arrived. I swear you bring these ballplayers here just to tease me. You won't let me near the hockey players, who never flirt with me anyway." He rolled his eyes. "But the Emperors aren't owned by you, so they're fair game."

I glared at him. Something about the way he was appreciating Marcus rubbed me wrong. If I didn't know better, I'd say it was a flare of jealousy but that was ridiculous. I hardly knew Marcus.

Pascal narrowed his eyes to study me. They widened a moment later. "Oh, I see how it is. You didn't bring him here for me. You brought him for yourself. An early Christmas gift, perhaps?"

"Zip it, Paz."

I closed my door and locked the car before walking toward the building. Pascal was right behind me. No matter where I was working, regardless of which company, he was there. And not in a bad way. He was utterly dedicated to his job, which I appreciated more than he'd ever know. The part I hated was that he didn't have much of a social life. No matter how much time off I gave him, he still worked. We had long talks about it and he assured me he was happy. I didn't miss the longing in his eyes when he'd see a couple together, though.

"There's no need to be testy," he said, catching up to me. "Who am I to judge you if you want Marcus?"

"I don't want Marcus," I said, trying to infuse as much boredom into my tone as I could. Paz was like a dog with a bone anytime I showed interest in someone.

"Whatever you say, boss."

I glanced over to find him grinning. I could never stay mad at him.

We wove our way through the offices of the arena and came to a stop in front of the owner's suite. Marcus wasn't the only one I invited today. My brother was here with his wife and their two teenage sons. Plus, two of my longtime investors were here with their spouses.

I didn't mind mixing business with pleasure, except when it came to my dating life. I was an incredibly open man when it came to my work, and what someone saw when they met me was what they got. My personal life was a different story. Only a handful saw the real me.

I opened the door and gestured for Paz to go in first. He did so with his tablet in hand, no doubt ready to list off more things I had to deal with.

The second I was in the room, Stock's arms were around me, holding me tight. I hadn't seen my brother in months and it was great to have him here. He brought his family to Espen for the holidays. They were staying through New Year's. I was so happy to have him around again.

I hugged my brother as Pascal smiled sweetly at us. Pulling back, I studied Stock. He had the same blond hair and hazel eyes I did, but he was two inches taller than me at six foot four and he wasn't as broad, though he was muscular.

I greeted his wife, Davina, and their sons, Ashton, who was fourteen, and Julien, who was seventeen, with hugs.

"How did you two grow so fast?" I asked the boys. I swore they each gained six inches since I'd last seen them.

"Right?" Davina asked. "I have to keep buying them clothes."

I loved my family. We might not see each other in person often, but we kept in touch over video chat once a month. No matter where any of us were, we got together and spent time with one another.

After talking with my family for a few more minutes, I made my way to the investors and did my usual speech with them, making sure they were happy, and asked how they were doing. No, I didn't have to sell them anything tonight since they weren't pulling their money from the team any time soon, but I still had to be a gracious host. Then it was on to Marcus. I gave him two tickets but was surprised to see him here alone.

Before I could get to him, the door to the suite opened and Dominic Truby stepped through. "Sorry I'm late," he said with a smile.

He looked around until his eyes landed on my brother. Dominic's mouth dropped open as he stared at Stock.

Here we go.

"Holy shit, you're Stockton Wilder," Dominic said in surprise. "How are you... Why are you..." He turned toward me. "Holy shit, your brother is here."

I smiled. "That he is."

"I can't believe Stockton Wilder will be sitting near me watching a hockey game. How fucking cool is this shit? Marcus, why didn't you text me?"

Marcus smirked. "And ruin this moment?" He didn't seem nearly as excited as Dominic was, which was surprising since everyone loved my brother. Not only was he exceedingly talented but he was one of the nicest guys I knew.

My brother extended his hand. "Dominic Truby, right?"

Dominic's mouth dropped open again. "You know who I am? Marcus, he knows who I am."

"I heard," he replied with a smile.

"Wow, this is just... Wow."

I went over to Marcus, leaving Dominic and Stock to talk. Davina took the boys back to their seats. She was used to this. She also was very down-to-earth and never tried to take advantage of the career Stock built. It helped that they were high school sweethearts.

Sticking my hands in my pockets, I stopped in front of Marcus. "I'm glad you could make it."

His lips lifted in a half smile and fuck me, it did something to me. Something I had to push really far down and not evaluate right now. "Thanks for the tickets, though I think Dom is going to kiss you when he comes over here. I can't tell you how many times he's made me sit through Stockton's movies."

I laughed. "Stock's got the whole badass thing down on screen."

He watched me and thought for a moment. It seemed like puzzle pieces clicking into place as he remembered something. "I'm sorry about your parents."

Even though it had been fifteen years since their deaths, it still hurt to think about them at times. My parents died when their small plane crashed shortly after takeoff. My dad loved to fly and had been a pilot for many years. All his training and skills weren't enough to save them when there was engine failure.

"Thanks. It was a long time ago," I responded.

"That doesn't diminish what happened."

"No, it doesn't. You're right." I glanced toward the ice to see the players skate out while the announcer came over the speakers.

Dominic stepped to us and threw his arms around Marcus and me. "This is one of the best days of my life. If I'd have known your brother was going to be here, I would have been on time."

Marcus rolled his eyes. "The only time you show up when you're supposed to is for our games. Everything else is hit or miss."

Dominic wrapped his arm around Marcus's neck. "Shut it or I'll drag you back to my place after this for a movie marathon."

"I'm sure Cheryl would appreciate that."

"Just you wait. I got a selfie with Stockton. As soon as my ass hits this seat, I'm texting my wife. She'll know she's in for a late night movie when I get home." His smile was big. "I can't believe I just met him. Fuck, this is amazing."

Paz cleared his throat beside me. It was my cue to wrap it up and make my way around the arena. I had more people to visit with outside of the ones in this suite. Though, I would have loved to spend the game talking with my family, Marcus, and Dominic.

Not wanting the night to end after the game, I said, "What do you two say to coming back to my place after the game for drinks?" I leaned in close to Dominic. "I'll even invite Stockton." I had enough rooms for everyone to crash at my place if need be.

Stock had a house outside of the city he stayed in every time he was here. He liked having the comforts of home for extended trips.

"Are you serious?" Dominic's eyes bugged.

"Absolutely." I smiled.

Chapter 3

Marcus

I lifted the bottle to my lips, watching Dominic fawn all over Stockton Wilder, who seemed to have the same close relationship with Kasper that I had with my sister. Dominic's squealing had died down throughout the game, his attention drawn to the ice in a close call win for the Jetties. Now they sat in a deep discussion of Stockton's films, dissecting the decisions directors made and analyzing the stunts he'd performed on his own. I'd questioned getting in the car with Dominic to ride over to Kasper's. With his excitement overflowing, I worried we wouldn't make it in one piece.

Even as the conversation surrounded me, I wasn't fully invested. Stockton's movies were great, I just didn't have the same obsession Dominic did. Instead, I glanced around the room, taking in Kasper's home. I couldn't believe I sat in *the* Kasper Wilder's penthouse having a beer like it was a normal Monday night. There was having money and then there was having Kasper's kind of money.

I chuckled to myself. This had to be what fans felt like meeting me, even if I didn't see myself as any more than a guy doing what he loved for a living.

The two-story penthouse in the middle of the city was beyond anything I could have imagined. A few of the players who did have penthouses usually shared the floor with one other person, not two entire floors to themselves.

A large gas fireplace sat on one side of the room with a flat-screen TV mounted above it. The Christmas tree, brightly decorated in the corner, added a warmth to the space that even the glow of the fire, as it reflected off the glass table in front of me, could not. And that was only half of the spacious room.

There was a bar built into the wall, the sliding door open with many different types of liquor on display. In the far corner I could see the entrance to a formal dining room and another I assumed led to the kitchen. The entire place had been tastefully decorated for the Christmas season.

The spot on the couch next to me sank down and I turned my head to see Kasper taking the seat beside me. When we arrived at Kasper's place, he had already changed into a pair of jeans and a beige sweater. He'd gone from the uber wealthy executive to a guy relaxing for drinks with his friends in the blink of an eye. Barefoot, he leaned against the back of the couch and propped his foot on the opposite knee, a glass in his hand.

"Sorry about that." He nodded his head over to where Stockton and Dominic sat in wingback chairs across from us. "Davina knows once Stock gets into these conversations, it won't be over for a while. She wanted to get the boys home before it got too late."

"No problem. I'm amazed they're still going."

Kasper's deep rumbling laughter filled the room. "They'll be on that topic for as long as Stock can talk or we interrupt them."

It was my turn to laugh. Kasper had no idea how big of a fan Dominic was. At one point, I remembered him trying to make us sit through a twenty-four-hour movie marathon before Stockton's latest movie came out. "Dominic can go just as long."

We sat there, quietly drinking, watching the two of them start their analysis of Stockton's last film and directorial debut.

"I've been hearing your name a lot on the possible free agent market," Kasper said suddenly.

I froze and moved my gaze slowly to him. My chest tightened and butterflies took off in my stomach. As an owner of another team in town, I had a feeling he knew more about my upcoming years with the Emperors than I did. I bit the inside of my cheek to keep from showing the fear I had they wouldn't sign me again. Espen was the only place I wanted to be. Having to play in another city would just be second best.

I gripped the bottle tighter in my hand. "I'm not surprised. I have one option year left after this upcoming season. There's lots of speculation about what the Emperors will do when my last option comes up. Guess it depends on how much salaries cost next year."

His brows drew together. "You think they'll trade you?"

I shrugged and took a sip to hide my anxiety about the entire conversation. "I honestly don't know. They haven't mentioned anything to my agent yet." Of all my friends, Kasper had to be the first person I admitted that to. The fear of what it meant if I admitted it out loud kept me silent.

Kasper nodded. "That isn't a complete surprise. With another year, I'm sure they're focused on the free agents that are already out there and the upcoming draft."

"I know but depending on who they pick up in the off-season will determine whether they'll be willing to pick up my last option year or even offer me another long-term deal to stay in Espen."

"You're one of the top catchers in the league. There's no way they'd get rid of you if they want to keep winning championships." Kasper clasped me on the shoulder. My body relaxed with his words and touch.

A smile lifted the corner of my lips and the pressure in my chest eased a bit. "Thanks. I hope you're right. I'd hate to leave Espen. It's truly become my home."

"I can't imagine being anywhere but here. Every time I have to travel for work, I can't wait to come home." He gestured around the room.

My gaze followed his movements and chuckled. "I can't imagine why."

He smirked. "Too much?"

I shook my head. "No. I think your place is amazing."

"Thank you. It took me a while to find what I wanted and even then, it didn't exist. I had to buy the building so they would let me renovate the top two floors into this." I choked on the beer I'd just swallowed. Kasper smacked me on the back. "You okay?"

I sputtered for a second until I could catch my breath. "You bought the building so you could have the top two floors?"

"Yes." He shrugged like that was a completely normal statement.

"Fair enough." What else could I say?

We talked more about the features he'd added into his remodel, including a full chef's kitchen and a fireplace in his bedroom, which had to be nice on cold nights. After a while, Stockton and Dominic joined the conversation. We laughed and joked and drank.

Eventually, Dominic stood, stretching his arms high. "As much as I would love to hang out longer, I need to get back home."

Kasper was quick with his offer. "I have plenty of rooms if you'd like to stay the night."

Kasper was probably worried about Dominic driving after how much he'd had to drink, but I knew he never got behind the wheel after more than a beer or two. Usually, he called a car to take him home.

"Thanks, man, but I need to get home to Cheryl. She doesn't give me shit about all the time I'm away from home, so I always make sure to get home and into our bed at some point in the night. I'll call a car." Exactly like I thought he would. Dominic pulled out his phone. Stockton stopped him before he could finish dialing.

"Don't worry about it," Stockton cut in. "The car service I have will bring an extra driver to take your car home. You can ride with me."

"Are you sure?"

He nodded. "Absolutely. You can tell me more about your World Series win on the way."

"Oh man," I muttered only loud enough for Kasper to hear. Asking Dominic to talk about the World Series had to be on the same level as asking Stockton about his movies. The car ride wouldn't be long enough.

"Works for me." Dominic pocketed his phone.

Stockton made his own call as Kasper turned to me. "I hope you'll stay. I wouldn't be able to forgive myself if something happened to the Emperors' star catcher on his way home."

"I don't want to intrude. I can just call a car." It was how I'd gotten to the arena in the first place. I hadn't expected to end up at Kasper's penthouse.

He covered my phone, our fingers brushing as he pushed it down. "I insist, then I'll drive you home in the morning."

Dominic spared me a passing glance, but his focus was once again consumed by Stockton and their discussion about the World Series.

"Okay."

Kasper walked Dominic and Stockton to the door. When he came back into the living room, I stood, following him toward the stairs. My knee cracked a few times on the way up, but I kept my mouth shut. Last thing I needed was anyone else knowing about my knees.

Kasper showed me to a guest room the size of my own bedroom at home. The large king bed was the focal point of the room, with cherry dressers along one wall. He pointed out the en suite bathroom and promised to return with clothes for me to change in to, even though I told him I'd be fine in the morning in what I was wearing, but he insisted. Minutes later, he was back, handing me a pile of things to wear to bed and more for tomorrow.

"There are towels in the closet and an extra toothbrush and toothpaste in the drawer." He chuckled. "Actually, if I'm not mistaken, the bathroom is probably fully stocked with everything you need. My housekeeper says it's rude not to have everything guests may want when they stay the night."

"Thank you. These," I lifted the clothes "and a toothbrush are perfect. I'm a pretty simple man."

Kasper watched me for a moment before smiling and taking a step back toward the door. "Sleep well, Marcus. I'll see you in the morning." Kasper looked like he wanted to say something else but didn't, instead, he opted for stepping into the hall and shutting the door behind him.

Standing in the middle of the room, I laid the pajama pants on the bed and clothes for tomorrow on the dresser. The shower called my name. I went to the bathroom and turned on the water. My knees were still sore and the hot water would do them some good. I discarded my clothes on the bathroom floor. I'd pick them up later. Normally, I didn't sleep in anything, but staying at someone else's house made me feel like I needed to pull on a pair of pants before I climbed between the sheets.

After a hot shower, my body more relaxed, I snuggled into the covers, the bed extremely comfortable, and let the excitement of the night lull me into a deep sleep.

***

The room seemed too bright. Had I left a light on? I opened my eyes and squinted into the room, blocking out the early morning light seeping through the windows. It took me a few moments to recognize where I was when I remembered Kasper insisting I stay the night.

The clothes he'd given me the night before sat neatly folded where I left them on the dresser. I sat up, moving my feet over the side of the bed, my knees still aching this morning. This long after the season, I should be fine. Callen was right, I needed to see someone about it before spring training. Hopefully, Spencer would be able to help. The last thing I needed was for Tim, the owner of the Emperors, to worry about my knees when I was trying to stay through my option years and get a new contract.

After doing some simple stretches, I pushed myself from the bed and went to the bathroom to splash water on my face and brush my teeth. Clean teeth in the morning always made me feel better, no matter how much I drank the night before. Surprisingly, there weren't many lingering effects from all the beers I had. I tugged on the jeans and long-sleeved Henley Kasper had given to me and folded my dirty clothes into a neat pile. Once I had everything in hand, I headed for the door.

Kasper had already been accommodating enough, I didn't want to mess with the rest of his day by making him wait around to take me back to my place. I went in search of him to thank him for letting me stay. The minute I opened the bedroom door, the scent of bacon filled my senses.

I treaded lightly down the stairs, mindful of my knee. When I reached the bottom, I wandered through the now empty living room, admiring the view from the floor-to-ceiling windows. The room had gone from warm and cozy to bright and cheery with the rise of the sun.

Following the scent of bacon and freshly brewed coffee, I made my way to what I assumed was the kitchen. I stopped dead in my tracks.

Kasper stood at the counter in low slung sweats and no shirt with his back to me, mixing something in a bowl. It was hard not to admire the well-defined muscle of his back and shoulders. I spent hours in the gym to get that kind of tone to my body, and all of his were hidden behind a suit most of the time.

In the center of his back, between his shoulders, was a large tattoo of a compass. The points on each direction were sharp, the work intricate. It was colorful with a different shade for each point. The color stayed within the lines of the compass. Red for north. Blue for south. Bright green for west and a vibrant hue of yellow for east.

There wasn't a single hair out of place on his head, which had me reaching up to smooth down the bed head I no doubt had. He swayed to the Christmas music playing in the background and suddenly I felt awkward watching and not announcing my presence.

I stepped farther into the room. "Good morning."

Chapter 4

Kasper

That saying about playing with fire certainly applied here. Inviting Marcus to spend the night, almost pressuring him to do so, was not one of my smartest moves, but it was emotionally driven. I liked him in my space. Wanted to keep him there. Which was so fucking foolish of me. I was going to get burned. I knew it and yet I couldn't help myself. I kept fanning the flames.

Cooking breakfast shirtless was not only a test of my resolve but of Marcus's as well. I had to see if he'd show any interest in me. To see if he really were straight. Also, my sweatpants left absolutely nothing to the imagination. Then again, I was in front of an athlete who had no doubt seen as much dick as porn stars, thanks to being around other guys often.

Marcus's deep voice slid over me. "Good morning."

I swallowed and willed my dick to behave when I turned around. Marcus looked damn good in my clothes. They fit him well. We were pretty evenly matched in size. Same height. Similar build. There was something about seeing him in them that brought out the possessive part of me. The one I shouldn't be entertaining.

Lusting after Marcus was a bad, bad move. I had to keep reminding myself that not only was he an athlete, but he was straight. Those were two strikes against him. He was also a solid twelve years younger than I was. I wasn't counting that as a strike because I didn't want Marcus to be out of the game. What would he want with a gay, older man anyway? Nothing, that's what. We had fun drinking and hanging out last night. That was it.

"Morning," I finally replied. "Hungry?"

"I could eat." He smiled.

"There's some acetaminophen and ibuprofen in the cabinet over the sink if you need it. I'm not sure how well you handle drinking."

"I'm feeling pretty good."

I nodded. "I'm glad."

I turned back to the bowl of pancake mix, acting like it was the most interesting thing in the room, though it was far from that. Instead of thinking about how Marcus held my eyes, and not how they never strayed from my face, I went to work making pancakes while the bacon cooked on low. It was almost done and I didn't want it to burn.

The pancakes cooked fast, thanks to the hot griddle. I served up two plates piled high with food and pointed Marcus to the coffee and whatever he needed to make it how he liked it. Instead of eating in the formal dining room, we sat on the stools that were by the raised counter on the island in my kitchen.

It should have been easier sitting next to Marcus instead of being able to look at him. It wasn't. I could smell his undercurrent of rich, spicy masculinity. A scent that was unique to him. One that was slightly masked by the detergent and fabric softener on the clothes of mine he was wearing.

And his warmth... I could feel him beside me. Fuck, this was so bad.

Then he moaned when he took his first bite of pancake. That was it. I was done for. Fucking obliterated. Now I could picture what he sounded like when he came.

"Oh my god, these are delicious," he said. I glanced over and noticed his eyes were closed as he savored the food. He had stubble along his jaw and cheeks. I wanted him to rub it against my bare skin.

Shaking my head, I willed myself to stop thinking about sex. I needed to change the subject. "You probably thought I couldn't cook." I didn't look at him but could feel his gaze on me.

"Honestly, I thought you'd have someone cook for you."

"I do but only dinner. The other meals I handle on my own."

"Do you have to work today? I was surprised to see you down here cooking. I figured you'd have to run off to a meeting or something. It's Tuesday, after all."

"I knew Stock would be at the game and wasn't sure if he'd crash here or not. I cleared my morning."

"So you're not rushing to shove me out the door?" he joked.

"Not at all. Take as long as you'd like."

"Don't tease me, Kasper. I could get used to this life."

I offered him a weak laugh but couldn't bring myself to reply. If he were mine, I'd give him everything. Although, I had a feeling that wasn't the type of man Marcus was. He wasn't someone who wanted to be kept, and deep down it wasn't what I wanted either.

My type wasn't someone who was always compliant. Granted, I was an alpha when it came to my businesses. I had to be. I wouldn't have made it as far as I had if I weren't. But at home, I wanted a partner. Someone who could give me advice. Help me when I needed it. And I wanted someone who desired the same in return.

In the bedroom, that was a different story. I needed to be dominated there. I wanted to be owned. That was a problem for some of my lovers. They saw me as this muscular, powerful, rich guy and thought I wanted to pound them into the bed. Every once in a while, I liked control in there. However, most of the time, I want to relinquish it. I wanted someone else to lead. I did it all day long in my work life. I didn't want to do it when I got home. And that was something hard to find.

I did with Hunter. He was all too happy to take control. He also thought that control was absolute and used it to his advantage. He found out I wouldn't tolerate it.

After breakfast, we both stood to take our dishes over to the sink but Marcus moved slower. I noticed him wince in pain, which he quickly tried to mask.

"Are you okay?" I didn't like seeing him hurting. It brought out the protective side in me. The one that wanted to care for him. And that one, I wasn't going to try and bury. I could play it off as a friend caring for another.

"Yeah," he said as he walked to the sink. "My knees get stiff. It's fine."

"It's not fine. You're a catcher. Your knees are valuable. Have you had them looked at?"

"Not yet, but I'm going to make an appointment."

I pulled out my phone and tapped a quick text to Spencer Matson. He'd be able to help Marcus. Hopefully, he had time to fit him in soon.

"What are you doing?" Marcus asked.

"Reaching out to Spencer and seeing if he can get you in."

Marcus stepped closer, causing me to focus on him instead of my phone. In his gray eyes I saw so many things, however, each went by too fast for me to latch on to and dissect. "I can do that myself, Kasper."

"I'm sure you can, but I know Spencer personally."

"I'm a big boy. I don't need someone taking care of me." There wasn't any anger in his voice. But it wasn't kind either. "You've already done enough by inviting me to the game, your house, and cooking for me."

"I like doing those things." My voice sounded so small and I hated it. I had insecurities like everyone else, and being rejected was one of them. Also, not being liked for who I really was. Not the guy on the magazine covers who was a good-looking, eligible bachelor. I didn't care about that stuff. It was superficial.

Marcus studied me for a moment before speaking again. "Do you always have to be in control?"

"No, there's one place I relinquish it." I snapped my mouth shut before I said more. What the hell was I thinking saying that out loud?

Marcus's eyes went wide. "Uh…"

"Shit, I'm sorry." I turned and put my phone on the counter. It vibrated with a text but I ignored it. Instead, I focused on washing the dishes, which was stupid considering I had a dishwasher. If I were cleaning them, I wasn't focusing on Marcus.

A warm hand on my bare back had me pausing my movements and tensing. "Thank you." I turned and Marcus was right there, a breath away. He backed up a step and cleared his throat. "For reaching out to Spencer, that is. I was going to do it, but if he can get me in, I'll take whatever appointment he has." He was flustered and a blush crept over his cheeks.

I decided to ignore it and washed my hands, dried them, and reached for my phone. Sure enough, there was a text from Spencer. "He said he can see you tonight at six. He can stop by your place if you don't want to go out, or you can go to his practice."

"Six works. Tell him I'll come to him. There's no reason to make him drive to me."

Nodding, I replied to Spencer. Once that was done, I didn't know what to say. I found everything magnified in Marcus's presence. Sounds. Sights. Scents. And I became someone I didn't like when my nerves kicked in.

Luckily, Marcus saved me from speaking when he said, "I should get going."

"Right." I nodded. "Give me a few to get dressed and I'll drive you home."

"You don't have to do that. I can call for a car."

"I insist. I have to get to the arena anyway. I'm meeting with my head of PR to discuss how the campaign she launched is going."

"I saw some of that. It was a great idea. Nice way to engage the fans."

I smiled, almost preening under his compliment. "Thank you."

With that, I hurried upstairs and got changed. I didn't need to shower since I'd done that before I came down to make breakfast. After putting on a tan suit and a crisp, white button-down beneath the jacket, I opened my drawer and grabbed a pair of cuff links that used to belong to my father. My mother had given them to him on their anniversary before the plane crash. They were gold with a single, small diamond in the center of each one. Every time I wore them, I felt closer to my parents.

I grabbed my wallet and went down the stairs, my shoes clapping on the hardwood. At the bottom of the stairs, I found Marcus perched on the arm of the couch. He stood as I approached.

"You're like Superman. You change in the blink of an eye to a different persona."

I chuckled. "If only I had his abilities."

"I don't know. It seems to me you can do a hell of a lot most can't."

"Money does that. I still think it's a shame it rules our society. We should be judged by our character, what we do for others, how we live our lives, not by the number of zeros in our bank accounts."

Marcus watched me for a moment. I thought he was going to say something, but in the end, he gripped his phone in his hand and started walking toward the door. Maybe I wasn't the man I'd like to think of myself as and I was the business mogul the world saw. I didn't need them all to see the real me. I didn't care what their opinions of me were. I had to be strong to keep my businesses running so I could pay my employees well. They depended on my success for their income.

But Marcus... I didn't want him to see me as the world did. I wanted him to see me as Evan did. As Spencer had come to. As my other close friends and family had. Fuck, I couldn't spend time unpacking this right now.

I took my keys and phone and strode to the elevator. We got to the garage and I unlocked my Aston Martin. Marcus paused for a second, staring at the car.

"You have plenty of money, Mr. Warnes. You can afford a car just like this."

"Yeah, but I'm not as fancy as you." He smiled then slid inside.

I got in the driver's seat and closed the door before meeting his eyes. "I may be fancy on the outside, but I assure you, I'm a very simple man within, who has simple needs. Although that doesn't mean I don't like to indulge and appreciate the good fortune I've created."

Marcus didn't reply and I decided to break our gaze before he could. Maybe once he was away from me I could put my filter back into place. I didn't like this need to impress him. Though, it wasn't necessarily impressing him with my wealth. I didn't think Marcus would care as much about that as he did about the person he was speaking to. And that was another tick in the pro box for him.

My friends knew the real me and I was starting to think of Marcus as a friend. If only I could get my dick on the same page and stop it from trying to reach out so Marcus could grasp it.

Chapter 5

Marcus

I pulled into the parking lot, trying to keep my hands from shaking on the steering wheel. Freaking out before I walked into Spencer's office was ridiculous. When I was home for Thanksgiving, I'd gone to our family doctor for an official diagnosis, out of fear the team would get wind of it and question my last option year. My hope was that Spencer would be able to deal with the problem before I had spring training.

I dropped my head onto the wheel and sucked in a deep breath. Last night, admitting my fears to Kasper had somehow made them more real. The end of my contract had seemed so far away. Now, here I was, one season away from my fate, maybe less if they decided to trade me instead of taking the option.

Could I play for any team in the league? Sure. But not every team had the camaraderie and cohesion the Emperors did. My luck, I'd end up with a team that were acquaintances at best.

No. I wouldn't let that happen.

I needed to walk my ass inside Spencer's office and get the process started, then I'd have this season to prove why they should keep me even past the last option year. Why they would want me for another five years or more. Blowing out a breath, I stepped out of the car and winced when I straighten my leg.

Time to get this shit fixed.

The moment I stepped through the door, I noticed the man sitting behind the reception desk. I thought I'd seen him before at a game maybe, but the fluorescent lights made his hair seem lighter than I remembered. The waiting room sat blissfully empty. The fewer people I had to explain my visit to the better. When I reached the counter, the receptionist looked up and immediately stood with a smile.

"Hi, Mr. Warnes. Spencer said I should take you back as soon as you arrived. He's waiting for you."

I gestured to one of the clipboards. "No paperwork for me to fill out?"

He shook his head. "Nope. He said he'd take care of it. Follow me."

He moved from behind the desk and waited for me by the entrance to a long hall. I followed him past a few exam rooms to the next to last one on the left. The door sat slightly ajar, a sliver of light slipping through the crack. He pushed the door open.

"Spencer, Mr. Warnes is here."

"Marcus, please."

He smiled again. I didn't miss the way his eyes danced from my lips to my chest to my arms.

"Thanks, Keenan. You can take off for the night since everyone else is gone. Thanks for waiting for Marcus to arrive."

"No problem." Keenan gestured for me to step inside. "I'll see you tomorrow."

"Enjoy your night."

Keenan turned down the hall with a wave.

Spencer stood from the chair on the side of the room. There were a couple of tablets sitting on the table. I stepped inside and Spencer closed the door behind me, which confused me since no one else seemed to be in the office.

When I glanced at it and back at him, he shrugged and smiled. "Habit."

"Fair enough. I thought there would be more people here."

"I figured you didn't want many people to know you were having issues." Spencer collected two of the tablets and placed them into slots on the wall. "Sorry. Trying to update some of the records of the Jetties players into our systems."

"It's fine. With time on my contract winding down, I wouldn't want to give the Emperors any reason not to pick up my last option year."

"Option year?" He patted the table I assumed I was supposed to sit on.

I shrugged out of my jacket, setting it on the chair and took a seat where he indicated, my legs hanging over the side. "The three years on my contract that were negotiated, but it's up to the club if they want to keep me for those. They've kept me for two of the three, but next year is a toss-up. They could want to trade me before I become a free agent. Or they could pick me up for another long-term deal."

"So you agree to a contract with possible extra years? Let me guess, if you don't play well enough, you don't see those extra years?"

"Exactly. They have to pay me through this upcoming year or find someone to pick up the last year of my contract. Which, if they were going to do, they would have already done it by now. But the last year they decide what they want to do. They could easily trade me and let another team deal with my contract."

Spencer frowned. "That sucks."

"It does. At least Callen has three more years before the two option years on his. Not like they won't keep him anyway."

He picked up the remaining tablet. "Well, let's make sure they don't have any reason not to keep you." He typed a few things into it then looked back up at me. "What diagnosis are we dealing with?"

"Umm, it's jumper's knee. At least, that's what my family doc near my parents' house told me before Thanksgiving."

Spencer arched a brow. "You have patellar tendonitis and you still helped us move the other day?" He shook his head and went back to his tablet.

"I didn't think it was a big deal."

"For a professional athlete who squats for at least half the game, it's huge." He reached for my leg. "It's the right one, correct?"

"Yeah."

"I'm going to do an evaluation first and we'll make a plan from there."

He lifted my leg, forcing it straight while he held it above the floor, then moved it back and forth. He had me stand and sink into a squat, among other things. The pain shot up my leg the moment I started down into a position I moved into almost as much as walking. I gritted my teeth and pushed through it. Spencer needed to know how bad things were. After about twenty minutes, he asked me to get back up on the table.

The butterflies in my stomach took off while I waited for Spencer to tell me the deal. When he studied the tablet without saying anything, I had to ask, "So what do I need to do to get back into playing shape?"

Spencer chuckled. "You're already a better patient than Callen."

I laughed with him. "Callen doesn't listen well."

He glanced up at me then. "No. No, he does not."

"Me, on the other hand, I listen really well."

He grabbed the rolling stool from the side of the room and brought it next to the table. "That's good. Your range of movement is stiff, and I could see the pain on your face when your leg moved in certain directions. Thank you for not trying to hide it, though I also don't want to push you to the point of that pain. These are things that are important to be honest about. I can't help you if you hide when it hurts."

"I won't hide anything as long as I can fix this."

"We can fix it. It's going to take a few visits a week to get you back in playing shape. But I'll have you ready to go before you need to report for spring training."

"That's all I need to hear."

"Good thing you came in when you did. Otherwise, we'd have run out of time before then."

I ran a hand through my hair. "I honestly thought it was the normal stiffness and knee pain that I deal with at the end of every season. I didn't think anything of it until it didn't go away after a week or so."

"Then, I'm glad Kasper sent me that text, even though I was surprised to get a message from him instead of Callen or you."

"Oh yeah. Well, I'd... uh... spent the night at his place after we left the Jetties game. I'd had way too much to drink." Why the hell was I babbling like such an idiot? Spencer didn't care about why I'd slept in Kasper's guest room. "Anyway, what days should I come?"

He regarded me for a minute before picking up his tablet again. "Why don't we try for Tuesdays and Thursdays for now? Those are our early nights. Our last appointment is at five. You can meet me here at six for therapy."

"Man, Callen will kill me if I keep you from getting home early in the off-season."

Spencer stood and walked over to the wall, placing the tablet in an open charging dock. "Nah, he'll be fine. I think he'd rather have a healthy you behind the plate. He'll survive me being late for a while."

"As long as you say so." I moved off the table and held a hand out to Spencer. "Thanks for seeing me. I'll be back on Thursday to start."

Spencer shook my hand. "Perfect. And I'll thank Kasper for sending you my way before things got too bad."

"I'll make sure I thank him the next time I see him, too." I made my way to the door, Spencer right behind me.

"Let me grab my bag and I'll walk out with you."

I waited outside the room while Spencer stepped into the office at the end of the hall and emerged a few minutes later, his coat and bag in hand. I tugged on my own jacket. The one downfall of living in New Jersey was the temperature changes. It could feel like all four seasons in one day, and this time of night we usually got hit with winter.

He hiked the strap of his bag on his shoulder and started flipping the lights off. "Did you get to sit in the box seats at the Jetties game?"

"Yeah. Kasper and I were going to head for drinks after moving you into Callen's, but when he got to O'Malley's he said something came up and he had to run. Offered the box seats to make it up to me, so Dominic and I went."

"That was the night with Evan." Spencer pushed his key into the door, locking it, then turning to the left of the building where the lot on the side was.

My feet stuttered. "Evan? As in Vander's boyfriend?"

Spencer sighed. "Yeah, he needed help with something. Kasper's such a nice guy, I'm not surprised he wanted to make it up to you."

The wind whipped around us and even in the coat, a shiver raced through me. "He's so down-to-earth."

"That he is." Spencer started toward a dark SUV at the end of the lot. "Have a good night, Marcus. I'll see you on Thursday."

"Thanks, Spencer."

I climbed in my car and started for home when my phone buzzed on the seat next to me. Once I hit a red light, I picked it up for a quick peek. The name on the screen had a groan leaving my lips. Yes, Dominic was one of my best friends, but one night of drinking with him was enough for me this week.

Dominic: Girls' night out. Hitting the bar with the guys, come join us.

I tossed the phone back on the passenger seat. I'd deal with it when I got back to my place.

When I opened the door to my condo, the emptiness hit me the same as it had the last few months. Coming home was extremely lonely. I used to be the guy who went out with whomever was going and found a woman to hook up with at any time, but at twenty-eight, it had gotten old. I wanted to come home to someone. Someone to share my life, my frustrations with. Someone I could talk to about the fears with my knee.

Dominic wanted to drink and party while he lived vicariously through the single guys on the team. He loved his wife deeply and would never do a damn thing to hurt her, so hanging out with the single guys and playing wingman fit him perfectly.

Except, I didn't want to be that guy anymore. The hookups and sneaking out before morning. There wasn't a chance in hell I'd find someone to spend my life with among the cleat chasers who found us wherever we went.

I sent Dominic a text that I couldn't make it and grabbed a beer from the fridge. Settled on the couch, remote in hand, I looked around the room and recognized the bareness of it. Not just the simple furniture and almost nothing on the walls, I was a simple guy after all, but seeing the Christmas decorations covering Kasper's place made my place feel even lonelier.

There never seemed to be a point to decorating for Christmas when it was only me. And there still didn't. It just made me long for that someone special to enjoy the holidays with even more.

My phone rang where I'd left it on the couch. My gut tightened. A pushy Dominic would be hard to ignore. He'd keep calling until I answered. Imagine my surprise when it wasn't Dominic's name on my screen but Kasper's.

Guess I'd get the chance to thank him sooner rather than later.

Chapter 6

Kasper

New Year's Eve was a time for parties. I knew it, but I didn't like it. I'd rather enjoy a quiet night on my couch, watching the ball drop in Times Square on TV, than entertain my family and friends. I loved them, though. And Evan had been saying he wanted a party. He and Vander just got back from Florida the day before after visiting Vander's aunt and uncle.

So here I was, on New Year's Eve, surrounded by those in my inner most circle and others who were on the fringe of it. Because of Evan. If I only invited the ones I fully trusted, Evan would be bored because that list wouldn't include his boyfriend. I very rarely let people all the way in. Evan. Spencer was an easy addition. That man was a vault and incredibly friendly. Pascal because he knew more about me than most and had to manage the business part of my life. Stockton and his wife and kids. A few others who gained my trust over the years like Brick. That was really it.

As I looked around the room and took in those here, some were moving up from the fringe to the inner circle. Slowly. At a snail's pace. Like Callen... And Marcus.

I shouldn't be thinking about Marcus. Sure, we'd had drinks a few times since that night he slept over, but that was it. I didn't ask him back here and he didn't invite me to his place. I didn't want to think about the times I'd driven past where he lived only to never allow myself to stop and see how he was doing. I also didn't dare ask Spencer. Not only was it a breach of privacy, but it wasn't my business.

Evan sidled over to me and bumped my hip with his. He had on a pair of black skinny jeans that were so tight they left very little to the imagination and a shimmery silver, short-sleeved top. It might be cold out, but with the way he couldn't sit still tonight, I had no doubt he was glad he wore something lighter.

"What'cha doing?" he asked as he followed my line of sight, which I quickly changed.

"Nothing."

"It's cute how you think I can't read you. I should have a master's degree in the University of Kasper Wilder." I raised an eyebrow at him, causing him to roll his eyes. "Okay, so there are some subjects I haven't taken and won't thanks to that hot piece of a left fielder over there, but I still aced the others. Now, no one else here may see you. I mean, really see you. I do because Vander and Callen started talking shop, and I'm so not in the mood to listen to more baseball stories. Hence, why my attention was diverted to you."

"Out of boredom."

"Right. So, Marcus huh?"

I shook my head. There was no way I could deny who I was looking at. Evan was right. He knew me best. If Spencer hadn't been talking to Marcus, he might be over here, too. I counted myself lucky he was busy. We'd grown closer since that first meeting. A love match it never was, but close friends, definitely.

Evan pushed on, knowing I wasn't ready to speak. "Normally, I'd say you're way out of the realm of possibility by checking him out. Like hauling your ass back down to earth kind of hell no. However, I haven't only been watching you. Seems our catcher has a wandering eye."

I immediately tensed. Who else was he looking at? Sure, there were some of Jetties' management here, as well as from my other company. Single men. And women. Lovely. I threw Marcus into the lion's den of hot, available people.

Evan placed his hand on my arm. "Chill out, Kas. You didn't let me get to the part of who he was looking at before you went all pissed-off alpha male on me."

"I did not."

He snorted. "Uh huh. Sure. Anywho, the Emperors' catcher has had his eyes on you as well. I don't know if he even realizes he's doing it. He's aware I caught him, though." Even leaned closer. "He has a cute blush. Don't let Vander know I said that."

I looked around quickly to make sure no one was near. Not that I thought they were. Evan wouldn't have said what he did if anyone could eavesdrop. "He's straight. I get it. But..."

"But you can't control who you desire, and let's face it, Marcus is damn fine. So what are you going to do about it?"

"There's nothing to be done. If I'm lucky, I get a good friend." Evan knew how I felt about dating athletes. Knew it was something I didn't want to do again. Yet, he didn't bring that up and I was grateful.

He nodded. "You could use more friends as long as you never replace me."

I smiled and slung my arm over Evan's shoulders. "No one could ever take your place."

"Damn straight."

Vander turned and watched Evan and me for a moment before coming over. He was a very attractive man. I could see what Evan loved about him. Most of all, it was the way Vander only had eyes for him. Evan lit up like the fireworks that would go off at midnight tonight when Vander set his gaze on him. Vander ate up the distance until he was face-to-face with Evan.

He didn't take his eyes off Evan when he said, "Got your arm on my man again, Kasper?"

"That I do." I liked to mess with him, plus, Vander was only teasing. He might be protective of Evan, but he wasn't possessive.

"Think you should be doing that?" I didn't miss the quirk of his lips.

"Oh, I don't know. He was my best friend first."

"Whose bed are you sleeping in tonight, sexy?" Vander asked Evan.

"Yours," he rasped.

I chuckled. It was fun screwing with Vander.

Vander tugged Evan toward the bar where I had hired someone to mix drinks for the evening. What good was the money I had if I didn't use it to spoil myself and the ones I cared about? I also had the evening catered. Dinner was served earlier and hors d'oeuvres would be served until eleven. I wanted everyone who I'd hired tonight to make it home before the crowds flooded the streets after midnight.

When I focused on the room in front of me again, Marcus was on his way over. I noticed the way his jeans hugged those powerful legs of his. The ones that squatted behind home plate. And the ones that were moving a lot easier than the last time I saw him. Spencer must be working his magic on him.

"Vander loves having his hands all over Evan at all times?" he said with a smirk.

"Vander and I like to banter back and forth in fun. Besides, Evan and I never crossed that line." I wasn't sure why I said it. That was a lie. I wanted Marcus to know there was never anything between Evan and me.

"So gay guys *can* be friends with other guys and not want to get them into bed?" he joked.

I elbowed him in the ribs. It felt so natural. "Very funny."

He stood beside me, shoulder to shoulder. I could feel the heat coming from him as well as smell that spicy scent of his. I shifted on my feet. I needed my dick to behave. I didn't want to get hard in a room full of my friends and family. With Marcus beside me, it was proving to be a test of my willpower.

Across the room, Stockton laughed at something Dominic said. He might have moved up from a Stock groupie to a friend. My brother liked to take off the month of December to spend in Espen with his wife and kids and me. I was sure he was working on something from here. He wasn't one to sit quiet for long, but family was everything to him. After we lost our parents, our relationship became even more important. He would drop everything if I needed him and vice versa.

"What's it like?" Marcus asked.

I turned to look at him but he was fixated on the room before us. "What's what like?"

"To be famous."

I chuckled. "I think you know the answer to that. You're not exactly unknown, Mr. Warnes."

Marcus turned and he was so close to me. A mere breath away. It caused my own to hitch and my eyes to widen. I wasn't easily affected by other people. If I did desire someone, it was rarely on this level.

"I have a following," he replied. "That I won't deny, but it's nothing compared to you and Stockton. He's beyond famous and you've built up a powerful name in both sports and aviation. The only people who recognize me watch baseball. You go out on the street and I'm sure you get lots of attention."

I shrugged and focused on keeping my breathing even. "The attention is nice to an extent. Every time I make the cover of a magazine, newspaper, or any kind of digital media, it helps my business. I keep all news positive where I'm concerned. There isn't room for screwing up when it can mean losing money. But that doesn't mean I always like it. Sometimes I want to go out for a meal. I want to walk along the streets of the city I love. I want to be like everyone else without people stopping me."

"You're nothing like everyone else." I wasn't sure if he meant it in the way I hoped or not. "And your dating life? That has to be on display as well."

I focused on the room again, not trusting myself to speak to him face-to-face about this particular topic. "When I have one. I work hard and I'm tired when I get home. Lately, it's hookups rather than a serious relationship." I wasn't going to say how even the hookups had been few and far between. I needed to change the subject, get us moving in a different direction. "Come on. Let's get another drink."

We walked over to the bar and each ordered something. Marcus had drank more than me tonight. I noticed the times he went to the bar and it wasn't for a beer. It was a little selfish of me to be offering him more. I didn't want him drunk, just buzzed enough that he shouldn't drive home. I could possibly persuade him to not call a car. It was stupid of me to want him sleeping in my home again, but I couldn't help it.

The night went on. I sipped my drink as I walked and talked among the guests. Marcus stuck to the people he knew, while I had to mingle with everyone. It was a shame and a blessing. I wanted to stay and talk with Marcus all night, but that wasn't smart. I was playing with fire and couldn't seem to help myself.

By the time midnight struck, I found myself beside Marcus as we, along with other guests, looked out the floor-to-ceiling windows and watched the fireworks light the sky. People rang in the new year with a kiss with their significant other, while I felt the ache in my chest at not having anyone. At least I didn't have to see Marcus kiss someone. He could have brought a date, yet he didn't. I wouldn't allow myself to read into that one. Lusting after the straight guy was bad enough.

An arm came around my waist a second before a kiss was smacked onto my cheek. "Happy New Year, Kas," Evan said beside me.

I smiled. Evan had that kind of personality. It was infectious and if he was happy, so was I. "Happy New Year, Ev." I pressed a kiss to his forehead.

Evan peered around me. "No one to kiss at midnight, Marcus?"

He shook his head. "No, but I'm fine."

"That you are but you should still get a kiss." Evan released me and went over to smack a kiss on Marcus's cheek as well. "There. Now you rang in the new year properly."

Before Marcus could reply, Vander came over and put his arm around Evan's waist to pull him close. "I wasn't done kissing you," he whispered into Evan's ear loud enough for us to hear.

"Are they always like this?" Marcus asked.

"Yes. Evan was never one to hide who he is and I think he's truly met his match in Vander." I smiled as I looked at the two of them still in their own little world, kissing like they were the only ones who lived there. It was sweet and full of love.

Marcus must have seen something on my face because next thing I knew, I was being dragged toward the bar. Marcus stood behind it, grabbing a bottle of vodka and two glasses.

"I shouldn't," I told him. I didn't want to get drunk tonight. Me drunk with a possible Marcus under my roof for the rest of the night and morning wouldn't be a good combination.

"It's New Year's Eve, Kas. Live a little." My nickname on his lips sent a shiver through me.

"Only one." I tipped the shot back, relishing in the burn it created. When I placed it on the bar, I saw Marcus watching me with a smile. I knew then and there I'd do anything he asked me to.

Chapter 7

Marcus

I poured two more shots, one for me and one for Kasper. Something about the way he watched Vander and Evan, a look of longing on his face, I figured he could use the shot to push it out of his head. At least for a little while. I knew how he felt. Wanting what your friends had and not being able to find it wasn't a great way to start a new year.

"Here." I handed him one of the shot glasses and held the other up for a toast. "Here's to new chances this year."

For a moment, Kasper looked like he wanted to refuse, but something in his eyes changed. Without a word, Kasper took the glass from me and clinked it against mine before swallowing the contents back in one gulp. Even the muscles in his neck were powerful as he drank down the liquid.

He set the glass on the bar and turned to face the people still mingling throughout the room. I did the same and stayed by his side, following the direction of his gaze to where Dominic and Cheryl were locked in a heated embrace.

He was quiet for a few minutes, just watching the crowd and the couples wrapped in each other. There were plenty of single people at the party, but it was hard not to notice the couples and wish that for yourself.

"I have to say that Cheryl Truby was not at all what I expected."

A great, gusty laugh escaped my lips, not expecting anything close to what Kasper had just said.

He turned to watch me. "What is it?"

"That's not what I thought you would say." I smirked and glanced over to where Dominic had Cheryl bent back, his tongue clearly down her throat. Not a man who was shy at PDAs, the alcohol helped spur him on. "But Cheryl is a saint of a woman. She's the only one who can put up with his antics and still love him at the end of the day."

Kasper moved behind the bar and poured a whiskey neat, then grabbed an IPA for me. Apparently, he'd been paying attention to what I'd been drinking throughout the night. He passed me the bottle. "I thought she may be quiet, letting him take center stage."

I stopped with the bottle halfway to my lips, a laugh bubbling out of me again. Seemed that Kasper was able to get a genuine laugh from me, something not many were able to do. When I finally could pull it back, I took a sip of the beer. "Nope. She's the exact opposite. Cheryl happens to be the only one Dominic listens to."

He glanced over at me. "He doesn't listen to you? I thought he was your best friend."

"One of them. But he doesn't listen to me for shit." We wandered away from the bar. "He's a guy who likes being famous. Likes people watching him and definitely doesn't mind being the center of attention." Kasper's nose scrunched up and I rushed to clarify. "He likes people watching him but would never take advantage of another soul. I've seen him use his influence to get so many things done to help people who have no power to help themselves."

Kasper nodded. He opened his mouth to say something else but got called away by someone I didn't know, probably someone he worked with. "I'll be back." He turned in the direction of the short guy waving him over.

I didn't know why it had been so important for Kasper to approve of Dominic, but it was. One of my best friends; he might be wild, but he did everything he could to help those less fortunate than himself. He hadn't grown up with a lot of money and knew how much someone in his position could make a difference in another's life.

I continued to mingle. Every so often finding myself in the same circle as Kasper until one of us was pulled in another direction. Slowly, as the crowd thinned out and people started to head home, I was surrounded by friends sitting in front of the fire. Spencer had his fingers entwined with Callen's, resting his head on his shoulder. In one of the brown leather chairs, Evan sat on Vander's lap. Every so often, I'd noticed them kissing, usually with a hint of tongue. We laughed and joked about Evan coming up for air to which we'd get the one-finger salute.

When Kasper had come back into the room after walking another guest to the door, he looked tired. I thought he might have been ready to get rid of everyone and have his house back, but at Evan's urging, he sat down across from me and laughed with the crowd.

What I noticed during that time was the way Kasper reacted to the conversation. He didn't say much. He would laugh with everyone else but never offered up any of his own stories. It made me a little sad for him. He was right; I knew fame but only among baseball fans. *Everyone* was in Kasper's business, which meant that even surrounded by friends he couldn't really be himself.

Friends?

I guessed that was what Kasper and I were becoming. We'd been out for drinks and he texted me every so often asking about my PT. Something that my other friends would have done had I told them anything about my knee problem. I figured the fewer people who knew, the better. At least, the better for me.

Eventually, the party was down to only me, Kasper, Evan, and Vander. I thought about leaving a few times when I saw my teammates and friends gathering their coats, but somehow I kept getting drawn back into a new conversation and ended up staying.

Then Evan brought out the shot glasses and a bottle of vodka from behind the bar. I knew it was a bad idea, but it didn't stop me from taking the first shot Evan offered, or the third. I noticed Kasper doing the same. The only one who seemed to be able to resist Evan's charm was Vander.

He sat patiently with Evan, watching him as if Evan hung the moon. It was exactly what I wanted. That connection. Evan almost fell out of Vander's lap when he leaned forward to focus his gaze on me.

"Are you ignoring me, Marcus?" I brought my attention back to what Evan was saying. I'd been so focused on the two of them together that I hadn't listened to anything he said.

"No. I zoned out for a minute." All the lights in the room seemed to have a halo around them. The alcohol warming me from the inside. "What did you want to know?"

"Where's your date tonight, silly? Everyone deserves to have someone on their arm for New Year's and I always see someone different on your arm at functions."

"Evan," Kasper warned. "He didn't need to bring a date tonight."

"No, it's okay." I rushed to break up the stare down. "I didn't want to bring a random girl." The warmth in my chest from the liquor also helped to weaken the filter from my brain to my mouth, admitting to things I'd normally never say to anyone. "I'm tired of superficial dates. I want to be with someone who I can build a life with. Have someone on my arm who loves me as much as the two of you love each other. I want what you have."

The words off my chest, I felt a little lighter and flustered for rambling on. I reached for the bottle and poured another shot. A glass slid next to mine and I looked up to see Kasper waiting for me to fill his as well. I poured the vodka, spilling some of it onto the table and passed it back. For the briefest moment, I wondered why Kasper was all alone on New Year's, but when I looked up again, Vander and Evan were kissing for the millionth time that night. And not just kissing. Evan had spun around and was currently grinding on Vander's lap. Kasper must have noticed it the same time I did because we both lifted our shots and tipped the contents back, avoiding the show.

Vander stood up with Evan in his arms like his ass was on fire. "I think it's time for us to go."

Kasper quirked a brow in their direction. "Ya think?"

Evan's hips moved against Vander's hands. It was obvious that Evan didn't seem to mind if he had an audience at the moment. As much as I didn't want to ride the elevator down with the two lovebirds, I knew it was time for me to get home. Kasper would want his peace after such a long night.

I stood, the room spinning a bit. I braced my feet and kept myself upright. "Guess I should get going, too."

Kasper jumped up as well, grabbing the back of the couch when he stumbled a bit. "No, please stay. There's no reason for you to go out and deal with the people heading home from parties."

I gestured to Vander and Evan on their way to the door. "But you're letting them leave."

"One, Vander is sober, unlike the rest of us." Kasper glanced over his shoulder, watching as Evan cupped Vander's cheeks, kissing with a lot of tongue. Then he brought his gaze back to me. "Two, my place may be big, but I do not want to listen to them all night."

I chuckled. "Good point."

"Stay." Kasper nodded his head toward the couch. "I'll see them to the door and lock up."

I sat down and watched as Kasper left the room, his steps a bit off balance. The sound of the door closing hit my ears while I watched the fire burn. It was simple yet seemed so much more relaxing than most of the night had been. I poured another glass as Kasper came back into the room.

"I'll take another." He sat down across from me.

I filled his glass, emptying the bottle. "We finished off the bottle. The morning isn't going to be pretty."

"Probably not. But it's New Year's Day. Do you have anywhere to be tomorrow?"

"Nope."

Kasper lifted his glass in a toast and drank it back. We set the glasses down and leaned back on our respective couches. I got caught up staring at the fire when Kasper spoke up again.

"You didn't have to answer Evan's question tonight."

I shrugged my shoulders, the edges of the room a little blurrier than they had been before. "Normally, I wouldn't have, but I feel relaxed here."

"I'm glad."

Silence descended over us once again, letting the question that had been plaguing me since Evan mentioned it force its way to the surface. I turned to face Kasper, who wasn't watching the fire but was watching me. "Can I ask you a question?"

He paused for a second then nodded.

"Why didn't you have a date tonight? I figure there must be a million men lining up for you."

Kasper closed his eyes and leaned his head against the back of his seat. "I feel the same as you. I don't want a superficial relationship. One based on sex and money.

The ones who want to find their way into my arms and bed aren't the same who want long term. I've had enough of them." A bitterness had crept into Kasper's tone. The kind you only knew from experience.

"Someone hurt you." The filter from brain to mouth wasn't just weakened but had apparently left the building with my sobriety.

Kasper kept his eyes closed and there was a slight hitch in his chest. "Yes." His voice so low I almost didn't hear it. "We dated. I thought what we had was forever. But he cheated and I couldn't forgive that. Ever."

"Fuck," I muttered.

Kasper must have realized what he said because he flew out of his seat, wobbling and almost falling back down before he managed to gain his balance. "I'm ready to turn in."

"Kasper, I'm sorry. I didn't mean to pry."

He shook his head as he started turning out lights. "It's not your fault. I'm just not used to revealing personal aspects of myself. I tend to keep everything close."

I stood slowly, knowing if I didn't, I'd face-plant to the floor. I followed him to the stairs and stopped him as he placed his foot on the first one. "You know I'm your friend, right?"

His eyes searched mine. "I hoped."

He turned and, holding tightly to the railing, we both managed to make it up the stairs without falling back down. Silently, I followed him to the same room I stayed in that first night.

As he went to leave for his own room, he stopped in the doorway and glanced over his shoulder at me. "Happy New Year, Marcus."

"Happy New Year, Kasper."

He shut the door and I heard his footsteps disappear down the hall. As I climbed into bed and tried to stop the room from spinning, I wondered what this year would bring.

Chapter 8

Kasper

"Goddammit!" I slammed my hand down on the desk after reading a headline on the sports feed I kept up with while I worked.

Hunter, my ex, was engaged. Not that I didn't think one day he'd get married, but I had hoped to beat him there. No, it wasn't a competition, but my heart couldn't get on the same page. That piece of shit, lying, cheating bastard was getting married before me. How did he find love so easily when I couldn't even find someone to date seriously? It was probably one of the many guys he kept on the side. I didn't think he could be faithful for the rest of his life.

"Fuck!" I threw the cupful of pens on my desk across the room.

Pascal opened the door and stuck his head in. He noted the pen cup on the floor and the dozen or so pens lying near it. "Now what did they ever do to you?"

"Did you see it?" I asked, still seething. I wasn't mad at Paz. Never. But he knew me well enough that by coming into my office when I yelled, it was like taking his life into his own hands.

He stepped in and shut the door behind him. In no way was my office soundproof, but the only one who sat near me was Paz. His desk was right outside, so he heard me even with the door closed.

"Are you sure you don't want to try out for the Emperors?" he asked. "You have quite an arm."

My office wasn't small. It was a big, open space with dark wood bookshelves on one wall. The other had the door to my private bathroom, which included a shower and a walk-in closet. There was a long conference table that seated ten on that side of the room. My desk sat in the middle near the tall windows with my back to them. When I threw that cup, I launched it across the spacious room.

After gathering my pens and putting them back into their place in the cup on my desk, Paz sat down in front of me. I had two chairs on the other side of my desk. "Did you read the whole article?" He knew without even asking.

Paz had been with me for many years. He witnessed the up and inevitable crashing down of my relationship with Hunter. He was also someone who never bullshitted me. Paz always gave it to me straight, which I greatly appreciated.

"No." I shook my head. "I didn't get past the headline."

"Good. Don't read it."

"Now I want to know what it says."

"I'll tell you. Don't go and dig. It mentioned who his fiancé is, someone none of us have ever heard of. Apparently, someone from his past. Blah blah blah, fuck him. Anyway, that's not what I didn't want you to read. Seems him getting engaged has the press dredging up your past relationship with him, so you're mentioned in the article."

"When did you read it?"

"An hour ago." Paz had an alert set so that anytime my name, my company's name, the Jetties, anything that pertained to me was mentioned, he knew about it. He was probably more in tune with what the media said than our PR department.

"Why didn't you tell me?"

"And deal with this an hour go? I was eating. I knew once you heard, my lunch would be long forgotten. You know I love food." Paz wasn't heartless. In fact, he had one of the biggest hearts of anyone I knew. He was trying to lighten my mood.

"Paz," I groaned and rubbed my hands over my face. "I don't want to deal with this."

"There is nothing for you to deal with. The media will find something else to latch on to soon enough. Hunter will be long forgotten."

"You know he's eating up the attention."

"That I have no doubt of."

Hunter was the kind of guy who was born to be a celebrity. He loved the fame. But that didn't mean he was a shit hockey player. No, he was damn good. No matter how much I hated him, I couldn't forget the power he had on the ice.

My phone vibrated on my desk. I dreaded looking to see who was texting me. That article had been out there for an hour. Plenty of time to get around. Luckily, only friends and family had my personal number. And those who wanted to talk to me at work had to go through Paz. He even had someone who worked for him to help with administrative tasks and backup phone support. That was how it was easy for Paz to be in here with me. And travel with me. And basically have no life outside of me. I really needed to give him another raise. Or a vacation. His entire trip, wherever he wanted to go away to, I'd happily pay for.

"You have that look again," he said.

"What look?"

"The 'I'm a hard-ass boss and Pascal deserves so much more' look." Fuck, he really knew me well.

"I do not."

He rolled his eyes dramatically. "Whatever you say. And before you offer, I'm not taking a vacation this year until you do."

I scoffed, "So, you're going to live and breathe work three-sixty-five, twenty-four seven? Hell no, Paz."

"You need a vacation, Kasper."

I grunted in response. I did need one. That didn't mean I was going to take it.

"Since you won't be going anywhere like an island with no internet, I arranged for a dinner for you tonight."

"I don't feel like dealing with anyone."

"This isn't what you think. It's not business but pleasure." He got this wicked gleam in his eyes.

"What did you do?"

"Something that will make you happy."

"I wonder what your version of making me happy is right now."

He scoffed, "It's like you forget who I am. I know you, Kas. As much as anyone else close to you does."

"Yet you skipped out on my New Year's Eve party." I couldn't help the dig. He had a previous engagement with friends, prior to me deciding to throw a party.

"Holy shit, still? I told you I had plans."

"Uh huh."

He shook his head and smiled. "Whatever. You're not going to divert my attention. You have reservations at Reese's at seven." I started to open my mouth but he held up a hand so I wouldn't cut him off. "Chef's table. No one will see you but Reese and Mari."

For all the shit Paz put up with, he still took good care of me. He knew me inside and out. Knew what I needed before I did. I had a feeling tonight would be no different. Whatever he did, I was sure it would make me feel better, if even for a little while.

"You're not going to tell me who I'm meeting?" I didn't like to dine alone. If I were going out to eat, I wanted someone to talk to, relax with, which left very few on the list of people who could be joining me tonight.

"It's a surprise and not the blowjob under the table kind."

"Fuck's sake," I muttered. "Fine."

He nodded. "Park around back. I know you don't want to be seen out tonight."

My need for privacy was high at the moment after hearing about my name all over the media again and not for the reasons I wanted it to be. I'd take good press any day, but that wasn't what was happening.

A knock on the door had us drawing our attention toward it. "Come in," I called.

Alivia, the woman who was Pascal's assistant, peeked her head in. Her orangish red hair was cut short. She had the look of someone completely fragile and innocent, which was the furthest thing from the truth. I'd heard her put someone in their place more times than I could count. People didn't work this close to me if they didn't have a backbone.

"Brick is here for your meeting," she said to me.

"Thank you. Give me five minutes then send him in."

She nodded and left, closing the door quietly behind her.

"Tell me who I'm meeting." I figured I'd try again.

"That's why you're making Brick wait?" Paz laughed. "I have too much work to do." He stood from the chair and went to the door, not paying attention to the number of times I asked him to reveal who my dinner was with as he walked away.

I still hadn't calmed all the way down by the time Brick entered the room.

"Tough day?" he asked. His charcoal suit was perfectly pressed and accentuated his light blue eyes.

"I take it you saw the article."

"I did. I know you're not still hung up on him, so what's really getting to you?" Brick had to have seen the anger on my face. The tension in my shoulders. The way I held my damn pen to the point I thought it was going to snap.

"He's getting married before me."

Brick snorted out a laugh. "Who gives a fuck? It's not like you had some unspoken competition with him where whoever got married first won. Kas, the man is a piece of shit. Sure, he plays hockey well, but there is nothing else of value to him. And for the way he hurt you, he's lucky I didn't show up on his doorstep and knock his teeth down his throat."

"You know I love it when you threaten violence on others on my behalf."

He smiled. "That I do."

Brick wasn't all bluster. If I would have let him, he would have put some serious hurt on Hunter. Brick was six foot even and spent his mornings before work in the gym.

Letting the topic of Hunter drop, Brick got down to business. I welcomed the opportunity to talk about something else.

My friends were in my life for a reason. As pissed as I was hearing Hunter was getting married, Brick was right. It didn't matter. I had my own life to live.

The rest of the day went by quickly and I stayed in the office until I had to leave for dinner. If I went home first, I wouldn't want to leave again.

My stomach growled, reminding me I skipped lunch today. Maybe going to dinner wasn't such a bad idea. I could use the meal, even if I had no idea who I was dining with.

I didn't think it was Evan. He was the one who texted me earlier. Followed by Spencer and Stockton.

As I drove to the restaurant, I thought about my brother. He was back in California. I missed him already. While we didn't see each other every day while he was here, it was at least every weekend. Having him and his family here made things better. Not so lonely.

I pulled up behind the restaurant and parked. I had taken my Audi Q8 out this morning since there was snow on the ground. The city streets were plowed well by the time I left home, but I didn't want to get salt all over my car. Plus, the Audi SUV had all-wheel drive.

When I approached the back door to the restaurant, Mari was there with a smile, holding the door open for me.

"Mari, hi," I said and leaned down to hug her. She was a good eight inches shorter than me.

Mari's mom and I had been friends most of our lives. Stockton knew her as well and loved her like I did. She knew me before I was on a magazine cover or in news articles. But over the years, we didn't stay in touch as much as we should have. Reese was busy running her restaurants. She had one here, as well as ones in New York City and Philadelphia. Her home base was Philly, so she wasn't here as often. And with me running my businesses, our schedules rarely aligned. It was more like we'd been friends, but we'd drifted apart over the years. Not because of an argument or falling out, but because of life.

If Paz sent me here tonight, it meant Reese was in town.

Mari walked with me back to the chef's table in its private room. The way Reese had it set up, it wasn't in view of the kitchen staff. It was much more secluded.

As I stepped into the room, I came to a stop and my breath faltered.

Marcus stood. "Kasper, hi." He looked a little shy. Something I'd never seen him like before.

Was he remembering the night a couple weeks ago when we got drunk well into the morning and I mentioned Hunter? Not by name of course, but I let slip I was once with someone seriously. Though, all it would take was a simple internet search to find out who was in my past.

"Hey, good to see you." I walked forward and took a seat near him as he sat as well. I wasn't about to sit at the far end of an eight person table. Mari took our drink orders and asked Marcus if he had any allergies or if there were any foods he didn't care for. He said no to both and she left us.

"I'm guessing I don't get to pick my food tonight?" he asked with a smile.

"Not when Reese is cooking. She's not in town much, but when she is and I come here, I'm not allowed to have a menu. She feeds me what she feels like."

"So you know the owner, then?" I nodded. "I figured when I was escorted back here to eat."

"I'm sorry Pascal dragged you out tonight."

Marcus cocked his head a little. "Why are you sorry? He said you could use a friend and I'm happy he called, though I wasn't sure how he got my number." I felt guilty for interrupting his evening.

"You didn't have any other plans, did you?"

"Just to eat dinner alone and do the exercises Spencer gave me. I'm not exactly living the life."

I smiled and it felt good. It was the first time I had all day. "Thank you," I said softly. "Also, Paz has access to everything of mine and if he didn't get your number from my contacts, my guess is Evan gave it to him. I hope you don't mind."

"Not at all."

Before we could continue our conversation, the door to the room opened and Mari came in with drinks, followed by Reese with two plates of appetizers. I immediately stood and took them from her to set on the table.

Reese's hair was dirty blonde and pulled up in a messy bun. She was dressed nice in a pair of black slacks and a fuchsia sweater. We hugged and stood close after, me keeping my hand cupped on her elbow.

"You're not cooking tonight?" I asked.

"I am but didn't think you'd want to hug me with the jacket I wore covered in food."

"You know I don't care about that." Clothes could be cleaned or replaced. I wouldn't miss hugging a friend because I could get dirty.

"Well, I care. Besides, I'm not cooking for everyone in the restaurant. Just you two."

"You didn't have to do that." I was going to have words with Paz tomorrow if Reese came in specifically for me.

"Don't even think it," she chastised, apparently reading my mind. "Paz called to see if I were around. I immediately offered to cook. I was here visiting Mari and checking in on the restaurant."

"Fine, but don't go to any trouble. Everything you make is good. We don't need something special."

She scoffed then turned to Marcus without replying to me. Holding out her hand, she introduced herself, which was something I should have done. "Reese Rockford, nice to meet you."

Marcus stood and shook her hand. "Marcus Warnes. You have a great place. I've been here a few times. The food is always amazing."

"Next time you come, ask for me or Mari. If I'm not here, she is. She runs this place, even when I'm here and cooking." She winked at her daughter.

Reese had Mari early in life when she was only seventeen. At forty-two now, Reese didn't look like the mom of a twenty-five-year-old. She looked young herself.

"Thank you. I'll do that." Marcus smiled warmly.

The moment Reese and Mari left, Marcus and I settled into comfortable conversation. It was kept light, which I appreciated. No talk of Hunter. I had no doubt Marcus knew. If he were like the other ballplayers and hockey players I knew, he followed many different teams and sports. Hunter making the news today wasn't going to be buried unless something major happened. Tomorrow, hopefully some other big, exciting news knocked him off his pedestal, but I wasn't stupid enough to hope for that tonight.

Dinner was fantastic and so was dessert. We stayed long after the plates were cleared away and shared stories of our youth and how we got involved in the sports we were in. Even though we were in different areas, him a player and me an owner, we had a lot in common.

By the end of the night, as we walked out into the crisp, cold New Jersey winter air, I realized I parked a few spaces down from Marcus. I didn't notice his SUV earlier. We both stood awkwardly for a moment. I wasn't sure if I should shake his hand to thank him for coming out tonight. What I wanted to do was wrap him in my arms and find out how the wine he had tonight tasted on his lips. Instead, I settled for a smile as we agreed to have dinner again soon.

Marcus was almost fully into my inner circle. The question was, what was I going to do once he got there? He was straight and much younger than me. Someone I desired on a primal level, even though I shouldn't. And with every encounter, he was coming to mean more and more to me. I was so fucked and not in a good way.

Chapter 9

Marcus

Sweat dripped down my temple. I loved the burn in my muscles as I pushed the weights above my head for the final rep of the day. Sitting up, I set the weights on the floor and grabbed the towel I'd left at the end of the table to wipe the sweat from my face.

Spencer still didn't want me to run, but there were plenty of other workouts he'd given me to strengthen my knees. This time of year would usually be filled with a lot of cardio for me. Anything to make up for all the holiday foods I'd spent the last month indulging in. With cardio on hold, I had to use weights to do the job.

The pain in my knee was practically gone. Something I was incredibly thankful for. With only about three weeks before pitchers and catchers would need to report for spring training, I finally felt like I was on track to return at a hundred percent. And no one in the clubhouse would be any the wiser about the issues I had at the end of last season.

I twisted the cap off a bottle of water when my phone started ringing from the other side of the room. The minute I saw *Brat* on the screen I answered.

"Hey, brat. What's up?"

Sienna groaned and I could practically hear the eye roll through the phone, along with a chuckle. "I could be ninety-years old and you'd still call me brat."

"Yep. You will always be younger than me." I wandered out of the workout room then farther down the hall to my bedroom.

"By like eighteen months, Marc."

My hand froze as I reached for the dresser. Only two people had ever called me Marc. One of whom decided I wasn't worth his time anymore. "You know I don't like that name," I snapped, struggling to keep the annoyance out of my voice.

I couldn't really blame her for saying it. For the first sixteen years of her life, that was all she'd called me. Then jealousy destroyed a friendship and I couldn't stand hearing that name anymore.

"You do realize it's been ten years since Zach dumped your friendship because you got the scholarship and he didn't, right?"

I snatched a clean pair of boxers out of the drawer. "And it's also been ten years since I've gone by anything other than Marcus."

She huffed. "Fine. If it will make you feel better, Marcus. I actually just called to see if you were going to head home at some point before you had to report to spring training."

I scrubbed a hand down my face. The attitude prominent in her voice. "I'm sorry. It's been a rough couple of weeks. I didn't mean to take it out on you. But things are looking up."

"Is this about the knee?"

"Partly. The knee is getting better. But watching my teammates in these serious relationships... I guess I'm just tired of being alone all the time."

Sienna giggled and it was nice to hear the happiness seep back into her tone. "You do realize you need to date if you don't want to be lonely. You're never going to find someone amongst the cleat chasers."

"Don't I know it. Look at all the shit Ayden had to deal with," I scoffed. "But I haven't had a lot of time for dating. Between physical therapy and hanging out with Kasper, plus the outside of therapy workouts, my days are a little crazy."

"Who's Kasper?"

I almost smacked myself in the head. How did I forget to tell Sienna I had become friends with Kasper Wilder? She was going to lose it. According to her, he was one of the sexist men on the planet. She didn't care how much older he was or that he wasn't into women. In her mind, it was perfectly acceptable to drool over magazine covers.

"Callen and Spencer introduced me to Kasper Wilder a few months back and I've been hanging out with him a bunch since then."

"Holy fucking shit! You mean *the* Kasper Wilder?"

"One and the same."

"You asshole. How did you not tell me this before? It would have given me the perfect reason to fly out and visit you."

I chuckled. "Maybe it's a good thing I didn't tell you."

"Shut up. Is he as hot in person as he is on a magazine cover?"

Surprisingly enough, I actually had an answer for her. "He is." Never in my life had I noticed if a guy was hot, but I had to agree with my sister on this one. Kasper was an attractive man.

"See? Even for the ladies' man to notice, he has to be hot." She laughed then sobered. "We'll definitely be talking about this later, but I have to leave for a shoot in a few minutes. Now, are you coming home before you head to Florida?" After college, Sienna decided to use her design degree to become a photographer.

"Yeah. I figured I'd come for a week and fly home on that Friday so I have the weekend to pack before my flight on Sunday night."

The echo of her hands clapping together reached my ears. "Perfect. I have plans for us."

"Oh god, what trouble are you going to get us into this time?"

"None, but I'm not telling you what we're doing either."

"Fess up, Sienna."

"Oh, look at that, I have to run. I'll see you soon."

Before I could continue my protest, the other side of the line went dead. My sister and I were close, and I knew she had something up her sleeve. But I also knew she wouldn't give up a thing, which meant I'd just have to wait until I got there to find out what insanity awaited me.

I flipped on *Sports Center* in my bedroom while I waited for the water to warm up in the shower. There was still a couple of hours before I was supposed to meet Callen and Ayden for drinks.

It would be nice to relax together before Ayden Thompson and I had to spend an extra grueling week in spring training while everyone else had the time off. As the star of the starting pitchers, Ayden would want to push himself when we got to Florida, so I'd get to join in the fun, too, at least while we practiced.

I was toweling off after my shower when the mention of the Espen Emperors from the TV caught my attention. I scrubbed the towel over my hair and walked back into the bedroom. There was a picture in the middle of the screen. I couldn't believe what I was seeing and hearing.

Today, the Espen Emperors made an interesting move in preparation of the upcoming season. In a surprise to everyone, the Emperors have signed free agent catcher, Micah Pena, for a—

I muted the TV, unable to listen to any more, simply staring at the picture of the man on the screen. Another catcher? My heart raced in my chest. Doing the math on the salaries in my head, I tried to imagine what they might be able to offer me next year. But everything in my brain was too much of a mess to put the numbers together.

It took me a few minutes to realize that my phone was vibrating in my hand. I hadn't even remembered picking it up. There were already a few missed calls from my agent, plus multiple calls and texts from Callen and Dominic. My agent I'd deal with tomorrow. I needed to process everything first before I went to him so we could figure out how this impacted me. I texted Dominic that I'd call him tomorrow.

Next, I opened Callen's text, ignoring his pleas to pick up the phone. My mood for going out with them tonight had disappeared in an instant.

Me: Not really feeling like going out tonight. Talk later.

Not even a second passed before my phone lit up again.

Callen: That move doesn't mean shit. Call me!

I dropped the phone onto my bed and went to get dressed. No longer needing the jeans I'd grabbed, I tossed them back in the drawer and pulled on a pair of track pants and a long-sleeved T-shirt.

Callen knew me well enough. When I didn't answer, he would give me space. There was no doubt he'd be beating down my door tomorrow with Dominic and probably Ayden in tow. And I would deal with them both then. For now, I didn't want to be around anyone. It wasn't like I would be good company. Barefoot, I padded out to the living room.

A few hours later, as I sat on the couch staring out of the floor-to-ceiling windows along one side of my living room, beer in hand, I decided I didn't really want to be alone any longer. But I didn't want to deal with my teammates either. The desire for someone to talk to and take my mind off the disaster of the day settled in my chest. Without really thinking about the why, I picked up my phone and sent a text. The response was almost instantaneous.

Kasper: I'll be there in a half hour.

I set the phone back down and waited. True to his word, a knock sounded on my door thirty minutes later. I'd already warned the front desk security that Kasper would be arriving soon. When I opened the door, he held a pack of my favorite IPA, the same one I'd had at his house on New Year's Eve.

"I thought you might want a drink."

I reached out and took the package from his hand. "You would be right. Let me put this in the fridge. Whiskey neat?"

"Please."

I led Kasper to the living room and quickly went to the kitchen to get our drinks. Kasper had already made himself comfortable on the couch when I returned. His jacket and tie discarded on the recliner and the top few buttons of his shirt opened. I handed him the glass and took a seat at the other end of the couch, turning to the side to face him.

He nodded toward the discarded jacket. "Sorry, I was still at the office when you texted me."

"Don't be. Thank you for coming over."

"I'd already seen the news when I got your text. I figured you could use the company. Are you okay?"

"No." I lifted the beer to my lips and took a nice, long pull from the bottle. "But I want that to be tomorrow's problem. Tonight, I want to talk about anything besides my career in baseball."

Kasper swirled the liquor around in his glass. "And I guess your friends would only want to talk about it?"

"Yes and no. Eventually, they'd stop, but I knew hanging out with you would make it easier to focus on something else."

"Let me say one thing. As an owner, those moves mean nothing in terms of your contract." Kasper took a sip of his drink. "With that being said, what would you like to talk about?"

"Thanks. Well, since you brought up being an owner, what made you buy the Jetties? I know you told me about playing hockey as a kid and loving the sport, but you already owned your aviation company. Why did you get into owning a team?"

Kasper turned his body, bending one leg on the couch to face me. "The aviation company was my first jump into being a business owner. My dad loved to fly, and in turn, I loved it as well, having grown up around planes with my parents and brother. Dad was a successful businessman himself, but his investments were smaller yet still very fruitful. He went into the aviation industry with me. He put up the money once I graduated college. We built something from the ground up. Together."

"Can you fly?"

"No, I never had a desire to. The business side was what excited me."

"I'm sure he was proud of you."

Kasper nodded. "He was. But back to your original question, once I had grown the company into what it is today, I had made quite a name for myself. When the Jetties became available for sale, I thought why not. I'd played hockey in middle and high school. I was never good enough to get a scholarship or go pro but it was fun. I already knew how to run a business and the Jetties gave me a new challenge by adding in a professional sports team."

"Do you miss it? Playing?"

"Sometimes, but I could never do what the players do. The grace and agility they show, the sheer power and skill they have, it's a sight to behold."

"It's a way more fast-paced sport than baseball." And just like that, my brain was right back where I was trying to avoid. The beer in my stomach started to sour.

"Tell me more about your sister."

When I looked up again, Kasper watched me expectantly. Somehow, over the last few months, he learned how to read me better than many could. He knew without me making a move or saying a word exactly what I was thinking.

"Sienna? I just got off the phone with the brat earlier."

Kasper chuckled. "It makes me laugh that you're both adults and you still call her a brat."

I laughed along with him. "She said something similar, but I'm pretty sure she wasn't laughing. Just arguing that I was only eighteen months older."

"Oh, she even broke out the extra months? She must have been serious."

The straight face Kasper held had me laughing even harder. I had a feeling he didn't let many people see this side of himself, but I was glad that he'd opened up to me.

"Very serious. Hopefully, she's nice when I fly out for the week before spring training." I winked.

"Hopefully."

We spent the rest of the night talking and joking about my trip to see my family and anything else that had nothing to do with baseball. By the time Kasper left,

I felt lighter than I had before I'd seen *Sports Center* and I knew I had Kasper to thank for that.

Chapter 10

Kasper

By the time I got home it was nearly eleven. I wasn't tired, but I couldn't exactly stay with Marcus all night talking either. I wanted to. I could have easily learned more about the man I was growing to care about. But that wasn't something we did in our friendship. At least, not when we were sober, which I was. I only had one drink earlier.

And that was the crux of the issue. He wasn't just a friend, not to me. Sure, on his end that was how he saw me. I, on the other hand, was developing strong feelings for Marcus. It was beyond lust at this point. The more I got to know him, the more I wanted to be with him. To spend more time with him.

"Fuck," I muttered as I scrubbed a hand over my face. I was lying in bed with the lights out, staring at the ceiling as if it held all the answers.

Reaching over, I grabbed my phone off the nightstand and sent a text to Evan. I wasn't sure if he was still awake since he had to work at the school tomorrow.

Me: Any time tomorrow for a friend?

The reply was almost immediate.

Evan: Always. Stop by before I leave for work. Vander will still be asleep. Bring breakfast, then I'll let you drive me to work.

Me: How gracious of you.

Evan: I know! Anyway, I need to get some sleep. You're lucky I was still awake. Well, I was lucky because Vander was doing some pretty phenomenal things to my ass. We just finished when you texted.

Me: Fuck's sake, Ev. Goodnight.

Evan: Night, Kas.

I wasn't sure how late I stayed up after that. I avoided looking at the clock. If I checked it, then I would countdown how little sleep I'd get. I had meetings late morning and throughout the afternoon.

Eventually, I drifted off to sleep with Marcus on my mind, exactly where he shouldn't have been.

***

Bright and early the next morning, with a minimal amount of sleep, I was in the elevator on my way up to Vander's condo. The man had chosen a nice building to live in. It wasn't flashy or screaming money. It suited Vander really well. He wasn't someone who liked to flaunt what he had, outside of Evan, that is.

I knocked on the door and it was quickly opened by Evan. He was dressed in a pair of dark track pants and a loose, long-sleeved T-shirt. Seeing Evan like this, no one would guess how he dressed when he went out to the clubs or when he was out on the town with Vander. Flashy Evan wasn't present at school, though that didn't mean he hid the rest of his personality or the man he loved. His students knew about his relationship with Vander and most were happy for them.

"Morning," Evan said as he shut the door quietly behind him.

Dropping a bag on the counter, Evan didn't wait a full minute before he was diving in to it to see what I brought him. He pulled out two large containers and popped the lids on both.

"I'm guessing the bacon one is mine?" he asked.

"Mmm hmm." He needed to eat better than he did and usually I'd push him on that, but I came here seeking his advice. Bacon would butter him up.

He grabbed a couple forks from the drawer and handed me one. He waved his hand over my container. "That has too much green going on for me to like it." He scrunched up his nose.

"God forbid you eat spinach," I deadpanned.

"Don't say the dreaded S-word in this house," Vander muttered as he came into the room still in sleep pants that hung low on his hips. He was shirtless and reminded me why I'd lusted after athletes. I had to wonder if Marcus looked that good shirtless up close. Sculpted to perfection.

Fingers snapped in front of my face. "You better not be doing what I think you are," Evan said with a touch of irritation in his voice.

"Appreciating your man?"

"Yeah, that."

"What if I were but also thinking about someone else who I really shouldn't be?"

Without missing a beat, Vander yawned and said, "You should visit us in the locker room once the season starts, Kasper. Then you could get a great view of what Marcus has to offer."

It shouldn't surprise me Vander knew I had a thing for his teammate. After all, Evan didn't keep secrets from Vander. I just had to hope it didn't get back to Marcus. Evan assured me I could trust his boyfriend, but that trust wasn't something I easily gave.

I groaned. "Who else knows?"

"No one," Evan replied. "I don't think Spencer and Callen have figured it out yet. Marcus sure as hell doesn't have a clue."

"I only know because Evan wondered if Marcus was bi," Vander stated as he filled a glass with water.

I pushed my untouched breakfast toward him. "Here. I didn't think you'd be up or I would have gotten you something."

He waved me off. "I'm going back to bed. I need more sleep." He walked over and kissed Evan's temple then dragged his feet as he went back up the hall.

Evan poured us each a cup of coffee then motioned toward the breakfast bar where we sat and ate. At first, we were quiet. I still couldn't wrap my head around everything I was feeling.

Evan was simply waiting me out, letting me take the lead. But I took too long and he couldn't take it anymore.

"Okay, since you're obviously not going to start spilling, I'm just going to get right to the point. I think you and Marcus could be really good together. He seems like he's lonely, and I rarely see him with a woman on his arm. Sure, when he needs a date for an event or something but no one ever serious. And I've witnessed how well you two get along. You two could build something special."

"Except you're leaving out one crucial part: he's not gay."

"Gay schmay. He doesn't need a label. He definitely has some sort of feelings for you. What I can't figure out is what they are exactly. Now tell me why you needed to come here this morning instead of just hashing this out over text."

I ate another bite of my veggie omelet. It gave me a minute to formulate my thoughts. Not that anything was going to change. I'd been thinking too much lately. Way more than I should about a straight ballplayer. I had businesses to run. Yet Marcus occupied so much of my mind.

Putting the fork down, I turned on the stool and faced my best friend. "What do I do, Ev? I don't have many choices here. I could bury my feelings and never broach anything more than friends with Marcus. I could continue lusting after him in the hopes that one day he'll miraculously find me attractive, even though he's never been with a guy before nor shown any interest in one. Or I lay it all out there and tell him I want him. The third option isn't one worth considering. I don't think I could ever say that."

"Well, that and you'd scare him away. We don't want him to pull back from you. We want him closer."

"I love spending time with him. He's comfortable, easy to speak to. We get along great."

"Comfortable doesn't make for dick on dick love."

I rolled my eyes, which was a total Evan move, but it was only us, so I didn't give a shit. "You don't fucking say."

He pointed his fork at me. "No need to get testy with me." Then he chuckled. "Testy. Testes. Balls. Did I ever tell you how much I love sucking on Vander's sac?"

"Enough," I cut him off. "There are some things I don't need to know."

"Nonsense. You're my best friend and I like to share."

"Share with Spencer."

Evan scrunched up his nose. "I love that man, but he's only gay for Callen. You have experienced many gay men, so you can relate to how glorious balls can be when they're in someone else's mouth."

"Thanks for making me sound like a slut."

"Please. You and I both know that's not the case."

"Can we get back on topic?"

"We can but I have a feeling you're not getting your balls sucked like you should be." He winked and took another bite of his omelet.

We finished up breakfast and I downed the rest of my coffee. I got nothing accomplished by coming to see Evan this morning, outside of his good company. No matter how much he might drive me up a wall at times, I loved him fiercely. I'd do anything for him. And him being in my life was one of the best things I had.

"What did you drive today?" he asked as we walked toward the parking deck.

"The Aston Martin."

"Oh, good," he all but purred. "I want you to drop me off like I'm one of the students."

I turned toward him. "Why the hell would I do that?"

"You're Kasper Wilder!" he said loudly as his voice echoed through the space. "To have you dropping me off at school will give everyone something to talk about. Plus, it's not every day someone rides up in a car like yours."

"Do you want me to get out and open the door for you when we get there?" Sarcasm dripped from my voice.

Evan's eyes widened, not caring that I wasn't serious. "Yes! Do that! It will piss off some of the other parents in line, since they're supposed to drop and go, but maybe you could bend over a little and give them a view they won't soon forget."

I shook my head and got into my car.

So, there I was, sitting in the car line at Espen High, waiting for our turn to drop off. Evan was bouncing in his seat like a kid waiting to see Santa.

Next thing I knew, he pulled out his phone and leaned close to me.

"What are you doing?" I asked as I stopped again. We slowly inched forward toward the school.

"If you think I'm not taking a selfie with you and posting how my daddy is dropping me off at school, you're sorely mistaken."

I reeled back. "You're what?"

"Shut up and go with it."

"It's a good thing you have Vander to protect you," I muttered.

"Empty threats. Now get back over here and smile."

I leaned in but there was no way I was smiling because Evan was going to write that in the caption on social media. I had no doubt.

My phone pinged with the tag and I waited until we moved up in line again before looking at it. If I were easily embarrassed, this was a time I would have turned bright red. But I wasn't and this was par for the course being friends with Evan. He liked to have fun and knew I was in a hard spot. So, while he wouldn't come out and admit it, he did this for me as much as he did for himself. And it worked. It was a hell of a distraction.

"Seriously?" I asked.

He beamed. "You read the hashtags?"

"Yes, the #kasperismydaddy and #bigdaddykas are especially lovely," I drolled.

There was also #kasperwilderismybff, #vanderknowsandiscoolwithit, #evanandkaspersdropoff, #mychauffeur, #arrivinginstyle, #eatyourheartout, and #wilderisntjustanameitsalifestyle.

"Oh my god!" he exclaimed. "Do you think we can get Big Daddy Kas to trend? I need to post this on my other sites to cover all the bases."

"Sure. We wouldn't want you to forget to do that. Katie is going to have a field day with this, by the way."

"Please. Katie loves social media. We follow each other, so she's bound to see it."

"Of course. It makes sense that the Jetties' PR person follows my best friend."

"I can hear that sarcasm in your voice again, Kasper Wilder. Don't think I missed it."

My phone vibrating with social media alerts from Facebook, Twitter, and Instagram kept me from replying. But it was the text from Paz that caused me to mute the thing.

Pascal: What the hell is this?

Pascal: *attached screenshot of Evan's Instagram post, including the photo and hashtags*

Pascal: *attached picture of himself laughing with tears running down his face*

"I need to fire Paz," I said aloud.

Evan took my phone from my hand and started laughing. "This is fantastic."

I stole my phone back and continued to move up in line. By the time we got to our turn, Evan pivoted in the seat with expectant eyes.

"Only you," I growled low. "No video or photos."

He smiled wide. "None."

I put the car in park and got out, rounding the hood and going to Evan's side to open the door for him.

He stepped out with a flourish then hugged me tight and kissed me on the cheek. "Thank you, Daddy."

I grumbled and resisted the urge to growl at him again as I stalked back to the driver's side. As quickly and as safely as possible, I left the drop off line and made my way back toward downtown so I could get to work. My phone had more text messages coming in, but I ignored them until I parked in my spot at the Jetties' arena.

There were more texts from Paz as well as others from Callen and Spencer. But it was the text from Marcus that made me smile.

Marcus: Big Daddy Kas?

Me: Don't ask.

He didn't reply right away and my nerves set in, which was not something I was used to feeling, so I texted him again.

Me: You're not going to laugh?

Marcus: Oh, I am. I'm just hiding it... Big Daddy.

I groaned loudly. I wasn't sure if it was because Evan gave ammo to everyone to tease me with or because there was a part of me that wanted Marcus to call me that in bed. I wasn't a daddy, not by any means, but Marcus could call me whatever he wanted as long as he was mine.

I shook those thoughts away. They wouldn't do me any good.

Me: Now that I know where you live, I can kill you in your sleep.

Marcus: No way! Big Daddy Kas in my bed?!

Me: I hate you.

Marcus: Nah, you love me.

If he only knew just how deep my feelings for him were beginning to run.

Chapter 11
Marcus

Enjoy your trip.

I saw the text from Kasper right as I was about to board the plane. The gate attendant waited with her hand out and a perky smile on her face. I handed her my ticket and watched as her short, blonde bob bounced when she gestured through the door. I shoved my phone into my pocket as I started down the jetway. It would be easier to answer Kasper once I got onto the plane. The flight attendant showed me to my window seat. After stowing my bag in the overhead compartment, I settled in for the short flight home.

I tugged my phone out of my pocket and put my headphones in. Before I could find something to watch, I needed to answer Kasper. His text still sat on my screen. People continued to board the flight, but I kept my focus on my phone. I never expected to feel a little bummed about leaving Espen when I was heading home to my parents, even if it were only for a week. I'd miss Kasper's company.

Me: Thanks, Big Daddy.

I could practically hear him groan in my head. Ever since Evan had posted that picture a couple of weeks ago, I found myself unable to stop teasing Kasper about it when we texted. Even if he didn't want to admit it, I knew it made him laugh. A cloud hung over Kasper. I didn't know what it was, but it was there in his eyes. There was a weariness in them I hadn't seen when we first met. And if making jokes was a way to brighten his day just a little bit, then I was in for it.

Kasper: I'm never going to live that down, am I?

Me: Maybe... eventually... LOL!

Kasper: You fly back Friday, right?

Marcus: Yeah. My flight gets in around seven.

Kasper: Text me when you land in Cleveland. I have a strange question for you.

The pilot's voice filled the cabin, asking us to put our devices on airplane mode. It didn't really give me a chance to think about what question Kasper had. I sent one last text that I'd text him when I landed before turning my phone off and pulling out my tablet. The flight was a little over an hour. Enough time to catch up on my favorite show.

Halfway through the second episode, the notification came that it was time to turn off our devices and put the tray tables up. I turned the tablet off and put it back into my bag. I sat back and glanced out the window, watching the city below us grow larger and larger. Minutes later, we were on the ground waiting to disembark. The second I stepped out of the terminal, I immediately scanned the room for my parents. I stopped dead at the sight before me.

Mr. Swinger.

Jesus fucking Christ. My sister stood in the middle of the Cleveland airport holding a sign that said Mr. Swinger. When I could get my feet working again, I raced toward her and grabbed the sign. It shouldn't have surprised me, but somehow she always managed to catch me off guard.

"Shit, Sienna."

She doubled over, laughing so hard she couldn't even stand straight to walk. I stood watching her with my arms crossed over my chest, knowing we were drawing a crowd. It was normal to get requests for autographs when people realized I was in the airport. I'd gotten used to being recognized, but this was something else altogether. Most of the time, people had to see me as I walked through to the baggage claim. This time, Sienna's outburst of laughter was drawing the crowd all on its own.

"You should see your face right now. I must've really got you if you're using my first name." She wiped the tears from her eyes.

"Funny. But I think you just increased our time at the airport by at least a half an hour." I discreetly nodded my head at the few people who started to approach.

She shrugged. "Totally worth it."

I wouldn't admit it to her, but she was right. The sign was hilarious and totally Sienna. Honestly, had I been picking her up, I might have done something very similar.

"Then, you can go get my bag from baggage claim while I sign this stuff."

A young boy with an Espen Emperors baseball cap had almost reached us.

"You can't tell him no."

"Never, but I also don't want to have to go to security to pick up my bag when it isn't claimed."

"Didn't think about that."

She took the escalator down and I turned to face the boy with a smile on my face. Hopefully, some day that boy would have the same chances I had.

About forty minutes later, we stepped out into the cold Ohio air on our way to Sienna's car. I tugged the edges of my jacket closed. "Shit. I always forget how much colder it is here this time of year."

Sienna shook her head as she unlocked the doors to her car. "You've gotten weak living in New Jersey all this time."

"And California before that." I tossed my bags into the back seat of her SUV, knowing the trunk was probably filled with her photography equipment.

I'd entered the draft at the end of my senior year at Notre Dame. My parents had made me promise to finish school so I'd have something to fall back on if I needed it. The California Redwoods drafted me. Two years later, I was traded to Espen and it was my dream city ever since.

"Ugh. It's a wonder you can survive any temperature below fifty."

"Very funny, brat. Mom and Dad failed to mention that you'd be the one picking me up." She glanced at me out of the corner of her eye as she pulled onto the highway to take us to Carson Run.

"Pretty sure if you check your messages, you had advance notice." A smirk lifted the corner of her mouth.

"Shit, I never turned my phone back on when I got off the plane." I reached into my pocket and flipped it back on.

The notifications started immediately. They always did when I flew home. My social media pages lighting up with tags from all the pictures and autographs in the airport. A few texts waited right below it. One from my mom, warning me Sienna was on her way to the airport to pick me up. Too bad I hadn't read that sooner, then I'd have been prepared. There were a couple from Kasper. The last one from ten minutes ago.

Kasper: You should have landed already. I'm starting to worry. I know how planes work better than most.

Totally my bad. It was probably better to call him at this point. I reached forward and turned down my sister's favorite radio station, hitting send on the call at the same time. And maybe just a little was the payback of talking to Kasper while my sister was in the car.

"Who are you calling?" I smirked at her and waited for the other end to connect.

"Full disclosure, I had Paz checking into your flight to make sure it landed safely." The fact that he jumped right into the conversation told me how worried he had been.

"Sorry, Kasper. I forgot to turn my phone back on." The whole car jerked forward and quickly threw us back again. I turned to Sienna. "Are you trying to kill us?"

"Who's trying to kill you?" Kasper's growly voice came over the line at the same time Sienna snarled at me.

"You're the one talking to Kasper Wilder while in the car with me."

A laughed escaped my lips. "My sister, Sienna, is trying to kill me because I decided to call you and she thinks you're hot. Seemed like pretty good payback."

Kasper let out a breath and chuckled. I could hear Sienna mumbling under her breath about paying me back later. "Okay. But what are you paying her back for?"

"She decided it was a good idea to wait for me at the airport with a sign that said Mr. Swinger on it."

Kasper's chuckles turned into great, gusty shouts of laughter. "Mr. Swinger?"

I smiled. I really liked hearing him happy. "Guess I'm not living that one down for a while."

"Maybe not ever."

"Looks like we both have our own names now." I settled against the seat.

"I think yours may be better, but thank you for calling. I really was starting to worry."

"Brat thinks she's funny and it took us an extra forty minutes to get out of the airport."

"You don't say no to an autograph, do you?"

Sienna seemed to overcome her embarrassment. "Never. He really doesn't say no to anything. Which is why he gets to judge the Mr. CRHS contest tonight."

My head snapped toward Sienna. "What the actual fuck, Sienna?"

"Mr. CRHS?" Kasper asked.

A groaned passed through my lips. "It's the local high school contest. Think of a pageant but the guys' version."

"And since Bethany needed another judge, having a former Mr. CRHS seemed like the perfect solution." I could feel the smugness radiating from her on the other side of the car.

"Sounds like you have some things to discuss with your sister, but I'd love to hear about this Mr. CRHS later. I'd also like a photo of you winning such a prestigious title."

I rubbed down my face. "Only if I have to."

"You definitely have to. Enjoy your time with your family."

After Kasper and I said our goodbyes, I immediately turned on my sister. "Judging Mr. CRHS? You've got to be kidding me." Pain radiated down my arm. "Ow. Good thing that's not my throwing arm."

"Ha! Like that actually hurt. You just told Kasper Wilder that I think he's hot. You deserve way more than a punch to the shoulder."

I shrugged. "I told you we've become friends. Besides, I think we're more than even. Between the sign at the airport and being a judge, I owe you more than a simple phone call."

"Don't even think about it," she said as she turned into the parking lot of my favorite diner. Being on the phone with Kasper, I hadn't even realized we passed into my hometown.

She pulled into a space next to a familiar car. "Mom and Dad meeting us for lunch?"

"Yep. They took the rest of the week off. They've probably been waiting but you know Mac won't care how long they're here."

I followed Sienna out of the car and into the diner. When we stepped inside, people glanced up and waved, immediately going back to their meals. The best part about coming home was the way the people treated me. They didn't fawn and drool or beg me for tickets and signatures. In Carson Run, I was the same as everyone else. A guy who was having lunch with his family. My mom waved from a corner booth. Mac, the owner of the diner, sat with them, chatting away with Dad.

As we approached the table, smiles filled both of my parents' faces. Mac stood and held his hand out to me. I reached out to take it. "Marcus, good to see you in town. I hear you're here for the week?"

"Yep. Gotta report to Florida next Sunday."

He used his free arm to clasp me on the shoulder. "Good thing I increased my order this week."

"You know it." Mac knew I'd be down to the diner for at least one meal a day every day I was here.

"Good. Good." He let go. Sienna and I slid into the booth across from our parents. "I know what Marcus wants, is everyone else ready to order?"

Mac took the rest of the orders and went back to the kitchen to get everything started. My dad turned to me. His brows drawn together.

"How are you feeling? The knee good?" Back in Jersey, or anywhere else for that matter, I would've worried about who would hear the question and the answer. But not here. I could say anything and it would never leave town.

"Good. Really good actually. I'll be one-hundred-percent when I arrive in Florida."

Mom blew out a breath. "That's wonderful, honey. We were so worried about you. As much as we'd love to see you home, we know you love playing for the Emperors."

"I do. And I'm going to play my ass off this year. Pena isn't going to need to come off the bench, except on my days off."

"I have to say, that was a bullshit move on the Emperors' part. They have you and a backup, why do they need another catcher?"

That had been a question I'd asked myself a million times since seeing the report, but I still didn't have the answer. For some reason, I found myself holding back from saying anything like that to my parents. Normally, I told them everything. This time, Kasper had become the person I put my trust in.

Mac saved me from having to dive too deep into the conversation about my career by bringing our plates. So, I pasted a smile on my face and muzzled the voice in the back of my head. "Who knows, but I'm sure they have a reason. Whatever it is, you'll still see me starting behind home plate."

Hopefully, it wouldn't be my last season doing it for the Emperors.

Chapter 12

Kasper

Valentine's Day was tomorrow. It was a day I loved at one time then hated. Now I was indifferent. Mostly.

Evan talked Vander into hosting a Valentine's party. Since the holiday fell on a Sunday, they were having it the night before. Evan told me it was a small gathering. There would be drinks and plenty of food. I asked if he needed any help and he quickly told me there was nothing for me to worry about, except for making sure I showed up.

I arrived on time since the party started before the hour when the city really kicked its nightlife into gear.

This wasn't a business affair, so I opted for a pair of jeans and a cream-colored cable knit sweater. It was so cold outside, to the point my balls tried to retreat up into my body. The sweater and my coat at least kept my upper half warm.

Knocking on Vander's door, I put one hand in my pocket while the other held the bottle of whiskey I bought for the party. I could hear noise inside and wondered for the hundredth time if Marcus were invited. I could have asked him. We texted once he came home yesterday and again today. But if he weren't invited to the party, I didn't want him to feel bad about it, so I kept quiet while hoping Evan knew me well enough to invite him.

The door opened, revealing a very festive Evan Ashland. He had on a pair of skinny jeans, a red T-shirt with *Vander is my Valentine* across the front in white script, and a headband with two hearts on springs adorned his head.

He scowled when he saw me. "You're not wearing red."

I glanced down with mock surprise. "Really? I could have sworn I had an outfit just like yours on when I left the house."

"Now you're just being a smart-ass. I'll let it slide since you brought the good stuff." He took the whiskey bottle from my hand.

"When have you known me to buy cheap liquor?"

"Never, now get inside." I stepped around him and he shut the door behind me. "You can put your coat in the first bedroom on the left."

I nodded and said hi to the others nearby before I walked down the hall. Callen and Spencer were here. Dominic and his wife. I also recognized Ayden Thompson and Jose Olivera. There were some friends of Evan's I only knew in passing, teachers he worked with and some others I'd never met.

The living room and kitchen were decorated with red streamers, balloons, and hearts. Just about every Valentine's decoration I could think of was there. I even saw some in the hall bathroom.

As I was stepping into the bedroom, I noticed Marcus with his phone in his hand, standing next to the bed. I relaxed seeing him. He was a great friend and, no matter how much I desired him, I wanted to see him. To talk to him. To just be near him. That was so fucking pathetic but apparently also my new mantra where he was concerned.

I took a few seconds to drink in the sight of him. Jeans that fit him perfectly. His thighs were strong and, while the denim didn't give everything away, they showcased him perfectly. If he turned around, I'd get a prime view of that gorgeous ass of his. He was wearing a dark red, long-sleeved shirt fitted to him and not in the least bit baggy.

Damn he was beautiful. Masculine. Fit.

His head lifted and he smiled when his eyes met mine. "I was hoping you'd be here. I was just typing out a text to you."

I returned his smile. It was infectious and I was helpless against it. "There's no way I could have skipped it. Ev would have dragged me from my place kicking and screaming."

"I doubt anyone could do that to you. You're not a small man, Kasper."

My body warmed at the thought of Marcus noticing my size. I was proud of the body I had. "You'd be surprised. Evan is really strong."

Marcus slid his phone into his pocket. "No red?"

I slipped out of my black wool coat and laid it on the bed. "Not one of my favorite holidays."

He stepped over and put his arm around my shoulders. "You miss having someone at your side?" He was joking, but damn I had to swallow down the urge to put my arm around his waist and anchor him beside me.

Instead, I kept the mood light and teased him back, only it came out more serious than I intended. "Looks like you're filling the role for the night." Shit, why did I say that?

Luckily, Marcus smirked and said, "The arm candy of Kasper Wilder? Who wouldn't want to be by your side? Adored by many. Lusted after by more. Maybe being seen with you will up my popularity. Get more asses in the seats at the home games."

I scoffed, "Like the Emperors have tons of empty seats. You sell out almost every game."

"We could always do better."

I hip-checked him and stepped toward the door, his arm falling away. The longer I stayed that close to him, the longer his scent had a chance to infiltrate my very being, the more risk I had of blurting out things I had no intention of saying to him.

I was almost to the door when Spencer filled the space. "I was wondering where you went. You have to save me." Spencer wore jeans and a shirt the same color as Evan's, but his read, *Callen is my Valentine*. "Do you see what he made me wear?" He tugged at the shirt.

"You look damn good with my name across your chest," Callen said, stepping up behind him and wrapping his arms around his stomach.

Spencer melted against him but didn't lose the irritation in his eyes as he held on to Callen's arms. "Yeah, I get how you like it, but there was nothing wrong with what I had on. I even wore red because I knew Ev would make me change if I didn't." He looked at my sweater. "What the hell?"

I shrugged. "I do what I want."

Next thing I knew, Evan was shouldering into the room, past Callen and Spencer. "Here." He shoved a red shirt at me, causing me to immediately blanch. I could actually feel the color leaving my face.

"No." I refused to unroll it, certain there was something about Marcus on it and in no way, shape, or form was I announcing to a roomful of people I had feelings for the Emperors' catcher. Nope. Fuck that. If I couldn't even admit them to the man himself, everyone else was off-limits.

Evan rolled his eyes. "Trust me and open the damn thing."

I trusted Evan. I really did. In that moment, I was shaking with nerves wondering what the shirt said. Did I think he'd embarrass me? Not intentionally. What he would do was give me a nudge toward Marcus. That I had no doubt.

Taking a deep breath, I held the shirt up and let it unroll. It was the same color as Evan's and Spencer's, but the shirt in my hands read, *Will you be mine?*

Subtle.

I lifted my gaze and met Evan's. He was smirking, knowing full well what he did. He didn't betray my trust, just gave me that nudge like I knew he would.

"I'm comfortable with what I'm wearing," I told him.

Evan reached forward and ran his hand over my arm. His nose scrunched up. "No, you're not. You like T-shirts, not sweaters. Quit being so damn formal and put on the shirt, Kas." With that, he turned, shoved Spencer and Callen out the door as he asked Spencer where his headband was. Evan even shut the door behind them, leaving me and Marcus alone. In the bedroom. With a closed door. It was a true test of my willpower.

Marcus's hand pressed against the center of my back as he came up beside me and looked at the shirt I was still stupidly holding. "Let me guess, he'll keep harassing you until you put it on?"

I nodded, not trusting my voice with Marcus so close. I could feel his warmth. The strength in that single touch. What I wouldn't give to turn my head and kiss him.

He stepped back and motioned toward the shirt. "You better do what he said." My eyes met his. He didn't leave the room. Didn't offer to give me privacy to change.

I tossed the shirt onto the bed and quickly lifted my sweater off, not bothering to look at Marcus again. It was bad enough my dick was on board with us being alone. I didn't need to give it more ammo by seeing the man when I was stripping out of my sweater.

The visual my mind created was mouthwatering. Me opening my jeans and taking my dick in my hand to stroke it slowly. Marcus dropping to his knees, eager for a taste. I could paint his lips with my precum. Watch as he licked it away, taking a part of me into him.

Fuck, that was not helping.

I reached for the shirt. The material was soft and stretched taut across my chest as I put it on. I let it hang down over my hips to help cover my half hard dick then finally took a chance to glance at Marcus.

His arms were crossed as he appraised me. I had no idea what he was thinking. Yes, I'd gotten to know him well but not to the point where I could read him easily.

"He's trying to set you up."

"What?" It was like I was struck dumb when the man talked. I was well educated, powerful, successful, and yet in front of this man, I could hardly remember where I was.

"Evan. He obviously wants you to meet someone tonight. I did notice a couple of guys who came alone, though I don't have any idea if they're gay or not. You may like them."

I shook my head. "I'm not here looking for a hookup."

"Why not? We talk all the time and I never hear you speak about other men. No dates. No nothing."

I wanted to tell him that was for a reason. That I hadn't found anyone else attractive since he and I became close. But I couldn't say those words. Couldn't confess everything I was feeling, especially not tonight where just beyond the closed door was a condo full of people here for a party.

"I work a lot. My businesses need attention. The people I attract seem to be after me for my money or to be recognized by being with me. As far as hookups, I have no interest. I can get myself off just as well as some random guy can do it for me. It's not what I want. Those are all empty and meaningless connections."

Marcus took a step closer, dropping his arms by his side as his face became serious. "You talk to me all the time. We hang out. We have fun. Don't tell me you don't have time. I know you were hurt, but hanging out with me won't get you want you really want. You need to put yourself out there. Open yourself up to the possibility of being with someone."

His words were a sobering reminder of what I would never have. What was right in front of me but wasn't mine to touch. To claim. To make love to. He saw our friendship as me hiding behind him when it was the furthest thing from the truth. I was so intricately caught in his web, I didn't know how to break free. I didn't struggle. Didn't try to find a weak spot so I could flee. No, if anything I let the web wrap tighter around me to keep me bound to him.

Stepping back, I knew I had to get out of the room. Marcus would never see me as anyone other than a friend. He was straight and I was the fool falling for him.

"You're right," I said. "I need to put myself out there."

With that, I turned toward the door, opened it, and stepped out into the party where I had to pretend like I wasn't hurting inside over a man who was never going to see me as a love interest.

It was amazing what my mind could do to me. To trick me and get my heart involved in the deceit.

Marcus held more power over me than he would ever know. Something no one had held since Hunter. Here I was repeating the pattern all over again. Only Marcus and I were never an item. He was nothing more than a dream I had in a world that wasn't my reality.

I plastered on a smile and started mingling with the others in the room. I introduced myself to people. And I used the shirt Evan had given me as a shield for my heart because I wasn't sure if I could survive any more heartache, even if it was something I brought on myself.

Chapter 13

Marcus

Kasper's retreating back hit me in the center of my chest. The dullness in his gaze as he stared at me screaming loud and clear that something was wrong. I'd upset Kasper. Not exactly my goal in life. I preferred him smiling and happy.

Snippets of our conversation from New Year's Eve paraded through my mind. I hadn't thought about our confessions since that night, probably trying to bury the loneliness to the back of my mind. I hadn't felt alone in a while, ever since spending time with Kasper. And now, tonight, I insulted him by suggesting he find a hookup for the night when he'd made it clear on New Year's Eve he'd been hurt. He wanted long term, not a weeknight fuck. God, I was an asshole.

Scrubbing a hand over my face, I walked out of the room and down the hall to the living room of the condo, where most of the guests were gathered, and searched for Kasper.

Eventually, I found him on the other side of the room talking to a group of people I didn't know. I needed to find a way to apologize. He wore a smile, but I could see in the rigid stance of his posture the front he was putting on. It was probably best that I let him finish whatever conversation he was having and catch him again in a few minutes.

I wandered farther into the living room, close to where Kasper stood surrounded by, what I could only assume were friends of Evan's, and sat down next to Ayden.

"Are we on the same flight tomorrow?" He lounged against the back of the couch with one foot propped on the opposite knee. As a starting pitcher, Ayden would have to report the same day I did.

"If you have the six o'clock flight, then yeah."

"Thank fuck. I don't feel like dealing with Powell yet. Not on my last day before the season starts."

Karl Powell never wanted to talk about anything besides baseball stats. There were points in the season when it was great and incredibly helpful, but Ayden was right, not on my last day before the heavy workout regime began.

"Fucking seriously. He needs to binge watch some Netflix and talk about that for a while. I still have to pack and check on the arrangements for the cleaning service while I'm gone."

"Same. I gotta get up early to make sure it's all done before I leave for the airport."

Movement to my left drew my attention and I noticed Kasper moving away from the group he'd been talking to. I wanted to catch him before he got pulled up in another conversation.

"I'm gonna go grab a beer." Ayden nodded and lifted his bottle toward his lips.

I pushed off the couch and moved in the direction Kasper went. I made it to him just as he began another conversation with a different group of people. This time I stayed, joining the conversation myself, hoping I'd get the chance for a moment alone.

The chance never came.

Kasper moved with purpose throughout the room, actively avoiding me at all costs. The knot that had started in the pit of my stomach, when Kasper left the room earlier, continued to tighten each time he switched from one group to the other. All after only a few minutes of me walking up to him.

I wanted to be pissed at every single person he talked to who wasn't me, but that was a completely irrational thought. I wasn't some jealous ex. We were friends. After the fourth blow off, I went back into the main part of the living room to hang out with my teammates. Apparently, Kasper needed more time and I'd give him that.

I drained the rest of my beer, only my third for the night, when a hand landed on my shoulder. I glanced back and found a smiling Ayden.

"I'm heading out. The thought of getting up early with no sleep sounds shitty, especially when Joe will have our asses up early the rest of the week."

I glanced at my phone and knew it was long past time for me to go home. I nodded and waved at the guys behind me.

"We're out," Ayden whipped his finger above his head in a circle.

"Don't get too bored without us next week," Dominic taunted.

Ayden flipped him off before I could.

"Let me grab my coat."

Before I made it to the bedroom, Spencer stopped me. "How's the knee?" he asked, low enough only I could hear.

"Never better. Thank you for everything."

Spencer shrugged. "You did all of the work, but if you need me while you're down there, call. You have my personal number. I can talk you through whatever exercises that could help."

"I will. Thanks." He smiled and went back into the mass of people, no doubt in search of Callen.

When I emerged from the bedroom a few minutes later, coat in hand, I looked around for Kasper. I really didn't want to go home before I apologized to him, but no matter how hard I searched, he was nowhere to be found. Ayden was getting antsy by the door, and I knew I had to get going. I'd send him a text once I got home.

After pulling into my parking space beneath my building, I took the elevator to my floor, the list of things I had to handle tomorrow running through my head, alternating with thoughts of Kasper. Had I ruined our friendship tonight? I really fucking hoped not. It was nice to spend time with someone who either wasn't living in the happy world of coupledom or wanted to spend every night out partying.

I locked the front door and went to the bedroom to strip out of my clothes and climb beneath the sheets. It felt like I stared at the phone for an hour before I decided exactly what to send to Kasper. Eventually, I gave up and just spoke from the heart. If our friendship was as important to him as it was to me, he didn't need perfectly worded apologies. Honesty would be fine.

Me: I'm sorry about what I said tonight. You're not the kind of man who takes random guys home. I know this and I'm sorry I suggested it. You're a man who deserves someone to love him and take care of him. I hope you find that man soon. You deserve to be happy.

I hit send on the text and waited. And waited. And waited some more. Kasper's responses had always been almost instant. When ten minutes had passed and not a peep, I figured he still wasn't ready to talk to me. I set my phone to silent and dropped it on the night stand, curling under the covers and letting a restless sleep take me.

***

The shrill sound of the alarm in my ear pulled me from sleep much earlier than I wanted to be awake. I'd tossed and turned most of the night, dreaming about my last conversation with Kasper. I reached for my phone on the nightstand to shut off the obnoxious buzzing. The first thing I noticed was a text from Kasper. With slightly shaking hands, I unlocked the phone and opened the message.

Kasper: It's my fault, too. I should have known better than to go to Evan's Valentine's party.

The tension in my muscles eased some seeing his text and my fingers flew across the screen after I noticed that his text had come in last night after I'd gone to bed.

Me: I wasn't kidding. You deserve to have your very own Valentine.

The three little dots appeared then disappeared only to reappear again. I sat there staring at my phone to see what he would say next.

Kasper: What time is your flight?

Not exactly what I expected, but if Kasper wanted to put last night to rest, I was happy to follow suit.

Me: Six.

Kasper: And you report to the stadium tomorrow morning, right?

Me: Yeah. Our workouts begin right away. We have the nights off as long as we're on time the next morning.

Kasper: That's good. At least you'll have time to rest.

Me: And text you.

Kasper: I like the sound of that.

The conversation didn't seem to come as easily as it had before I shoved my foot squarely in my mouth the night before. Hopefully, we'd be able to find our way back to that easy banter. I'd keep trying until we did. My phone buzzed again, but this time it wasn't a text from Kasper but a reminder about what time I needed to leave for the airport to make my flight.

The to-do list that had started in my head the day before raced through my mind. As much as I wanted to continue my conversation with Kasper, I had to get my ass out of bed and get my things together.

Me: I have to go and get ready to leave, but I'll text you when I get to the airport.

Kasper: I'll keep my phone on.

That was a positive. He hadn't completely shut me out. What amazed me the most was how devastated I'd been thinking about losing Kasper's friendship. I'd been friends with Dominic and some of the other guys for years, and while the loss of their friendship would hurt, I didn't think it would have nearly the same gut-wrenching impact losing Kasper would.

I threw the covers off and climbed out of bed, ready to begin another season in the majors. This season was different than the others since it would determine my place in Espen for the future. I went straight for the coffee machine. The caffeine would be vital to getting everything done before I had to leave.

It had taken me all day, but with minutes to spare, the car I'd called pulled up outside the airport. Thank fuck the club had already shipped my equipment down to Florida. I grabbed my one bag and threw it over my shoulder then reached back into the trunk for my suitcase. A quick tip for the driver and I was making my way through security and toward the terminal where I saw Ayden waiting to board the plane.

Wanting to send one last text to Kasper before I left, I stopped a few feet away and pulled out my phone.

Me: Having a little déjà vu here.

Kasper: I hope not. The last time I had to wait almost an hour after you landed to hear that you were okay.

Me: Scout's honor I'll text you as soon as we land.

Kasper: Were you actually a Boy Scout?

I couldn't stop the chuckle that left my lips.

Me: Not exactly, but it sounded good.

Kasper: It did. Keep in touch while you're away. We'll have to get together when you're back in Espen. I'm going to miss you making me laugh.

Me: Don't worry. I'll find a way.

A voice came over the loudspeaker calling my group to board.

Me: I gotta go. They just called my group. But I promise to text when I land.

Kasper: Safe travels.

I shoved my phone back into my pocket and made my way to the gate. I exited the jetway and stepped onto the plane. My third flight in a week. To say I was tired of flying was an understatement. Ayden was already seated and playing on his phone when I joined him.

"Ready for another year?" he asked as I sat down.

"As ready as I'll ever be. It needs to be a good one."

He smirked. "With the two of us together? It will be."

"I like the sound of that. I need them to take my last option year and offer me another long-term deal."

"They'd be stupid as hell not to do that. There aren't many catchers of your caliber in the league. I know I need you behind the plate."

The rest of the plane filled up while we talked about the upcoming season. Before I knew it, the flight attendant had started the safety instructions as the plane taxied toward the runway.

Ayden and I were both engrossed in our screens when one of the flight attendants came over the intercom.

"Happy Valentine's Day, everyone. We'll begin beverage service shortly."

Ayden groaned. "Fuck, I never want to deal with this holiday again. Six years of getting bitched out about how I had to leave around Valentine's Day or was already gone. Good fucking riddance."

I chuckled and ordered two beers from the flight attendant. "I take it your divorce is final."

"Hell yeah. Biggest mistake of my life, marrying one of the cleat chasers. I'm never getting married again."

The flight attendant handed each of us a can and a cup if we wanted to pour it. The usual for a short flight when the entire team wasn't on board.

"Never?"

"No. Not worth it, man." He lifted the beer to his lips and closed his eyes, leaning his head against the headrest. "She only wanted me for my money, otherwise, she wouldn't have cheated on me."

I felt bad for Ayden, but I still refused to give up hope of finding the right person for me. Dominic, Callen, and Vander had all done it. As much as I told Kasper he deserved someone to spend his life with, I knew I did, too.

Chapter 14

Kasper

Evan had reached a point where he couldn't stand being away from Vander any longer. He was twitchy and irritable. Not his normal Evan self. Being around him was starting to bring my mood farther into the abyss it was already skimming the rim of. With Marcus gone for a month now, I was miserable. I worked, ate, and slept. It was all I'd been doing to keep my mind off the fact that one of my closest friends was in Florida.

I tried so hard in those early days of him being gone to stop thinking about him as anything other than a friend, but it was pointless. I felt sick to my stomach keeping him at arm's length.

My resolve was shit. I didn't date, though I should have. Didn't look for anyone else, even if that was my goal after leaving the bedroom at the Valentine's party. I couldn't do it. It would be more faces of people I didn't want to wake up in the morning next to. More people I didn't have a connection with like I did with Marcus.

Our text and phone conversations got back to normal by the end of that first week he was away and, while I knew it wasn't good for my mental health, it was better than struggling to only talk to him every now and then. I missed him. I missed my friend.

Every night I thought of him when I was trying to sleep, and it was damn hard to keep those thoughts PG and not where I wanted them to go. With him in my bed. Him over top of me, pounding into me. I knew he had a lot of strength. His muscles said as much. In bed, he would be amazing.

And that led me to spilling everything to Spencer one night after I had too much to drink when he was at my place with Evan. It was a Saturday. I invited them over for dinner in hopes of cheering them both up. Since none of us had to work the next day, I broke out a bottle of expensive wine and started the spiral into an evening of drinking.

Once I was good and drunk, my filter was gone. I knew I could say anything to my friends and they would never judge me or think poorly of me. I was safe in their presence. So, the words spilled from my lips that I had kept to myself. Yes, Evan knew I wanted Marcus, but he wasn't aware of just how deep my feelings ran.

It wasn't my proudest moment, but they both hugged me and told me I wasn't alone. How no matter what, I'd always have them in my life. It meant everything to me.

That night, I went to bed with tears in my eyes and pain in my heart. No matter what, I knew I had them, though. They would lift me up as I would always do for them.

While Evan loved how close Marcus and I were, Spencer was concerned about me getting my heart broken. Normally, Evan would worry, too, but he'd become a hopeless romantic and kept saying anything was possible and maybe Marcus wasn't as straight as he thought he was. His logic was that no straight man spent that much time messaging with another man, close friends or not. Then he proved his point by asking how much I texted Spencer. It was minimal and I adored Spencer. Even Evan and I didn't text that much. Then there was Brick, and it was the same. His point was made.

Spencer wouldn't be himself, though, if he weren't watching out for his friends' well-being. Being with both him and Evan, they balanced each other so well. Normally, I was the friend who felt the need to take control. To handle any and all problems. But that night, I let every one of my guards down and it felt good to pour my heart out.

I knew better than to get my hopes up but I was like a teenager with a crush, hanging on to any tiny thread I could get in hopes Marcus could become more to me.

Then I got an idea on Monday. I was going to fly the three of us down to Florida for the weekend. We could surprise the guys and have fun. If, by the end of the weekend, Marcus gave no inkling that he had any feelings for me, I would let him go. Pack up my feelings for him and put them in the little box in my mind where shit I shouldn't think about went, then I'd cement that bitch shut.

Evan had screamed louder than I'd ever heard another person yell when I told him my plans of flying us south. He threw himself into my arms and thanked me with kisses to my cheek for giving him a chance to see Vander. Spencer smiled wide as I watched the tension slowly leave his body. He might not have been as vocal as Evan about how much he missed Callen, but he did. It was evident in the bags under his eyes and the rigid way he held himself. It wasn't easy being involved with ballplayers, but love made it worth it for them.

It was Friday morning. Both Evan and Spencer took the day off. Evan used one of his many sick days he had banked and Spencer had a lighter than normal schedule, so he was easily able to have others on his staff handle his patients.

As for me, well, Pascal was a master at rearranging my calendar and did so with ease. He asked if I wanted him to travel with me, but I told him to take the day and weekend off. I could see how excited he was. He still reminded me that no matter what, he was only a call away. I didn't deserve an assistant as great as him.

It was ten in the morning and we had just arrived at the small, executive airport my jet was taking off from. Once inside, Micki was there to give us drinks and help us get settled. She was married to my pilot, Holton. It worked well since this way they were never away from each other. Plus, they decided years ago they didn't want to have children, so flying around with me and my team, they got to see the world. I always put them up in great hotels and covered their expenses.

Evan and Spencer sat in the seats facing mine. Evan was practically bouncing out of his in excitement.

"You know you have to sit through a game before you can get your hands on him, right?" I asked.

He dramatically rolled his eyes. "Yes, I know. But tonight, after dinner, I'm going to do very wicked things to my man."

"We fully expect you to start dry-humping him as soon as the game is over," Spencer stated and patted Evan's thigh.

Evan shoved his hand away. "Don't even start with me. You're going to be doing the same thing to Callen."

He smirked. "Maybe, though I'd like to think I could at least wait until we're away from others."

I sat and watched them banter back and forth, wishing I could add in my own comments, but I couldn't. I was going to Florida to see someone who was only a friend. I had plans to gently push that envelope this weekend. To flirt a tiny bit. Nothing overly obvious, except to those who knew me well, which were few and far between.

The flight wasn't long and, before I knew it, we were touching down and then in the SUV on our way to the hotel. While Evan and Spencer would no doubt be staying with their significant others, I didn't have such a luxury. Instead, I booked a suite at a hotel close to where the Emperors trained.

No matter how many times I'd told myself I wasn't going to date an athlete again, here I was hoping with everything in me I would get close enough to Marcus for him to give me a chance. For him to let me show him just how great we could be together. It was just another box checked in my *Reasons Why Kasper Wilder is an Idiot* list.

Callen, Vander, Marcus, Dominic, and Ayden rented a house together for the duration of spring training. It was more cost effective and gave them a sense of home rather than living out of a hotel room.

By the time we were back in the SUV and on our way to the field, the game had started a half hour ago. I didn't want us to show up before the game began. I really wanted that element of surprise and Evan and Spencer were excited about it.

When I first got the idea in my head earlier in the week to do this, I called up Tim Deary, who owned the Emperors, and asked for three tickets to all three games while we were in Florida. He said it was a great time to call because he had something he wanted to discuss with me. We set something up on the calendar for after I returned.

When I was considering buying the Jetties, I had already known Tim since we ran in the same social circle. I called him and asked for a meeting. I wanted to get his advice, even if he owned a baseball team instead of hockey. Tim gave me his professional opinion, which I valued greatly. His advice was sound and helped me in my decision to buy the team.

Since then, we'd grown closer and he became someone I could trust, though our relationship wasn't one of close friends like I had with Evan and Spencer. He was more of a business friend than personal.

Tim wasn't down here for spring training, instead leaving it up to the coaches to handle. Thanks to him, our tickets to the game were easy to get and further lent to our surprise.

We walked through the stands until we found our seats and I laughed at seeing they were right behind the Emperors dugout. People looked at us as we walked by. I knew we'd draw attention, not only because of who I was but with Evan and Spencer as well. Their faces were known by fans since they appeared in the media alongside their men.

The Emperors were up at bat against the Saddle Harbor Silver Maples. Lance Wilson was at the plate pitching to Jose Olivera. There were two strikes and one ball. Andrew Hudson was on second.

The pitch was thrown, Olivera swung, and the bat connected with the ball perfectly. It went high and far, right over the wall.

Players in the dugout cheered, as did fans, while Hudson and Olivera came into home and scored two runs for the Emperors.

We watched as multiple players came out of the dugout to congratulate them. And that was the point when our surprise paid off.

Callen turned and looked into the stands as the fans cheered. His eyes landed on us before facing Olivera again. Then he did a double take with his mouth hanging open. A wide smile spread over his lips. It was great to see.

Without taking his eyes off Spencer, he started slapping Vander on his side until Vander turned with a scowl and smacked him back. Then, when Callen wouldn't look at him, he followed his line of sight. Vander's eyes widened and he beamed. He started walking toward us, but Callen held him back. He must have forgotten where he was and that they were playing a game.

The best part was after they started going back to the dugout and Callen leaned over Marcus's shoulder and whispered in his ear. He suddenly turned and the smile he gave me was the most beautiful thing I'd ever seen. Fuck, Marcus was gorgeous and I was so helplessly gone over him.

He waved to me and I smiled like a fool and waved back. I was sure others were wondering what the relationship between the two of us was. After all, I came here with two of the Emperors' significant others. However, I didn't care. No one else mattered but the ones I kept in my circle. People would talk. They always did. Gossip was aplenty in professional sports. They couldn't take or sully this moment from me, though. It was mine and I was always going to remember it.

Callen gripped Marcus's shoulder and turned him toward the dugout while talking to him. Beside me, Spencer and Evan were so damn happy. Everything I'd done to get us down here today was worth it. I loved my friends and would go to the ends of the earth for them. Bringing them here so they could see the men they loved was one of the easiest decisions I'd ever made. It also might have been a little selfish on my part because I got to see Marcus.

Marcus

"Fuck, I can't believe he's here." The excitement in Callen's voice was palpable as he led us into the dugout. "No doubt that's Kasper's doing."

I thought about the kind man who took care of his friends, no matter the cost. "I have no doubt about that."

I dropped down on the bench so I could pull off my chest protector. Unless the next three batters went down swinging, which was unlikely considering it was a split squad game, I had a small break until I needed to put the equipment back on. With half of the team, mostly players who don't start during the regular season and ones who won't make the final roster, playing at the same time in another stadium about thirty miles away, we had all of our starters on the field today. Not always the norm for spring training games.

I leaned back against the dugout wall, not bothering with the shin guards. Those fuckers took too long to get back on when we had to go back on the field. The Florida sun could be brutal this time of year when you were used to the colder temperatures. Dominic passed by and sat down next to me, handing me a bottle of water.

"I see we've lost Callen and Vander to thoughts of fucking their men when we get back to the house. Glad I took one of the downstairs rooms now."

I groaned. My room was right across the hall from Evan and Vander. "Oh fuck, I'm going to have to listen to them all night."

He bumped his shoulder into mine, chuckling. "You can thank your boyfriend for that one."

My brows drew together. "My boyfriend? I think that collision with the runner at first earlier is messing with your head, or did you forget I'm single and straight?"

He hit my shoulder. Ass. "No, I know you're single and straight, but you have to admit you spend more time with Kasper than anyone else. It's all that secret sexting. One's gotta wonder if the gay gene is rubbing off on you."

I smirked as Callen smacked Dominic upside the back of his head. "Knock that shit off. Gay gene." Callen shook his head. "You're just jealous Cheryl isn't here and you won't be keeping Ayden awake with the sounds of you fucking across the hall."

"Oh, I'll keep him awake all right. Me and my right hand can make plenty of noise."

"No fucking way am I listening to that all night," Ayden called from across the dugout. "We're going out drinking until he's drunk enough that he'll just pass out."

Dominic punched his hand in the air. "Fuck yes."

And that quickly, the conversation switched to plans for the night while we watched Gian Martinez, the Emperors' second baseman, bat with Vander on deck.

But Dominic's words continued to echo in my head until I had to head back out behind the plate. The rest of the inning passed by in a blur. I was running on autopilot while I tried to digest exactly what was different about mine and Kasper's friendship. Yes, we texted a lot, but I felt like Kasper needed someone to confide in, someone to laugh with. We were both lonely, looking for our forevers, so there wasn't anything weird about spending time together when everyone else had a significant other to go home to.

The next time we stepped onto the field, I forced myself to shake off the thoughts and put my head back into the game.

Callen and Vander's game improved drastically with the arrival of their men, making the time that we were on the field much shorter. It only gave me more time to think in the dugout. I couldn't stop myself from leaning over the rail to peek over the top of the dugout at Kasper. Each time, his eyes were on me like he'd been waiting for me to appear.

The top of the ninth, with two outs and runners on first and third, I was over this shit. There were too many things in my head to keep playing the game. The runner at first took a bit larger lead than he had previously. I knew he was going for it. Right before the pitch, I adjusted my stance. There was a reason I had the fastest pop time in the majors. The ball came at me. The moment it hit my glove, I was up whipping the ball toward Callen, who tagged the runner, ending the game.

Catcher Interference

In a playoff game, that move would've been met with tackles and celebrations. In spring training, we did high fives, congratulations to the other team, and went to the locker room for showers. The Sliver Maples would want to get back to their facility. Callen and Vander were racing everyone through their showers. We'd rented a couple of cars for the time we were in Florida, but since we were all playing in the same game today, we'd only brought the Suburban.

My stomach fluttered as I followed everyone out to the parking lot. This was the first time I'd see Kasper face-to-face since the Valentine's Day party. Things seemed normal during our texts and chats, but that didn't mean everything would be when we were together again.

I stepped out into the warm spring air and found Vander holding Evan under his ass, kissing him passionately. Callen and Spencer were more reserved, but the love between them was obvious. When I looked to the right, I saw Kasper smiling directly at me and I knew everything was fine.

"Hungry?" he asked. "I've made reservations for everyone if you want to go out."

"I'm in," Dominic said with a smirk, walking up beside me and wrapping his arm around my neck. "I'm sure Marcus is in, too. Aren't you?"

I elbowed the asshole in the ribs, reveling in the *oomph* that left his lips. He was stirring up shit for no reason.

"Dinner sounds great." I glanced down at my clothes. "But I think we need to change first."

Kasper nodded. "I'm sure Evan and Spencer want to drop their stuff at your place anyway. I have it in the car. Mine's already at the hotel, so we can follow you over."

Ayden pulled up in the Suburban. "Hop in, everyone. I'm starving. The sooner we change, the sooner we eat."

"Then we drink," Dominic chimed in.

"You two can drink." Vander yanked open the back door. "The rest of us have a game tomorrow. Besides, I have other stuff to do tonight." His eyes were on Evan, who was currently shaking his ass as he walked to another black SUV.

"We'll follow you there." Kasper pulled a set of keys out of his pocket and turned in the same direction as Evan.

Once everyone was piled into the cars, we drove back to the house, only a few minutes from the stadium. On the beach, it had been perfect for what we'd been looking for. Five bedrooms. Two on the first floor and three on the second. We had a pool and every amenity we could need for the time we were in Florida. A beautiful gourmet kitchen we barely used. Not one of us enjoyed cooking.

Ayden pulled into the driveway next to the smaller SUV we'd rented. Behind us, Kasper drove in and parked. Evan and Spencer were out of the car with bags in hands in seconds. Dominic already had the door unlocked, waving everyone inside.

I turned to Kasper. "Just give us a few to change and we'll be ready to go."

Dominic was already pointing at Callen and Vander. "No, there is not time for a quickie right now. I've been on the field all day and I'm hungry. You all can fuck each other senseless after dinner."

I thought I heard a few grumbles from the four of them, but they agreed and went to change and put their bags away. When I came back downstairs in jeans and a short-sleeved, button-down, black shirt, everyone was ready to go. We split up into different cars. Dominic and Ayden took the small SUV to go out later and I ended up with Kasper, while Callen, Vander, Spencer, and Evan were in the Suburban.

"I'm glad you came down. Callen and Vander were getting grumpier by the day."

Kasper laughed. "Sounds like Evan and Spencer, but they weren't the only ones. I missed spending time with you."

"Me, too. I know things got back to normal when we talked, but I still worried I'd ruined our friendship." I looked down.

A hand landed on my shoulder and I glanced over to see we'd stopped at a red light. "That's something you never have to worry about. I was having a bad night and I let it affect everything around me."

I smiled and a comfortable silence settled over us until the car behind us blew its horn, breaking our connection. The light had turned green. Kasper winked at me then pressed his foot to the pedal, sending us down the road.

Kasper pulled into the parking lot of my favorite steak house when we were in Florida for spring training. I convinced the guys to eat there pretty often.

"I love this place," I said, climbing out of the car.

Kasper smiled. "I had a feeling you would."

Everyone gathered in the main entrance. At this point, the staff was used to seeing us in there for dinner, but add in Spencer, Evan, and Kasper Wilder, and the staff went a little crazy. The host immediately showed us to the large, round table they set aside for us. I couldn't help but notice the way Kasper lightly touched my back, directing me toward one of the chairs. I didn't get a chance to think about what it meant before everyone else took their seats. Kasper to my left and Dominic directly across from me.

Drinks and appetizers were ordered immediately. The waiters quickly left to give us time to browse through the menu. Out of the corner of my eye, I saw the way Callen and Spencer whispered to each other and how Vander couldn't keep his hands off Evan. A bit of jealousy ate at me watching what I'd been hoping for. Kasper patted my thigh, leaving his palm there for a few seconds before taking his hand back.

Once the waiters had taken everyone's order, I fell into another easy conversation with Kasper. The flow and company putting me at ease. Throughout dinner, I noticed the little touches to my arm when Kasper wanted me to pass him the salt shaker or when his leg brushed mine under the table. Normally, I wouldn't have thought anything about it, but Dominic's gaze seemed to be zeroed in on me every time it happened. At one point, he lifted a brow and moved his eyes to Kasper's hand and back to me. I pretended to ignore him and went back to my conversation, but my brain was now firmly focused on every little move Kasper made.

With dinner over and Kasper refusing to let any of us pay the bill, we walked back out to the parking lot and

I found myself disappointed that Kasper had to head back to the hotel while the rest of us went back to the house.

"Will you guys be at the game tomorrow?" I asked when we reached his SUV.

"I have tickets for all three games. I figured we'd fly back Sunday night."

I chuckled. "I guess that's the benefit of owning a plane. You choose your departure times."

"That and the food."

"I don't play on Sunday, but Callen and Vander do. Callen doesn't have off until Monday and Vander was off last Wednesday."

He winked. "I know. I've been keeping track."

For the first time in my friendship with Kasper, I didn't know exactly how to act, so I took a step back and waved. "I'll see you tomorrow, then. Thanks for dinner." Wow, that was fucking awkward.

"You're welcome."

Before I could sound like any more of an idiot, I walked over and climbed in the driver's seat of the Suburban, giving the lovebirds the two back seats. I hadn't felt that uncomfortable around Kasper since that first day in Callen's driveway. The others in the SUV were too caught up in each other to notice my inner turmoil.

Thankfully, they went right to their rooms when we got back to the house. Dominic and Ayden were god only knew where for the night, which gave me and my beer the living room to ourselves while I pondered what the hell was happening in my life.

The longer I sat in there, nursing my beer, Kasper's light, simple touches and Dominic's words rolling around my head, the more I became convinced that my relationship with Kasper wasn't exactly what my other friendships were. Maybe it wasn't only a friendship at all. But what the fuck did that mean? I was straight. Straight men didn't suddenly start liking other men, did they?

As far as I knew, Spencer had been straight before Callen. Did I find Kasper attractive? I thought about the couple of times I'd seen him with no shirt on and had admired the muscles on his back. The way I missed him when we hadn't talked during the party, even when he was only a few feet away. I cared about Kasper more than I cared about anyone else, but what did that mean?

I ran my hand through my hair and tugged on the ends. Sitting there drinking wasn't getting me answers. There was only one place I'd get what I needed. I left the half-empty beer on the kitchen counter and took the stairs two at a time.

My fist landed on Vander's door with a thud. "Put your clothes on. I need you for a second." When they didn't answer, I pounded on the door again. Just as I was about to knock for a third time, the door swung open to reveal Evan in only a towel. Before Evan or Vander could bitch that I interrupted them, I spoke. "Where's Kasper staying and what's his room number?"

Evan watched me for a moment, then a slow smile formed on his lips. "The Englewood Bay Resort, room 712."

"Thank you."

I heard the click of the door as I raced down the stairs and grabbed the keys off the table. In no time, I was taking the elevator up to Kasper's room. My hand shook as I knocked on the door. Knots formed in my stomach while I waited for him to answer.

When the door opened, Kasper stood in nothing but a pair of gray sweats and his brows were drawn together in confusion.

Time to figure it all out.

Chapter 16

Kasper

Pacing the length of my hotel suite for what had to be the fiftieth time, I couldn't get my mind to shut off. I flirted with Marcus tonight. Not much. Little touches here and there. I was testing him. Seeing what he would do. And he did nothing. He didn't push me away nor did he seem to lean in to my touch, which led me to believe he was either completely oblivious or liked them. I was leaning toward oblivious.

I hated coming back here alone. Not that I necessarily thought I could get Marcus to come with me. Had we been back in Espen, him hanging out at my place or me at his would have been no big deal. I was hoping for the same here. Unfortunately, that didn't happen.

On lap fifty-one of the suite, there was a knock on the door. I hadn't ordered room service and the only ones who knew where I was were Evan and Spencer. No way would they be coming over here tonight. They were both most likely in bed with their men.

I strode to the door and opened it without bothering to look through the peephole. If someone wanted to fuck with me while I was here, they picked the wrong night to do it. I was in no mood for bullshit. But who I found on the other side of the door had my heart beating faster and my breath faltering. What was Marcus doing here?

"Is everything okay?" I asked. First and foremost, I wanted to make sure my friend was all right. It wasn't late yet, but he had a game tomorrow, so he needed a good night's sleep.

For a moment, he simply watched me. Didn't come in. Didn't even blink. Just stood and stared.

"Marcus," I said to pull him out of his thoughts. "Why don't you come in and we can talk?"

He nodded and stepped inside. I shut and locked the door then led him over to a small sitting area with my hand on his lower back. It wasn't conscious, though. More natural to touch him like that.

The suite I booked was a good size. There was a separate living area, small kitchenette, and a bedroom with a king-sized bed and a small sitting area.

We both took seats on the couch, keeping a few feet between us. I was grateful the furniture in here was comfortable instead of looking nice and feeling like I was sitting on a two-by-four. Some places went for appearances over comfort, which I understood, but there should be a balance.

I waited for Marcus to talk. He still had on the jeans and black button-down that he did for dinner. It accentuated his muscles and let the bottom part of his tattoo show on his arm. It also made me feel really underdressed in my sweatpants and no shirt, but I wasn't about to get up and change or throw a shirt on. Marcus came here for a reason and I wanted to hear him out.

"Marcus, talk to me." He was starting to frighten me. I couldn't imagine anything had happened between the time we parted ways and now, but I wasn't certain.

"Were you flirting with me at dinner?"

I froze. I didn't see that coming.

Deciding to go with blunt honesty, because nothing else would get me anywhere, I admitted, "Yes. Did it bother you? I can make sure never to do it again." That was the furthest thing from what I wanted. It felt right touching him at dinner.

"No, but what does it mean? I know what the point of flirting is, but you and me... I'm not sure what to do with that."

"I enjoy spending time with you. I have from the start. The more I get to know you, the more I want to be around you. You already know I'm gay. It's a fact I never hide. And while I'm well aware you're straight, I also can't deny this energy between us. It could be one-sided and, if so, that's on me and I'll back off. But if it isn't, if you're feeling something, too... Shit, I'm making a mess of things." I shook my head.

Marcus leaned forward and gripped my wrist before I could rake my hand through my hair. "No, you're not. I came here for answers. I want to know how you feel."

I swallowed. My tongue felt huge in my mouth. The words I wanted to spill got caught for a moment. I was afraid if I said too much, I'd chase him away and ruin the friendship we had; however, if I didn't voice this, the strain was already there. I developed feelings for Marcus. It was sink or swim time.

"I..." This was harder than I guessed it would be. "I've developed feelings for you, Marcus. I didn't mean to. Didn't set out to try and see if you could be bi or something else. But somewhere along the way, our friendship became so much more to me. I love talking to you. Hanging out with you. I love it when we text and I can bounce ideas off you. You understand me. And you've become this big part of my inner circle, which you know I rarely let anyone into. But with you, I want you there. I want you by my side as more than a friend."

He watched me. This time, he was blinking at least, so that was an improvement. Then he inched closer. I held my breath, trying not to let myself hope. I didn't want to be an experiment for him, but at the same time, I would take any part of him I could get. I was desperate for Marcus and that left me completely vulnerable.

Here I was laying everything out there. My hands shook in my lap. He didn't release my wrist. His thumb slowly stroked the inside of it. Did he realize he was doing it?

"What about never being with an athlete again?" he asked quietly.

"You make me want to break my rules."

Marcus got closer. There were only inches separating us. "I'm not sure what I'm doing."

"What do you want?"

"Answers," he whispered

"You can ask me anything you want."

"What if words won't tell me what I need to know?"

My heart was going to pound out of my chest. Was this really happening? Was Marcus leaning closer like he was going to kiss me? If this were a dream, I never wanted to wake up.

"Whatever you want, I'm here." I meant it. Marcus could do anything to me, ask me questions, touch me, talk some more. I was open to whatever he wanted.

"Kasper." My name on his lips gave me the courage to make a move.

I leaned forward and very gently brushed my lips over his. It was slow and sweet and not nearly enough. Nothing more than a featherlight touch. I needed him to make a move, though. I needed to know he wanted this. Wanted me.

Dropping my forehead to his, I looked into his eyes. Up close, his eyes weren't simply gray. They had flecks of silver in them. They held so much intensity and uncertainty.

"Tell me," I prompted. He was angled toward me and I placed my hand on his thigh. I could feel his body trembling. "I need words, Marcus."

He studied me. Heard the words I said, but it was like it took him a bit to process them before he seemed to focus on me. He reached for the back of my neck, holding on but not pulling me toward him. Desire swirled in his eyes and I knew we both wanted the same thing. "Please."

This time when I brought my lips to his, there was no barely-there touch. Our lips met and I couldn't hold back. I'd wanted to taste him for far too long.

My lips parted and my tongue teased along his until he gasped into my mouth. I didn't want to push him too hard, too fast, so I eased my tongue into his mouth. Went in search of his. And the moment they touched, it was like he finally decided to give in and taste me back.

His tongue met mine as we battled for dominance. But the thing was, in bed I let others take over. I didn't want to run things there. I wanted to give everything over to the one I was trusting my body with. I hadn't fully relinquished control with anyone since Hunter. With Marcus, I trusted him completely.

My hands went to either side of his neck as I pulled us closer and angled my head to get more of him. He used his strength and his hold on my wrist to tug me forward until I was straddling his lap.

Not once did Marcus break our kiss while his hands started exploring me. I could only imagine what he was thinking. This was the first time he ever kissed another guy, let alone got to touch one intimately. I had to be patient. Let his hands roam wherever they wanted.

His hands skimmed down my sides and over my stomach. His fingers traced over my pecs, each finding my nipples. With a quick pinch, I let out a whimper against his lips. It spurred him on. He flicked and teased my nipples. Rolled them between his fingers then gave them another pinch. The sting went right to my balls.

Moving to my back, he slid his hands down until they reached the top of my ass then stopped as if he weren't sure how far to go. He teased along the elastic of my waistband. I wasn't wearing anything underneath. I didn't think I was going to have company tonight and as sexually frustrated as I'd been, having easy access to my dick tonight was a priority.

"Touch me," I whispered against his lips. "Anywhere. Everywhere. I'll love it. I promise." There was nothing he could do wrong. Every touch of his sent fire racing across my skin.

It must have been what he needed to hear, because the next thing I knew, Marcus's large hands were inside my pants, palming my ass. I bucked forward to rub my hard dick against him, needing the friction. That started a slow grind and, while torturous, it wasn't nearly enough.

I coasted my hands down from his neck, to his shirt, and started undoing the buttons. "If you want me to stop at any point, just say the word and I will."

He kept kissing me but didn't respond.

"I need an acknowledgement, Marcus. Did you hear me?"

He nodded.

I continued working his shirt until the buttons were all undone then I pushed it over his shoulders and off, loving his warm skin beneath my hands. He was all hard muscles, tattoos, and so damn sexy. Not just on his stomach, chest, and arms. His legs were works of art. They were flexing beneath me. I could feel every movement. The power this man had was a huge turn-on.

There was so much more of him I wanted to explore. The way his finger kept tentatively dipping into my crease let me know he wasn't done playing, so I dropped my hands lower and started working his jeans open. I broke away from his mouth and kissed along his jaw while I did so.

He was hard as steel behind the zipper. It was like Christmas morning. I got to open up the gift I wanted but didn't think I'd ever receive.

Tugging at his jeans, I couldn't get them to move, so I eased back as he chased me with his lips and hands.

"Lift up," I told him and tugged his jeans past his knees.

I looked up, worried I might see hesitation on his part, however, there was nothing there but pure desire. Marcus wasn't scared off. He wanted this. Here. With me. That made my decision to pull down my sweats and kick them off easier.

Then I was back on his lap. The moment our bare dicks touched, he groaned loudly and my hands held on to his shoulders for dear life. I was seconds from coming, more worked up than I'd been in a long time.

My body took over as my mind checked out. I started grinding against Marcus, chasing that high I so desperately desired. Looking down, I found Marcus's gaze on me. He was so fucking beautiful. So perfect.

"Please, Kas." His voice was rough with need.

I knew what he wanted, even if he couldn't find the words. I kissed him again as I collected precum from my tip and used it as lube. I brought us together in my hand, squeezing slightly, starting to jerk us at the same time.

Marcus gripped my hips and began fucking my hand. The feel of his dick against mine, along with the tight channel of my hand, had me right on the edge again.

"Come for me," I begged him. I could barely hang on. "I've got you. I won't let you fall."

One more upward stroke of my hand, his body tensed, and Marcus started coming in hot spurts over my hand, our stomachs, and his chest. I held out long enough for him to ride most of his orgasm out before I let go, too. I cried out his name then tugged his bottom lip between my teeth as wave after wave of white-hot bliss rolled over me.

When I finally came back to earth, I had released his lip and dropped my head to his shoulder. We were both panting hard.

I was scared to look into his eyes. Instead, I grabbed a handful of tissues from the box on the end table beside the couch and went to work cleaning us off before tossing them to the side.

Every insecurity, every doubt, started working their way into my head until my hand started shaking with fear. Did I just ruin our friendship? Did I push him too far tonight? Did he regret what happened between us?

Confidence was something I had in spades when it came to my businesses. In relationships, I was petrified to give my heart to anyone. Afraid they'd take it and walk all over it.

Marcus used his finger to tip my chin up until our eyes met. He kissed me once. Twice. Three times then wrapped me in his arms. It was exactly what I needed and he somehow knew it.

We had things to discuss. Words we needed to say. However, they didn't have to happen yet. I wanted to hold on to Marcus for as long as he let me, even if it was only for tonight.

Chapter 17

Marcus

The moon high in the deep black sky illuminated the room and the man lying in front of me. After more kissing, Kasper brought me into the bedroom where, for the first time in my life, I wrapped my hand around a dick that wasn't my own. In the heat of the moment, everything seemed right. Seemed perfect. I passed out with Kasper wrapped tightly in my arms.

Desire and lust ruling me, I hadn't thought twice about what I'd done with Kasper. Feelings and emotions ran my actions. Now, in the silence of the night, surrounded by the heat of Kasper's body and the scent of his cologne, I couldn't turn my brain off. His back to my chest, he was everywhere and I just couldn't think.

Gently sliding my arm from around his waist, I waited until I heard his soft snores continue. Then I slipped from the bed. The muscles in my back and shoulders were tense as I tiptoed from the room. Kasper deserved honesty about my feelings, something I was unable to give him while my mind wasn't on the same page as my body.

Memories of his hands in my hair, his lips on my neck, flitted through my mind. And I couldn't stop my dick from getting hard again. I pushed the memories down. Lust wasn't enough of a reason for me to crawl back into bed and curl up with Kasper again. I needed to work through the emotions on my own. Then I could be upfront and honest with him about what I wanted from our relationship.

Friendship *or more*.

But I also knew it wouldn't be fair to leave Kasper without saying anything. There was no point in waking him to give him words I didn't have. Maybe it didn't have to be something I said.

On the side of the room was a desk where I found hotel stationary and a pen. My hand trembled as I touched the point of the pen to the paper, and my heart ached as I began to write. A few weeks ago, I'd told Kasper he deserved his own Valentine, if that wasn't me, as much as it would hurt to lose him in my life, I'd have to let him go. Something I was nowhere near ready to do yet.

Kasper,

I had to be at the field early and didn't want to wake you. But I promise to see you after the game.

Marcus

It was definitely the chicken's way out, but it was better than leaving without anything. After I propped the note on the nightstand where Kasper was sure to find it, I quietly shut the bedroom door behind me. Clothing was strewn all over the room where we hadn't bothered to care where it landed. The car keys jingled in the pocket of my jeans as I pulled them on. Once I was fully dressed, I left Kasper's hotel room behind.

On the drive back to the house, I forced myself to focus. No need to get into an accident because I was currently freaking out.

Watch the reflectors on the road.

Make a left.

Make the next right.

I let the simple commands run on repeat in my head until I pulled into the driveway and turned off the engine.

Dominic and Ayden still hadn't returned home. At two in the morning, there was no doubt they'd feel like shit tomorrow, but that was their problem. I had enough of my own at the moment. The house was dark and silent. Part of me expected to still hear sounds of the guys with their men, even if I knew they'd be long asleep. The guilt of leaving had me looking for things that just weren't there.

I climbed the stairs as quietly as I could. With Dominic and Ayden both on the first floor, the only person coming upstairs would be me. I hoped after hours of whatever they'd been up to, *the same things you'd been up to with Kasper,* they'd be out cold. Having any kind of conversation about where I'd been was strictly off-limits. I didn't have answers for most of the questions myself.

The moment I shut my bedroom door, I walked over and sat down on the edge of my bed, holding my head in my hands. In the solitude of my room, I finally let all the fears and worries that had started earlier when I woke up with my arms around Kasper consume me.

What had I been thinking?

I'd gone to Kasper looking for answers, wondering about Dominic's comments and the way Kasper flirted with me at dinner. Not to end up kissing him. Getting off with him. It didn't help the way my heart raced at the look on Kasper's face when he gave over to the passion and let himself go. I had to wonder if some part of my brain expected exactly what happened. How could I go looking for answers about Kasper flirting with me and not expect my lips to end up on his, otherwise, why bother going to look for answers in the first place?

I laid back on the bed, staring at the ceiling. The night's events played through my head as a sense of déjà vu came over me. Only a few hours ago, I was downstairs doing the same exact thing. Even having the answers to the questions I'd wanted, I laid there with a million more unanswered ones.

There was no denying how hard I came with Kasper's hand wrapped tightly around my cock. And I definitely couldn't mistake him for a woman. But what did all of this mean for me? Was I gay? Bi? Or was it only Kasper who made me feel this way?

The longer I laid there, the more I realized that none of it mattered anyway. Labels or the why of it. The way I felt in Kasper's arms tonight was undeniable. It was passion and fire. Lust and satisfaction. But more than that, the connection we had ran deeper than any I had with another person. It was everything I'd been looking for, I just hadn't realized it.

Now the question became whether I was willing to give up that connection, that fire, because Kasper was a man. I'd always seen myself as straight. A man who'd find a wife and have kids someday. Slowly, in my mind, I could see that picture change. Two men could still have a family. Have everything I'd always wanted.

No. I wasn't willing to give up Kasper because he didn't fit the mold of what I was expecting.

Time to make a new one.

With my decision made, I stripped off my clothes and crawled under the covers, knowing I only had a few hours left of sleep before I'd need to be up. Nine innings before I could talk to Kasper.

***

It seemed as if only minutes had passed when the alarm went off and it was time to pull myself out of bed. Exhausted, I forced myself up and, in a zombie state, got ready to head over to the field.

Evan eyed me curiously as I came down the stairs, but surprisingly enough, he didn't say a word. Evan and Spencer were getting a ride to the game from Kasper, guaranteeing I'd get to see him before I got to talk to him. He deserved to know it all after the game and I'd make sure he did.

Every inning of the game dragged on as if each were a game of its own. I caught sight of Kasper in the stands in the middle of the third inning. He smiled at me, but I could tell it was forced. My stomach tightened. I had no doubt he was upset at waking up alone this morning and probably thought the worst. Soon enough, he'd know there was nothing to fear. From then on, if I went to sleep next to him, I'd wake up next to him.

When the game finally ended, excitement had me practically bouncing on the balls of my feet. Even the day's loss couldn't pull me down.

In the locker room, Callen stopped me. "Hey, Spencer and I have plans tonight and I think Vander and Evan do, too. Would you mind keeping Kasper company? I feel like shit knowing he flew them down here to have him sit in the hotel by himself tonight."

"Sure. No problem." Either Callen had no idea how close Kasper and I had become or he knew and was doing his own meddling. Either way, I had not a single problem keeping Kasper company tonight. If I had my way, after we talked, we'd be keeping each other company with no clothes on.

"Thanks, man." He clapped me on the shoulder and went to the showers.

I followed suit. This time, I'd been prepared with jeans and a V-neck shirt, hoping Kasper and I would be able to do our own thing tonight. I finished showering and came out to find most of the locker room empty. Callen and Vander were long gone, which meant Kasper was probably outside alone, waiting for me.

When I stepped out into the warm, evening air, everything felt different than it had just twenty-four hours earlier. Kasper stood next to his rental, glancing everywhere but at me. With confident strides, I walked over and stood directly in front of him. He reached up and rubbed his hand along the back of his neck.

"Callen and Spencer went somewhere for dinner and asked if I'd be able to take you home."

"How about dinner first?"

His eyes continued to dart around the parking lot. "Sure. Where would you like to go?"

"Can we order room service from your hotel? I want us to talk and I don't think we need an audience for that."

Kasper swallowed hard and nodded, turning to move around to the driver's side of the car. Before he took a step, I grabbed his hand, making him look back at me. "I promise, everything will be okay."

His smile was pained as he nodded again and moved around to climb into the SUV. I tossed my bag in the back seat and got in. The ride to the hotel was made in complete silence. I wanted to be face-to-face for this conversation, but with each mile that passed, I regretted even more getting out of bed and not having this conversation before I left.

Kasper still hadn't spoken a word when he unlocked his door and we stepped inside. He dropped the keys and room card on the coffee table and went straight for the desk to pick up the phone. "What do you want to eat? I'm not hungry but I'll order you something."

I walked over and took the phone out of his hand, put it down, and gripped his hand in mine, bringing him back over to the couch where I'd had the most explosive night of my life. "Let's talk first."

I took a seat and watched Kasper sit as far away from me as humanly possible. Well, that wouldn't do. Scooting closer, I placed my hand on his knee to stop him from moving backward.

He looked at my hand then back up at me. "What do you want to talk about?"

"First, I want to apologize. I'm sorry I left last night without waking you up. But there were so many things running through my head, I needed some time alone to process it." I moved my thumb back and forth over his knee. The stiffness in his shoulders relaxed slightly. "I didn't mean to hurt you, but I wanted to give you answers. I meant what I said about you deserving someone to love and take care of you."

Kasper tried to move again. "Let me guess, you think I'll find it, but it's not you."

When he tried to stand, I added more pressure to my grip. Keeping my gaze fixed on him, I laid it all out there. "Not at all, actually. I want to give this thing between us a try. Yes, I had to sort through my feelings for you. Why I'd never been attracted to a guy before now. How I'd never come as hard in my life as I had last night, and what it meant for me as a person."

He slid a bit closer to me and it seemed as though I was getting through to him. "What does it mean?"

"It means it doesn't matter that you're a man. All that matters is the way you make me feel. For years I've tried to connect to every single woman I dated. The physical attraction was there but the emotional one never was." I moved my hand farther up his leg and watched the heat spark in his eyes. "With you, it is. The emotional and the physical. If being with you makes me feel like I did last night, then I know I'm with the right person."

Kasper opened his mouth to answer and closed it. Instead, he grabbed me by the back of the neck and pulled me into the hottest kiss I'd ever experienced. Our tongues tangled for dominance, the heat overtaking us once again. I pulled back breathless, watching the quick rise and fall of his chest.

As our panting breaths returned to normal, he turned to look at the phone and back at me. "Guess we should get your dinner ordered."

I stood and walked toward the bedroom, tugging my shirt off in the process. "Or you could join me in here and show me again what it feels like to have your cock rubbing against mine. We can eat afterward." Kasper was up and around the couch in a flash.

Dinner could never compare to him.

We spent the next hour proving that we only needed each other to survive.

Chapter 18

Kasper

"What do you say?" Tim Deary asked.

I was sitting opposite him in his office. He just made a massive business proposal. Tim wanted to buy the Espen Sandpipers. The football team hadn't been doing well with their management nor their season. They needed an overhaul. Tim would be great at it, but he didn't have the money alone to pull off the purchase. I did, but taking on another sports team... I wasn't sure.

"This is a huge undertaking," I replied. "We're not talking about taking a strong team and making a few tweaks. Easily running a successful season. We'd have to go through every member of management, the players, and their contracts. The only good thing we have going for us is that it's their off-season."

Tim leaned forward. His salt-and-pepper hair was neatly styled and his dark eyes gleamed with ambition and hope. "We could do it. The Sandpipers aren't a completely lost cause."

"No, they're not. This is a lot to consider. I'm going to have to get back to you on it."

He nodded. "I understand. We have time. Word isn't even out that Kyle wants to sell. He came to me asking if I wanted it before he opened it up to others."

"How long will he wait?"

"A bit. That doesn't mean you can take months to decide."

"No, I get it. I'll think about it." I stood and extended my hand to Tim. He shook it as he stood as well. "I appreciate you bringing the proposal to me. I'll be in touch."

"Thanks, Kasper. I look forward to hearing from you."

As I walked back to my car, I knew I didn't want to take Tim up on the offer, but if I turned him down right off the bat, he would try to keep persuading me. I had no doubt he'd send over the financial information and other stats for the team for me to review. I'd go over it, but in the end, my decision would remain the same. I had one sports team. I didn't need another. I honestly wasn't a huge football fan. Hockey was where my heart was as well as baseball, apparently.

I headed back to my office for yet another meeting. One of the Jetties players had gotten into some hot water and it was plastered all over social media. Katie was trying to put out fires left and right, but I could tell she was drowning. I needed to help her with whatever I could.

Being the owner of the team didn't mean I let everyone else take care of things while I lavished in everything an owner had. I liked to be involved. I liked getting to know the management, the coaches, the players. I wanted to be in the nitty-gritty of things with them and use the business skills I'd honed over the years to help. After all, I needed to set an example for the team. I couldn't expect them to work hard if I wasn't willing to.

Hours ticked by and one fire spread into more. Seemed social media blowing up wasn't our only problem. Our goalie had gotten into a fight and fractured one of his fingers.

By the time I looked at the clock, I realized I was missing the opening game for the Emperors. I slammed my hand down on the desk. The sound reverberated through my office. "Goddammit!" Of all the things I wanted to do today, I needed to be at the game for Marcus. He'd even said there was a seat waiting for me. And I fucked up by missing it.

A knock sounded on my door. Of course, Paz heard me.

"Come in," I called.

Paz slipped in and closed the door behind him. "Everything okay?"

"I'm missing the game."

He nodded. "Yes. I tried to tell you an hour ago, but you yelled and told me to leave." Shit. He had.

I groaned and scrubbed my hands over my face. "Why do you put up with me?"

Paz smiled. "You pay me really well and I like to buy nice things."

"Be serious. You can't let me yell at you like that. Hand me my ass if you have to."

"You know we don't cross that line, Kas, no matter how nice your ass is."

I picked up a pen and threw it at him. He easily dodged it. He also managed to get me to smile. He was right. There was no way in hell we'd ever be more than friends and coworkers. "Marcus is going to kill me."

Paz walked over until I could see the sincerity in his warm, brown eyes. "I don't know Marcus well, but he's someone you let into your life and kept there. That tells me he's good people. And being as such, he's well aware of the businessman you are. He'll forgive you."

I hadn't told Pascal about my new relationship with Marcus. Paz handled my schedule and basically managed my life for me. Plus, I trusted him fully. I didn't want to out Marcus without his permission, though.

It had only been a couple weeks with Marcus, though they had been amazing. We hadn't seen each other much, thanks to spring training, but when he came home, we met up. Nothing more than shared kisses and touches. Cuddling in bed. We hadn't gone further than getting each other off and I was fine with it. Although, I wouldn't lie to myself and say I didn't wonder how it would feel to have Marcus finally take me. To have him inside me.

Paz waved his hand in front of my face until I focused on him again. He smirked. "I'd ask where you went just now, but I'm pretty sure I already know." I wondered if he guessed there was something between Marcus and me. "Do you need anything else?"

"Make sure I leave here in an hour, please. I'm missing the game but maybe I can make it up to him."

"I'm sure you'll think of something." He winked and turned on his heel toward the door. "One hour."

"Thank you."

I had to put Marcus out of my head and focus on the emails that piled up while I was busy today with other things. There was one from Tim, which I decided to put off for the time being. I started going through my messages and it felt like no time at all had passed before Paz was in my office, practically shoving me out the door. I made him shut his computer down as well and follow me out. He'd worked long enough today.

The sun had set by the time I walked to my car. After saying goodnight to Paz, I got in and made my way home. Since I normally didn't cook dinner, I knew there was something good at home waiting for me, thanks to the wonderful woman who helped keep my home in order. I just had to heat it up.

My first order of business when I entered my living room was to write a long, sappy, and overly apologetic text to Marcus. He wouldn't see it yet since they were still playing. They had a night game and when I flipped on the television, it was already the top of the seventh. The game would be over soon. It also made me realize how late I stayed in the office. I had to watch the clock better.

I ate dinner in front of the TV, barely tasting what was in my mouth, instead completely focused on the game. I jumped up and cheered when the Emperors won. No one saw me but I had to cheer on the team, especially Marcus. I sent him a text saying how well he played and I congratulated him, telling him to call when he could. The team was surely going to celebrate tonight, so I might not hear from him until the early morning hours when he crawled home.

Our relationship, if that was what we were calling it, felt very fragile. Marcus said he wanted to try this thing with me. Meanwhile, I jumped in with both feet. There was a part of me that said to be careful. To not sink too far, too fast, but it was already too late for that. I was in deep. Not that I could tell Marcus that. I'd scare him away for sure.

I had to hope, above everything else, I wasn't just a place holder until someone better came along. That I wasn't simply here for him to discover this other side of his sexuality.

Marcus was genuine in everything he did and that translated to the bedroom as well. He was passionate and caring. Patient and intense. It was those things that kept me hopeful. I needed something to cling to or else I'd let the doubts consume me, and I didn't want that.

Falling for another athlete wasn't smart. I knew that. I couldn't stop this thing with Marcus, though. It felt like the universe was telling me to take a leap. Of course, that leap could be off a cliff eventually. I wasn't on the precipice yet. I was still a good deal away from the edge. I didn't need to see the view from there. I liked it right where I was, safely back and not in danger of falling and breaking everything, including my heart.

An hour and a half later, there was a knock at my door. My heart started to race at the thought of Marcus being on the other side. Not many could come right up to my place. Anything business related, I would have been called or texted. Evan and Spencer were no doubt with their men or waiting for them.

I held my breath as I opened the door and revealed a very sexy Marcus Warnes. I stepped forward with a smile and embraced him. "Congrats on the win. You did great."

We pulled apart and I held the door open for him. "Thanks. It was a good game." He walked into the space as I shut the door. He didn't go into the living room or sit down.

I came around so I could face him. Was he angry I didn't show tonight? "Did you get my messages?" The insecure side of me appeared, waiting for him to be pissed and walk out.

"I did." He studied me for a second. "I'm not mad, Kas. I understand you have businesses to run." He stepped closer and cupped my jaw, slowly caressing my stubble. "I'm not going anywhere."

A shuddering breath left me. I closed my eyes and leaned into his touch. "I'm sorry. I really wanted to be there tonight, but King did something stupid and it was all over social media. Then Leslie got into a fight and broke a finger." I'd lost track of how many times Leslie Knoxton got into fights. The goalie was not a small man. Others seemed to love picking on him for his name. He was one of the calmest individuals I'd ever met, yet make fun of his name and the gloves came off. Leslie was his father's name and his grandfather's. It was one he proudly loved and embraced.

"Kas," Marcus said my name gently, causing me to open my eyes. "Stop. I'm not mad. You don't have to explain things to me. We both have demanding jobs. All that matters is we meet in the middle when we can. It's why I'm here."

"You didn't want to celebrate with the rest of the team?"

"I was with them for a little bit and, while I love the team and my friends, from the time my feet left the field, I only had one destination in sight. I wanted to be with you, not them."

Leaning forward, I pressed my lips to his and tasted the beer he had been drinking. It was a slow, drugging kiss. One where our tongues moved in languid strokes as we got as close as we could to each other with our clothes still on.

Marcus backed me up until I hit the back of the couch. Then his hands were everywhere. I was dizzy with lust as he owned me. He could take me down until I was nothing but raw need. He could ask me anything in those moments and I'd bare my soul to him.

With a quick movement I didn't see coming, he gripped the backs of my thighs and lifted me until my ass rested on the top of the couch and my legs wrapped around him. I had on a pair of sweatpants and a T-shirt I changed into after the game was over. I was hard and so damn eager for him. Whatever he wanted to do, whatever he needed, I would give it to him.

"Marcus," I moaned against his lips as his hand dipped beneath the elastic of my pants and he wrapped his strong, callused fingers around my length.

"Shh, I'll take care of you."

I pulled back, gulping in much needed air. "I should be taking care of you. You're the one who played hard tonight."

"Just because I play a professional sport doesn't mean I had a day more challenging or mentally exhausting than you did. You work hard as well. And tonight, we're going to play hard."

"Fuck," I muttered.

I dove back in for his lips. My fingers fumbled at the front of his jeans. He stepped away to take over and dropped them to the floor before kicking them all the way off. I did the same, standing bare from the waist down.

I'd wanted to get my mouth on Marcus since we first started this. I wanted to know how he felt on my tongue, but we'd kept it to using our hands and rubbing against each other.

Marcus stepped forward and gripped my shirt at the hem to pull it over my head. He did the same with his. Next thing I knew, he was spinning me around until I was naked and bent over the back of the couch. My hands gripped the cushions as his strong body curled over mine and his dick nestled against my crease. Maybe tonight wasn't the night I got Marcus in my mouth, but I was completely on board with the direction we were going in.

He rubbed there a few times before moving his dick until it was between my legs, nudging my balls with every thrust. I moaned and clenched my thighs, tightening the grip I had on him. In that moment, I was grateful for the leg exercises I did so I could hold him how I was.

His breath coasted over the shell of my ear as his hands gripped my waist to hold me in place. "One day,

I'm going to take you like this. Would you like that, Kas?"

"Fuck, yes."

"Mmmm... me, too." I didn't know what had gotten into Marcus, but if this was the way he celebrated, he could come over every damned time they won.

He kept up the movement between my legs and gripped my dick in his hand. He pumped me in time with every thrust. I was on the razor's edge, so close to coming.

Marcus swiped the precum from my tip and used it to make his palm slick. "Come for me," he whispered.

Two more tugs and I was spilling into his hand, onto the back of the couch, and the floor. My thigh muscles flexed, triggering Marcus to follow with his own orgasm. He groaned out my name as he came. His cum dripped down my legs, warm and sticky.

Damn, he really took to this whole being with a guy thing better than I could have ever hoped. And he hadn't forgotten what I said when I told him there was one place I relinquished control. Marcus was listening. He heard me.

He rested his forehead against my spine while he caught his breath. "This was so much better than celebrating with the guys."

Chapter 19

Marcus

Pinkish-orange lights seeped in through the blinds of my hotel room. Normally, it would piss me off to be woken up long before I had to get ready to head to the field. Not this morning. What the sun and my alarm didn't seem to realize was that I'd been up for the last hour or so trying to figure out a way to get my shit together.

A little over ten days into the season and I'd only had one good game to speak of—opening day. The excitement of that first game had a way of bringing out your best. Even if you lost, it was only because the other team's best was better than yours. The games after that did not have the same outcome. And for every mistake I tried to fix, it seemed like I made two more.

Ever since game two, when in the third inning I felt a small tug on the side of my right knee and fears of getting hurt had me being extra cautious with every move I made. No matter how hard I tried to get it out of my head, in those spilt second moments of decision-making, I always took the safest route.

In hindsight, I knew I should've made a different decision, but no matter how many times I told myself that, I continued to favor my knee. The team doctor and physical therapists all asked if I was all right. Time and again, I told them yes. We were barely two weeks in, I knew I could work whatever this was out of my head.

Then, to add to the stress over my job was also the stress about my relationship with Kasper. Not exactly the relationship part. Everything there was fantastic. More than I ever could have imagined. It sucked being away from home since that first series. Somehow, I knew being in Kasper's arms would go a long way to clearing my head. Unfortunately, our first two away series came right on the back of our first three home games.

I talked to Kasper every night, it just wasn't the same. The physical connection, the comfort was what I craved. And if I wanted that from Kasper, I had to be honest about what we were to each other. We'd kept everything to ourselves until I had time to talk to my family. They deserved to know from me, not from a tabloid or whoever else decided to exploit the information.

Grabbing my phone from the nightstand, I checked the time. Eight in the morning. Not too early for my parents. Sienna may not be awake, but I could just talk to her later. My neck grew damp as I scrolled through the contacts looking for their number. In a perfect world, this shouldn't be a big deal.

If only we lived in a perfect world.

In reality, this was a very big deal. I didn't give two shits about fans or any of that crap. My family was an entirely different story. We were close, and I was afraid to lose that.

I thought about Kasper's smile when I made him laugh and the feel of his head on my chest as we slept. A place I hadn't been for too many days. If I were honest, I would say it wasn't just my knee that had been affecting my performance. Even though our relationship was still new, I knew I had to make this call. And maybe I had avoided it until the day I'd be flying home to Kasper.

I sucked in a breath and hit send. By the time my mom answered in less than two rings, my hands had started to shake and my stomach felt queasy.

"Hello."

"Hey, Mom." My voice sounded a bit higher pitched than normal. Something she'd see through right away.

"Hi, Marcus. I didn't expect to hear from you this early. Don't you have to leave for the field soon?"

"No, it's a three o'clock game." The phone still pressed to my ear, I didn't know exactly how to start this conversation. Mom didn't have that problem. Like always, she knew exactly what we needed when we needed it.

"Marcus." Her voice held so much kindness. "I can tell something is bothering you. Dad and I have seen it whenever you step onto the field. You know you can talk to us."

I gripped the phone even tighter, hoping she still meant it when I was done. "I know. That's why I called.

Is Dad there? I want to talk to everyone together, but I'll call Sienna later."

"Actually, she's here. She had an early morning shoot and brought bagels for breakfast on her way home. Let me get Dad and I'll put you on speaker." I could hear my mom calling for my dad, but I couldn't sit still any longer. My feet moved across the floor of their own volition.

"Marcus, is everything okay? Is your knee all right?" My dad's voice came over the line.

Rolling my shoulders back, I sucked in a deep breath. "Yeah, Dad. My knee is fine. And everything is okay. Actually, things are better than okay. I just hope you guys think it is, too."

"If it makes you happy, then that's all that matters."

I forced my feet to stop moving and sat down on the edge of the bed. "This is definitely something I should be telling you in person, but I know it will be awhile before I can get home again." The words got stuck in my throat before I pushed them out in a rush. "I'm in a relationship with Kasper Wilder."

"Holy shit!" Sienna yelled, but other than that, there was dead silence.

I held my breath, waiting for an answer. Sweat beaded on my temple as I waited for anything. What was probably only a few minutes felt like hours. All while there was nothing on the other end of the line until my mom finally spoke up.

"Marcus, were you worried that we'd be angry that you're dating a man?"

I rubbed my hand across the back of my neck. "I didn't know what you would think. Hell, I didn't know what to think at first."

"Oh, dear, we're definitely surprised, but as long as our children are happy, we're happy."

"Damn, Marcus," Dad said. "You had me worried that the problem with your knee had gotten worse. This will be different but easier to deal with than you getting hurt."

The secret that had weighed so heavily on my shoulders for the last few weeks lifted almost instantly.

"So does this mean you're bi?" Sienna asked.

I shrugged, even though she couldn't see me. "Apparently."

"So unfair, Marcus. He's sexy as hell."

I laughed, but my dad interrupted, wanting to talk about my knee some more. We stayed on the phone for a little bit longer, me reassuring my parents that physically I was fine. They'd also noticed the struggles I had on the field. Things that were second nature to me. After promising them that I'd call again soon, I hung up and got ready to head over to the stadium.

A text from Spencer arrived right as I got to the stadium. He'd also noticed the stiffness in some of my moves and reminded me to continue with the stretches. He also gave me a few extra exercises that should help keep my knee loose through the entire game. By the time I finished the warm-up and the extra stretches, I felt relaxed and ready to face the game.

If only my day had continued on the positive note it had started on. Instead, I found myself behind the plate in the bottom of the ninth up by one. The rest of the team had done everything they needed to win this game. Me, on the other hand, I hadn't been able to connect with the ball the entire game. And while there hadn't been any mistakes, I still didn't feel like I'd been playing as well as I normally did.

Two more outs and we'd be on the road home. Out of the corner of my eye, I saw the runner at first take a commanding lead. I couldn't blame him. If he could get the steal, they had two runners in scoring position if they got a base hit. The moment the ball left Meller's hand, I prepared myself to pop up the second it hit my glove. Up I came and whipped the ball toward Callen, who covered second, but it was a little off and flew past his glove. Both runners bolted, making it to home before my team could get the ball back to me.

Fuck!

Another loss. This one squarely on my shoulders. I went through the motions, congratulating the other team. Showering. Getting on the bus to the airport. My teammates tried to talk to me. Even Callen tried to take the blame for my shitty throw. Jose and Gian claimed they should have been better backup. But I knew the truth. This loss was on me. We all made mistakes that might cost us the game, but mine seemed to be more frequent lately.

The short flight had us back in Espen in two hours. Callen and Dominic wanted to go out and get a drink, shake off the game. I just wanted to go home and figure out what the fuck was wrong with me.

I shut the door to my condo and dropped my bag by the door. It could stay there until tomorrow when we had the day off. At least, a day off from games. Joe wanted us down at the field for a workout midmorning. I grabbed a beer from the fridge before heading to the living room to relax on the couch and wallow in my own misery. Who knew I'd be having a career crisis at the young age of twenty-eight?

One beer down and I was on my way to the kitchen for another when there was a knock on my door. I groaned. Enough of my friends had access to my condo without a call up, so I could imagine them on the other side of the door trying to cheer me up. I popped the top on the beer and wandered slowly to the door. Maybe if I took long enough they'd go away.

Another knock. No such luck. I pulled the door open and was happy when they hadn't gone away.

"I thought you could use dinner and beer?" Kasper held up a bag of takeout and a six-pack.

I stepped back and held the door open. "I guess you saw the game."

He sighed and nudged the door shut behind him with his foot. "I did. And I knew you'd be here going over every play of the last two series in your head until you made yourself crazy."

I took the beer from his hand and followed him into my kitchen. He set the bag on the counter and wrapped his arm around my waist, pulling me tight to his chest. His lips touched mine and I sank into the kiss, trying to let all the things that troubled me fall away. He broke the kiss first, cupping my cheek and caressing it with his thumb.

"Let's get some food in you before the beer I know you're going to keep drinking does its damage on you." Kasper had been there enough to know where I kept everything. In no time, he had food on plates, open beers, and was guiding me out to the living room.

The food was good, but the company was better. Kasper knew I'd talk about it when I was ready. Until then, he sat there and his presence was enough. I finished my plate and sat it on the table, surprised at how hungry I actually was considering the mess in my head.

We sat in silence, drinking beer and watching one another. I twisted the bottle in my hands, trying to find the words.

"I can't get out of my head anymore. At first, I thought it was the fear of hurting my knee again. I'm favoring it at times, but I don't think it's enough to make as many mistakes as I have lately. Then, I wondered if it was because I hadn't told my parents about us yet, so I called them this morning."

Kasper's brows rose. "You told your parents about us?"

"I did. I told you, I didn't want to keep our relationship hidden. I just wanted them to hear it from me. Not a tabloid."

He slid closer to me and placed his hand on my thigh. "I know. I guess I didn't expect you to tell them so soon. I figured you'd want to fly out and talk to them."

I placed my hand over his and squeezed. "I probably should've waited to tell them in person, but with the season in full swing, who knows when I'd get a chance to go and see them. I didn't want to wait anymore."

"How did it go?"

I chuckled. "Well, Sienna is jealous as fuck since you're so hot." Kasper laughed with me. "And my parents were more worried about my knee than the fact that I'm dating a man. They said as long as I'm happy, that's all that matters."

"And what about your knee? I know you've told me it's fine. Is it really?"

"It is." I ran my hand down my face. "But that's what has me so frustrated. If my knee is fine and I told my parents, why the hell am I still playing like shit?" I lifted the beer to my lips and took a sip.

"Let me ask you a question. Have you ever overthrown second during a steal?"

I shrugged. "Sure. What catcher hasn't?"

"And you felt good going into today's game?"

My brows drew together as I looked at him. "Yeah. At least, until I couldn't hit the damn ball then lost the game for everyone."

"Stay with me for a second here. I know you think these events are connected, but maybe it's actually two different problems. Let's say the last few games had to do with the stress from your knee and telling your family about us. And today's game was just one of those games."

I took another swig from the bottle. "If it were only the overthrow, I could get behind that, but I couldn't connect the bat with the ball."

Kasper shook his head and ran his thumb along my lower lip. No matter how my day was, any part of his body touching my lips got my dick hard. It pushed against my zipper, begging to be free. I had to shove thoughts of Kasper's mouth around my dick to the side to bring myself back into the conversation. Things hadn't gotten that far yet, but goddamn if I didn't want them to.

"The score was two to three. Besides Callen and Dominic, their pitcher took out every single man on your team. Not even Vander hit the ball. Do you think he's home beating himself up about how shitty of a game he played?"

I scoffed. "I doubt that. More than a week away, he's probably balls deep in Evan at this point." We both shivered at the thought. "Sorry, I didn't need to put that visual in either of our heads." Thinking about being balls deep in Kasper was sexy. Thinking about my friends doing it were visions I didn't need in my brain.

"Agreed. Look, you need to let the last few games go. Everything that was bothering you is taken care of. Now you have a day off to regroup. I have no doubt you'll go out there and kick ass in two days."

"Do you really think so?" I knew I sounded young, I just needed the reassurance only Kasper could give me.

"Trust me, Marc. Everything will be fine." My entire body froze. Kasper sensed it immediately. He flipped his hand over to take mine and squeeze. "Did I say something wrong?"

I couldn't stop the instant reaction that name caused. It only served to remind me of a time when people didn't bother to stick around. When jealousy took years of friendship and flushed it. I tried to push away the negative feelings from that name to look at the man in front of me. The man who I believed wouldn't go anywhere unless I forced him out of my life.

I squeezed his hand back. "No, it's just been a really long time since anyone called me that."

"I'm sorry. I didn't mean to upset you."

I set the bottle on the table and pulled Kasper to me, taking his lips with mine for a brief, I wanted so much more, kiss. First, I owed him a story. "You didn't. The quick version of the story is that my best friend since kindergarten, Zach, was the only person to call me Marc besides Sienna. When we were young, he couldn't say my whole name and shortened it to Marc. It just stuck and since Sienna spent a lot of time with us, she picked it up as well. We played baseball our entire lives together. But when I got the full ride to Notre Dame and he couldn't get anything above a D3 school, he stopped speaking to me." We'd both hoped to get in Division 1 colleges, but the best offer he got was a Division 3. They had baseball programs, but the chance of making it to the majors from there was slim.

"I'm sorry. It slipped out. I won't use it again. I don't want to make you uncomfortable."

I let go of his hand and cupped his face with both of mine, tilting it for better access to his mouth. "I think I like you calling me Marc."

Our lips connected and lightning zipped through my veins. I missed the taste of him. The feel of him. Without everything else weighing me down, I was able to enjoy him. Kasper had a way of making me feel invincible. Wednesday, I'd go out there and kick ass. Until then, I was going to enjoy every touch and taste of the man before me.

The hard shaft in my jeans pulsed in time with the racing of my heart. I slipped my hands beneath his shirt, feeling the firm muscles of his pecs and tight buds of his nipples. His groan vibrated our lips. When I felt his fingers at the hem of my shirt, I broke the kiss and yanked my shirt over my head, watching as he followed suit.

"God, you're sexy." I laid my hands against his skin, feeling the hair beneath my fingertips.

"All I have to do is look at you and I'm hard." Kasper kissed down my neck, moving lower to slip from the couch and drop to his knees between my spread thighs.

My cock jumped at the sight and that was before he ran his fingers over my fabric covered dick. Heat blazed in his eyes.

My hips thrusted up into his hand. "Kasper, it's not enough."

He continued to stroke me. "I want to taste you."

"Oh god." My dick pressed against the zipper of my pants. "Yes. Put your fucking mouth on me."

Kasper's fingers moved to the button of my jeans, quickly undoing it and tugging down the zipper. I thought I might combust from the anticipation alone of having his mouth on me. It wasn't like I hadn't dreamed of being able to fuck his mouth.

"Up." He tapped my hip and I lifted so he could pull my jeans and boxer briefs down my thighs. My cock sprang to attention the moment it was free of its confines. "I've been dying to taste you."

I sank my fingers into the hair at the back of his head, knowing he liked someone else to take control in the bedroom. "Then taste me."

Kasper's mouth opened. The moment the warm wet heat of his mouth engulfed me, I thought I'd lose it. I shoved the orgasm down and enjoyed the way Kasper's mouth stretched around my dick. I traced my fingers around his lips, loving the way he looked on his knees before me. This strong, confident man wanted me. And it was more than just sex but the connection I felt to him in every touch.

As his mouth moved up and down my shaft, tasting, teasing, the pressure in my balls increased. Never one to be a quick trigger, I blamed it on the week we went without seeing each other. The missing time was why I tightened my fingers in Kasper's hair. It was why I thrust my hips up and down, pushing my dick into his mouth. And it was definitely why I cried out when he took me all the way into the back of his throat.

Who was I kidding? I was a horny bastard around Kasper. It could have been less than twenty-four hours since the last time I saw him and I'd still want to be buried deep in his throat.

Just as I felt the telltale tingling in the base of my spine, Kasper groaned around me, sending the most delicious vibrations around my dick. That was all it took. I came in a rush, mesmerized as Kasper swallowed down every drop.

Limply, I dropped back against the couch. I needed to get my wits together and take care of Kasper, but first, I had to catch my breath. When I could finally move, I sat forward to reach for him. I saw the wet spot on the front of his pants. He glanced up at me with his eyes glazed over and a smile on his lips.

"Sucking me gets you off, does it?"

"Yes," he moaned and pressed the heel of his hand to his dick.

I stood and held out my hand to him. "Good thing my pants fit you. Now, come on. It's time for me to see if I can get you off again in the shower."

Kasper took my hand and after helping him up, I led him to my bedroom. The whole time there wasn't a single worry on my mind.

Chapter 20

Kasper

I stood just inside of Marcus's condo, unsure of what we were doing. We were going out to dinner. That alone wasn't a big deal. But combine it with us being together and this being a date, that changed things.

Early this morning, I left here after spending the night in Marcus's arms. It was where I wanted to be. The only place I let go and allowed myself to feel. Before I left, I wrote a quick note asking if he'd go on a date with me tonight. It was pushing it. We hadn't had an official date out in public yet. I was taking a chance and it paid off when I got a text from him earlier saying he wanted to go.

However, this was the first time Marcus would be out on a date with a man. And the media loved me. I didn't say that to be conceited. It was a fact. When I was out in public, the media was tipped off and I was photographed. Being a very successful bachelor made anyone on my arm very enticing to them.

Marcus stopped in front of me and gently gripped my chin. "Hey, look at me." I did. The worry must have been written all over my face. He chuckled. "You're more concerned about this than I am. Shouldn't it be the other way around? I'm the one who's never been with a guy before."

"Are you sure you want to be seen with me?"

"With you? Hot as fuck Kasper Wilder? Hell yeah, I do." He kissed me hard to drive his point home.

I let out a breath. "Okay, so you're going to be fine when I hold your hand or kiss you in public?"

"Kas, you could bend me over that sexy car of yours and kiss up my spine in front of the cameras for all I care. Wait, no, don't do that. That shit is for us alone, but you get what I mean." Marcus got right to the heart of my issue and I appreciated it. "The media loves you. I just hope they deem me worthy of such a man." He winked, letting me know he was joking.

"Don't say I didn't warn you. They can be brutal."

Marcus scoffed, "You think I don't get people on social media ripping apart my plays after every game? Calling me names, saying I should do better?"

Reaching up, I cupped the side of his neck. "You're right. I'm sorry. This is new for me. When I go out with someone, they're usually out and everyone already knows it. This will be a shock for your fans."

"Maybe, but what do I care? Callen and Vander are gay. They have plenty of fans who don't care."

"You know what Callen went through. You saw it when he came out. Vander was already out when he came to the team."

"I did and that's why I'm meeting this head-on. No hiding. Me and you against the world." He grinned.

I had to bite my tongue to keep from letting those three words I wanted to say fly. There was no doubt I had fallen hard for Marcus. Every time we were together it reinforced it. Made me love him more. Instead, I said, "I'm damn lucky to have you."

"Yeah, you are." He winked again, causing me to laugh. I was grateful he made me feel better before we left.

The drive to Reese's was short. Marcus and I had been there before together, but it was in the private room and not on the floor with everyone else. I called ahead and made reservations. Reese wasn't in Espen tonight, although Mari would be there.

As we were walking in the front door, Marcus took my hand in his, surprising me. He said he was fine with it, but saying it and doing it were two different things. I smiled over at him and squeezed his hand tighter.

Mari was there waiting for us when we got inside. Her long hair was pulled back on the sides and top, letting the rest hang over her shoulders. She loved to play with the color of it and tonight it was a vibrant blue. She had on a pair of black pants and a black blouse with the restaurant's name above the left breast in a fancy script.

We walked right up to her and she immediately embraced me, breaking my hold on Marcus, then hugged him as well. He seemed a little shocked by the show of affection but hugged her back.

Leaning back, she smiled. "Kasper, you look happy."

I couldn't fight my grin. "That's due to the man by my side."

Marcus bumped me with his shoulder. "You say such sweet things to me."

Mari chuckled. "Come with me. I have a table for you."

She led us through the restaurant until we were at a corner table with the walls at our backs and we sat next to each other. Across the restaurant were floor-to-ceiling windows, but Mari would never seat me there. I didn't normally like being on display for everyone outside to watch me eat as they walked by.

"No menus?" I asked as we took our seats.

"You know better than that. Mom may not be here but that doesn't mean you don't get special treatment. The chef has a wonderful meal prepared for you two. I'll send your waitress over to get your drink order then start you with an appetizer."

"Thanks, Mari."

"Anytime."

We sat and talked. A few other diners looked our way. That was what happened when you were visible to the public like Marcus and I were. He was more of a star than me, though. The people of Espen loved the Emperors.

After we finished our meal and dessert, a couple of patrons came over to ask for Marcus's autograph. He grinned, talked with them a bit, and signed whatever they asked him. He was gracious and so good with them. I loved watching him interact with his fans.

Once they left, he reached across the table with his palm up in an open invitation to hold his hand. I didn't have to think about it. I laid my hand in his. It fit so perfectly. In fact, everything about us did. He caressed the back of my hand with his thumb, causing my mind to go to all the dirty things I wanted to do to him when we left here tonight.

The waitress coming over interrupted my thoughts, thankfully. I didn't need to be hard right now. She tried to tell me the meal was on the house, but I wouldn't hear of it. I politely asked her to go back and tell Mari she better send me the bill or I was going to make a wild guess at what our meal cost and put cash down on the table.

I wouldn't. I didn't carry that much cash on me, but it was enough to get Mari to give the waitress the bill and have it brought over. Since I asked Marcus out tonight, the meal was on me. It was nice to be with someone who wasn't after me for my money. Who made a damned good living on his own and didn't see me as a meal ticket or a ride to fame.

With the bill paid, we walked hand in hand through the restaurant. I was sure people looked at us. I didn't care what anyone else thought of me and Marcus. I was damn proud to have his hand in mine. He was going home with me tonight, no one else.

Before we reached the front door, Mari stepped in front of us. "There are photographers out there. I can take you through the back to make things easier on you."

I glanced to Marcus, who gave me a subtle nod toward the door. "We're good, but thank you for offering."

She hugged us both and told us to come back soon. She also told me to stop arguing with her over the bill. I laughed. That was never going to happen. I loved the food here and didn't come so they could feed me for free. I wanted to support my friend, her daughter, and their business. Plus, us being photographed outside would bring more attention to the restaurant. It was a perk of Marcus and me being visible tonight.

I was about to ask Marcus if he was ready, but he tugged me toward the door, making sure to keep his hand firmly in mine. The moment we were on the sidewalk, the cameras flashed bright against the night. Our names were called out. Questions were asked. Instead of answering any of them, Marcus pulled me to a stop in front of the photographers, brought our joined hands up to his lips and kissed the back of my hand while his eyes held mine. I smiled and no doubt looked like a lovesick fool. It was perfect.

On the drive to my place, Marcus couldn't keep his hands off me. It was hard navigating the city streets with his hand on my dick. Fortunately, I got us back in one piece and we quickly fell into bed, letting our bodies lead until we both fell asleep, blissfully sated.

***

I groaned and stood from my desk, facing the windows. I couldn't concentrate for shit today. My mind was so wrapped up in Marcus. The press had a field day dissecting our relationship, and moreover, the fact that Marcus was dating a man. Not just any man either. Me.

But that wasn't what was bothering me. It was that we hadn't defined who we were to each other. Dating? Sure. Sleeping together? Obviously. But were we exclusive? I wasn't seeing anyone else and I didn't think Marcus was either. When he had home games, his free time was spent with me or at his condo.

There was this part of me that wanted to know we were committed to each other. That we were in this long term. I didn't voice that to Marcus, though. He had enough going on with trying to play his games well. He didn't need my voice in his head screwing it up.

Groaning again, I sat back down and stared at my computer. Nothing was getting done. I should call it a day and get the hell out of here.

A knock sounded on my door then Pascal peeked his head in. "Are you okay? You sound like a grizzly bear carrying on in here."

"Come in and take a seat. Close the door behind you." I needed to pour my heart out to someone. Stockton was on set. Evan and Spencer were working. Paz was about to hear the brunt of my frustration.

Paz sat down on the other side of my desk, tablet in hand.

"You can put that down. This isn't work related."

He placed it on my desk. "I'm guessing this has something to do with the hot Emperors' catcher." Paz, as well as everyone who followed me and the Emperors, now knew about my relationship with Marcus.

I didn't bother reminding Paz that anything I said had to stay between us. Not only had he signed a confidentiality agreement when I hired him, but he'd been with me long enough that I trusted him. "This thing between Marcus and me isn't new. Well, not very new. We've been friends for a while and it grew into more."

Paz grinned. "So I saw on the front page of the sports section in this morning's paper." Espen had its own newspaper, *The Espen Times*. They did a great job covering the local teams. "I had an idea there was something going on between the two of you. You never cared so much about missing an Emperors game in the past when you did want to attend. Not only that, I can't remember another time when you took a spontaneous vacation. I'm glad I was right. You two look very happy together. I'm also going to need to meet him again to make sure his intentions with you are pure."

I cocked an eyebrow at him.

"Don't look at me like that, Kas. Someone has to look out for you."

"He's not like Hunter." I hated even bringing his name into this conversation.

"I should hope not. But you did say you weren't dating any more professional athletes and yet, here you are. Falling for the straight guy. Well, not so straight after all, but that's beside the point. I want to make sure you don't get hurt again."

"There's no way to guarantee that." I wished there were. I would give anything to know my relationship with Marcus was solid. That he wanted what I did. That we both had our eyes set on a long future together.

Paz leaned forward and folded his hands on my desk. "I may not know much about relationships, but I know you. You want someone to spend your life with.

Who will love you as fiercely as you love them. You deserve that and so much more. But you're not going to find it if you keep holding yourself back."

"You're right, but what if I bring up our relationship and tell him I'm in this with him no matter where it takes us and it scares him. I don't want to push him too hard."

"You know him better than I do. Do you think that will happen?"

"I'm not sure. I'm the first guy he's ever been with. He's happy. It's the unknown that worries me. We haven't talked about who we are to each other yet."

"Kas, I saw that photo. A thousand words were spoken with that one look. He wouldn't have let them take the picture and been so openly, adoringly enthralled with you if he didn't want everyone to know you're together. He doesn't seem to be the type to attention seek."

"No, you're right about that."

Paz sat back in the seat. "Okay, here's my advice, which I seriously don't think you need, but you don't want to open your eyes and see what's right in front of you. You need to talk to him. No one else can give you the answers you're looking for, except Marcus." I opened my mouth but he held up his hand to stop me. "If he doesn't say what you're hoping he does, then it's better to find out now before you get any deeper with him."

I looked at him then down at my hands where they sat on my lap. The only way I could get any deeper was if I put a ring on his hand and dropped down on one knee.

"You fell for him, didn't you?" Paz asked softly.

I nodded but didn't look up.

"You have to talk to him. You have to get things out in the open. You just said he's not like Hunter. Give him the chance to prove it to you. That he's not in this for the wrong reasons. That he's right where he wants to be. If shit hits the fan, you'll deal with it. You didn't get this far in life without battling your way over every obstacle in your path. Life isn't easy. As much as it sucks, you know that better than most." Leave it to Paz to give it to me straight. I didn't expect anything else from him. I needed this talk.

Finally lifting my gaze to his, I asked, "And when everything comes crashing down around me?"

"You'll have Evan, Spencer, Stock, and me there to get you through it."

Marcus

The crack of the ball connecting with the bat hit my ears, this sound off from what would normally be a base hit, if not a homerun. I saw the ball fly high into the air above my head. In seconds, I jumped up from my stance and threw the mask off my face to see where the ball went. Only one more out to end the game, and I was determined to catch the foul ball and win.

The ball grew larger and larger in my sight as it raced toward the ground. I lifted my glove and stood right below it, waiting for it to drop in. When I heard the sound of the ball smacking into the leather, I closed my glove tightly and watched the umpire call the final out of the game.

I threw my fist up in the air and pointed at Dave Meller, our closer, as we returned to the dugout. Another game, another win. And another sense of normalcy taking over the way I played. My entire body felt charged and ready to play. No more questions or worries distracting me. I focused on the game and it paid off. Kasper had been right. With everything else on my mind, there was no way I could play the way I always had.

The locker room was wild, as usual, with Dominic trying to get everyone to go out and celebrate. Guys ripping on each other for fun. Ignoring it all, I went to the showers. I told Kasper I'd meet him at his place once I left the stadium.

A few months ago, I never would have imagined this as my life. Finally having someone to go home to after a game. And not just anyone, but Kasper. He cared about how my day went like I cared about his. We could go out to eat or be just as happy relaxing in front of the TV at home.

But tonight? Tonight I wanted to stay in. Kasper and I had had plenty of orgasms together, but I still hadn't fucked him. I knew Kasper was going slow and letting us progress at a pace I was comfortable with. Comfortable with everything we'd done, I wanted to take it to the next level. I wanted to watch my dick sink into his tight ass. Having no clue how to do that without hurting Kasper, something I'd never want to do, I'd spent the last several days watching a shit ton of gay porn. While I learned a lot and jerked off more than I had as a teenager, I wasn't a hundred-percent confident, but I knew Kasper would help me find my way.

The day after our pictures were printed in the paper, I expected some razzing from the guys, but they hadn't blinked. It was like they'd known all along where things were heading with me and Kasper, even if I'd never dated a man before. Although, Vander did welcome me to the 'right' team. I'd laughed and told him that Evan was rubbing off on him. The moment he started talking about really rubbing off on each other, I left him where he stood. A few of the other guys were shocked to see me with a guy. Not that they cared. To them, it was my business.

I came out of the shower with a towel wrapped around my waist and went straight for my locker when Joe stepped out of his office.

"Hey, Marcus. Tim's upstairs in his box. He wanted to know if you could head up for a minute."

"Sure. Let me get dressed and I'll go up."

He nodded and turned back into his office and shut the door. On most teams, players would be nervous being asked to meet with the team owner after a game. It wasn't that way on the Emperors. Tim liked to pay compliments and talk about plays with his players on a regular basis. There were times he just wanted to talk about our families and lives. Tim went out of his way to make this team feel more like a family. You never knew who might get called upstairs. No one minded the extra time at the stadium.

I finished getting dressed and shoved my car keys and phone in my pocket. I left my bag inside my locker to grab on my way out. Getting out into the main stadium from the locker room was its own set of mazes. Eventually, I found myself on the elevator on the way up to the floor with the club boxes. The custodians were making quick work of cleaning the empty boxes as I passed for the next night's game. The only box that seemed to be quiet was Tim's.

Knocking lightly on the door, I waited, not wanting to interrupt him. The door opened and Tim's brother, Jamie, stood on the other side and gestured for me to come in. We'd all known Tim had a brother, but until Callen came out, we hadn't known he was gay. Afterward, we started seeing more of Jamie at the stadium. It was like he finally felt accepted there. He also made sure to get to know all the players on the team.

He held out a hand to me. "Great game tonight, Marcus."

"Thanks. It feels good to be playing well again. I feel settled." I wouldn't sugarcoat it. My first few games were ones I wanted to fade into memory.

"Well, if I were going home to Kasper Wilder every night, I'd feel settled, too." He winked and I couldn't stop the laugh that left my lips.

Jamie Deary was almost ten years younger than his older brother, and Tim was extremely protective of him because of it. But Jamie took it in stride, constantly ribbing his older brother about being so serious all the time.

"There are benefits to that, too."

"Come in. Tim's on the phone, but he should be back in a minute. I told him I'd wait until you got here before I left." He tugged his phone out of his pocket. "It's still early. Time for me to find some fun for the night."

I held both hands up. "Don't let me keep you."

He waved on his way out, looking like a younger more carefree version of his brother. I wandered through the suite and stood in front of the windows, looking down at home plate. My private office. The one place, besides with Kasper, I felt the most comfortable.

Like I was home. A few minutes later, Tim stepped into the room, his raised cell phone in hand.

"Sorry about that. I had to take that call." He gestured toward a set of couches facing each other. "Why don't you take a seat? What can I get you to drink?"

"Thanks. Water will be fine for me." I sat down and waited for Tim to return with a bottle of water and two beers.

He set one in front of me. "Just in case you change your mind." He took the seat across from me and took a sip from his beer. I reached for the water and did the same. "You played great tonight. It's nice to see you feeling like your old self again."

"It's nice to feel that way. I think I had so many things sitting on my shoulders that I just had to let it all go so I could focus."

Tim smiled. "I saw your photos with Kasper. Congratulations."

"Thank you. I can honestly say I never saw it coming, but I'm happy."

"I'm glad to hear it." Tim's smile fell a little, which had the hairs on the back of my neck rising. I was ready for a relaxing chat about the game and my new relationship. The serious, almost sad look on his face had not been what I was expecting. "Look, Marcus, there's something we need to talk about."

My heart started to race. "What's up?"

"Before I begin, let me say, we love having you as an Emperor."

Bile churned in my stomach. "You're trading me." The words slipped past my lips before I could stop them. They weren't a question but a statement. "Where?"

Tim sighed and leaned forward to rest his elbow on his knees, the bottle of beer caught between his palms. "We haven't decided if we're trading you, but it's a possibility." He looked me straight in the eye. "Marcus, you're a fantastic catcher. We know this. Probably one of the best in the league. You know me. I see us as a family, so trading one of my family away makes me sick, but this is also a business and I need to look at the bottom line."

So many thoughts were running through my head, I didn't know where to start. Not like I'd be able to get them out anyway. My throat felt tight.

"I know this isn't what you want to hear."

He had no idea. My relationship with Kasper had just started, and here I was about to be shipped to another city for at least six months of the year. Long distance wasn't exactly healthy for a new relationship. My chest tightened as I thought of telling Kasper this instead of celebrating tonight. How was I supposed to walk away and not see him unless the team who got me played the Emperors?

"We have to look at all of our options, especially with Gian retiring and having to find a new second baseman to replace him." Tim set the bottle on the table and sat up. "After a great game, I hate being the bearer of this kind of news, but I don't like leaving the hard conversations to someone else. And since I need to call your agent in the morning to discuss possible destinations, I knew it was imperative to talk to you tonight instead of letting him tell you tomorrow."

I stood and set the water bottle down on the table beside the untouched beer. No wonder he'd brought it over. What Tim didn't understand was that alcohol wasn't what I needed at the moment.

I needed Kasper.

"Thank you for letting me know. I'll contact my agent tomorrow afternoon before the game so we can make plans."

I turned and walked for the door, not seeing a single reason to keep sitting here and trading pleasantries. Apparently, I didn't have much longer to be part of the Emperors' family. What was the point in sitting and playing nice with the owner?

My hand had just wrapped around the handle when I heard my name. I glanced over my shoulder, refusing to walk back into the room.

"I wish business wasn't always so hard."

I nodded and opened the door, walking out and straight to the elevator. In a daze, I fled the stadium, forgetting about my bag until I reached my car and opened the back to toss it in. When I realized I left it in the locker room, I decided to skip going back for it and having to deal with people asking about my chat with Tim. That could be a conversation for tomorrow.

When I pulled out of the lot, I drove around the city, not heading in a specific direction, trying to think of exactly what to say to Kasper. He'd dated an athlete before, hell, he owned a team. He knew what it was like to have to travel to games, but this would be more than that. I'd be living in a completely different city and until they decided who to trade with, who knew where that could be. Completely across the country wasn't out of the question. My first trade had brought me to the opposite side of the country.

After almost two hours, I found myself staring at Kasper's door but still hadn't gotten up the nerve to knock on it. A few seconds later it flew open and I came face-to-face with a very worried looking Kasper.

"Where have you been?" He grabbed my hand and dragged me into the warm embrace of his arms, kicking the door shut behind me. "I was so worried. I've been trying to call and text but you didn't answer."

His body heat and the way he held me tightly to him had me melting into the warmth, accepting comfort from him he didn't yet know I needed. When I didn't answer and stood with my head resting in the curve of his neck, he leaned back and used his finger to tilt my chin up.

"What's wrong?"

I swallowed past the lump in my throat. The concern in Kasper's eyes was my undoing. His face blurred before me. "Tim told me tonight they're thinking about trading me."

Kasper sucked in a breath.

"He plans on calling my agent tomorrow."

Kasper took my hand and held it to his chest. "Did he say why?"

"Budgets and second basemen, blah blah blah. Does the why really matter? What matters to me is leaving you. Our relationship has just begun and now I could be shipped off to the other side of the country for the next six months."

Kasper wiped his thumb beneath my eye. The caring way which he brushed the tear aside made the pain in my chest grow.

How was I supposed to do any of this without him by my side?

Chapter 22

Kasper

The words coming from Marcus, the broken sound of his voice, the tears in his eyes, the trembling of his hands as they held on to me. It took everything in me not to fall apart along with him. I wanted to but couldn't. I had to be the strong one tonight. I had to be here for him.

I knew dating an athlete there was a chance he could be traded. He could also suffer a career-ending injury or decide to retire. But the trade was the most realistic of the three due to Marcus's contract.

I held Marcus in my arms as I thought about calling Tim and chewing him out. Screw that. I was going to do it to his face.

No.

I couldn't.

I knew better.

That was my personal side talking, not my business one. I knew this stuff happened all the time but to the man I loved? I wanted to punch something.

Pulling back, I took Marcus's cheeks in my hands and brushed away more of his tears. "I wish I could say something to make this better. I can't. I can't change Tim's mind. But what I can do is tell you that this changes nothing between us. I'm not letting you go, Marc. Do you hear me? You could play in California and it wouldn't make any difference to me. I own an aviation company, remember? I can go anywhere I want." Sensible, that was what I was going with. Not the irrational side that wanted to scream about how unfair this was.

Marcus blew out a breath. "Kas, you and I both know your businesses are here. You can fly out to see me, but you can't live with me wherever I go. You have too much to do here."

"I'll hire more people to help manage things." I could find a solution for just about anything.

He chuckled though it lacked humor. "You can't. You're hands-on."

"Listen to me when I say we'll make it work. I didn't get to where I am today by letting the hard shit fall to the side where I could ignore it. I take every single obstacle that comes my way and crush it. This is no different."

"What are we doing?" He looked so sad and his words hit me square in the chest.

I still didn't think he was ready for me to tell him I loved him, but there was so much more I needed to say. "You want to know what we're doing? We're in a relationship. You pretty much declared it to the world, by the way." I smirked, trying to lighten the mood, though I wasn't sure if it was possible.

I was confident in my words but inside, I was a nervous wreck. I knew we needed to have this talk but I didn't think it would be on the heels of the news that he might be traded.

"Are you sure that's what you want?" he asked. "It's not going to be easy." Marcus was vulnerable. He was wearing his heart on his sleeve. It was shredding me to pieces. Worse than my own inner turmoil.

"There is nothing in this world I want more than you by my side, in my life, and in my bed."

"I want that, too," he whispered. "I don't want to leave."

"I know you don't and I don't want you to."

"I want to be with you."

"Good. Then, no sleeping with anyone else or dating them."

Marcus reached up to dance his fingers along my bottom lip. "I'm not Hunter, Kas. I'm not going to leave you for someone else."

"How do you do that? Know what I'm thinking without actually voicing it?"

"I'm pretty fluent in all things Kasper Wilder. There's a lot to cover, but I'm an excellent student."

I shook my head. "You sound like Evan."

"He knows you well. I do, too. But I'm going to ask again because I could go anywhere if I'm traded. Long distance isn't easy for anyone, let alone two people who are so deeply entrenched in their jobs like we are. Are you sure I'm who you want?"

"I don't want to be with anyone but you. I don't care what I have to do, where I have to fly, how much money I need to spend, it's worth it if it means I get to be with you. If we're solid together, we can handle anything that comes our way."

"Even me being traded?" Marcus didn't want to leave Espen. He loved it here. He was comfortable. This was his home.

"Baseball isn't a year-round sport. You have an off-season and you can spend that here. When you're playing, I can fly wherever whenever I can. We can work out the logistics if you get traded. You're stuck with me."

"So I can call you my boyfriend, then?" His tears were gone and his eyes sparkled with mischief. I'd much rather see him like this than he was when he arrived.

"Boyfriend sounds so juvenile."

He rolled his eyes. "Only you. Okay, how about partner?"

"That's better." I nodded. "Sounds more mature."

"God forbid everyone sees the other side of Kasper Wilder. The only one they get is the serious, business one."

"Do you want to be my partner, Marcus?"

"In crime? Sure, that could be fun." He shrugged. "We could get in a lot of trouble together. Think about the kind of getaway we could make in a plane. Screeching down the runway trying to outrun the law."

I poked him in the side and started tickling him. "Are you done?"

He let out a laugh and was able to get away from me by a few feet since we were still standing. "Knock it off. I've had a shitty day and don't need you tickling me."

"What if I do something else to you? Or rather, you do something to me?" I prowled toward him with a confident gait.

Marcus kept me on my toes. He kept my mind on him all the time. And up until tonight, I was nervous about where our relationship—if we had one—was headed. But now I knew he wanted to be with me. If he didn't, he would have said so when I brought it up. He also wouldn't be so upset about leaving me if he got traded. I knew it wasn't just thinking about us being apart that upset him, although it was part of it.

He didn't move as I came for him. His body was coiled tight. The air between us charged like that moment before a thunderstorm was about to hit, when it was rolling in. The mood changed. My cards were on the table. I wanted Marcus for however long he wanted me, and I wasn't going to let him being traded get in the way of that.

I stopped when I was mere inches from him. Our bodies didn't touch, though they were damn close. "I want you to fuck me, Marcus. I want you to take me to my bedroom, strip me out of my clothes, drive into me, and make me forget everything but you."

My words were hitting their mark. His pupils were blown. His breathing was coming faster. Me talking about him taking me out of my head would also do the same to him. He wouldn't be able to focus on anything but us. How good we were together. How right.

He didn't respond, so I continued talking as I backed him toward the stairs. "When we go into my bedroom, nothing will exist but us. No talk of anything but you and me. And you're going to take charge. I'll do whatever you say and I'll enjoy it. Because it's you. I trust you. Understand?"

He visibly swallowed and nodded.

"Good."

Reaching for his hand, I threaded our fingers together and tugged him up the stairs with me. We entered my bedroom, which had the heavy curtains drawn, blocking out the entire world. Then I closed the door behind us. No, there was no one else here, but I wanted that feeling of letting everything go beyond these walls.

I stood in front of Marcus again and watched him. Without saying a word, he slowly unbuttoned my dress shirt. I hadn't gotten changed from work yet. I didn't know what Marcus's plans were going to be for us for the night since it was Friday. While I didn't need to go into the office tomorrow, he had a game to play.

With a gentleness I loved about him, Marcus slid my shirt from my body and went to work on my belt and slacks. The sound of the metal on the belt clanging was loud in the silence of the room. So was the rustling of the fabric as it fell down my legs and hit the floor.

Marcus palmed my dick and stroked it a few times, through the fabric of my boxer briefs, before sliding them down as well. He kneeled and took my clothes the rest of the way off over my bare feet.

When he stood he said, "Get on your back on the bed. Get yourself ready for me."

Fucking yes. Now this was the Marcus I'd been waiting for. Sure, he'd shown signs of being in charge when we fooled around, but the game changed tonight.

Everything changed. I had a feeling he was going to blow my mind.

I grabbed the lube and a condom from the nightstand drawer and tossed them onto the king-sized bed then positioned myself in the middle of it on top of a couple pillows.

My bedroom was big. There was a walk-in closet, a gas fireplace that was visible in here as well as in the en suite on the other side. I had two tall armoires that matched the dark mahogany of the bed and nightstands. And there was a comfortable seating area in front of the floor-to-ceiling windows, which were currently blocked by the curtains.

Marcus's eyes never left mine as he stripped out of his clothes with the same leisurely pace he rid me of mine. I returned his gaze, even as my slicked-up finger found my hole and started stretching it open. There was nothing in this world that had ever turned me on like Marcus had.

My dick was hard and leaking, begging for attention. I refused to touch it. I wanted Marcus to bring me off when he was ready.

As he walked toward me and climbed onto the bed with grace, I knew he was nervous. It was in the slight tremble of his hand when he slicked up his finger and reached for me as he sat near my hip. It was in the way his breath caught when he finally sank his finger inside, right along mine.

He was careful when he touched me, almost like he feared I might break. I would if he ever left me, but I couldn't voice that out loud. I had to trust Marcus and his desire to be with me, regardless of where his career took him.

Once I added a second finger and worked along with him, I was about to start begging for him to fuck me. I had to tell him I was ready. He'd never slept with a man before. This was new to him.

"I'm good," I told him, my voice needy and rough.

Marcus nodded and gently removed his finger when I did. He put the condom on, slicked himself up, then lowered himself over me. He didn't dive right into fucking me. Instead, he pressed his lips to mine and took his time assaulting my senses with his beautiful body, heady taste, gentle touch, rich, spicy scent, and his moans that vibrated up his throat to his lips.

His dick rubbed against mine and had me arching up to get more friction. I was so damn desperate.

"I've got you, Kas."

And he did. He drew away so I could pull my legs back. It was a very vulnerable position for me to be in. If there were anyone I would lay everything out there for, it was Marcus. He already had my heart. I had a feeling once he was inside me, he was going to own my soul as well.

Gripping his length, Marcus lined up and slowly pushed in. Once the head was inside, he braced his arms beside mine and held himself there to give me time to adjust. He watched my body for cues. Saw the moment I relaxed and could take more, pushing in a little at a time until he was fully seated and his balls were against my ass.

I hadn't been with anyone in a while. The burn was present but with it was raw need. The look on Marcus's face only amped up my own desire. Fuck, he was gorgeous. All tight muscles as he started to leisurely pump inside of me.

I reached for his sides and brought my legs down over his hips, trying to get the perfect angle. With every thrust of his hips, the pain lessened and pleasure took over.

Marcus leaned down to kiss me deeply then sat back, took my ass in his big hands, and spread me wider. He lifted me and started pounding into me in earnest. It was like lightning was zipping up my spine then shooting directly to my balls every time he grazed over my prostate.

No words were spoken as he fucked me harder than I'd ever been before. Maybe fucked wasn't the right word, because in that moment, I didn't think anything about what we were doing was just fucking. I loved him with every part of my being and knew he had feelings for me, too. I could see it in his eyes when he gazed down at me as sweat dotted his brow. I felt it in the way he held me close as he worked me over and used me to drive himself to the brink.

I reached for my dick, unable to take it any longer. The need to come was too strong. Marcus was on the edge and I wanted us to come as close together as we could.

But Marcus had other plans and pushed my hand away to take over with a tight grip. He leaned over me again, his lips a breath away. "You're mine to take care of, Kas. I'm going to be the one who gives you what you want. I'm going to be the one whose name you call out when you come. And I'm the one who you're going to remember tomorrow when your ass is sore every time you walk or sit."

Those words coming from him and his hand wrapped around my dick pumping me was all it took for me to climax. I called out his name as I went. I screamed it hoarsely while my body shattered with an orgasm so strong if felt like it was never going to end.

I heard him say my name as he pulled up taut and spilled into the condom. One day, I hoped there wouldn't be a barrier between us. I'd never gone bare with anyone before, not even my ex. But with Marcus, I wanted every part of him. I wanted to feel his cum drip from my ass, knowing he fully claimed me.

He lowered himself on top of me. Both of us were panting and covered in sweat. Marcus tucked his head in the crook of my neck.

When I finally could move again, I wrapped my arms around him and held on for all I was worth. The universe was trying to take him away from me and there was no way I was going to let that happen. Whether he lived here or somewhere else, Marcus Warnes was mine.

Chapter 23

Marcus

I rolled my eyes, listening to Charlie, my agent, complain about his call from Tim. Charlie was the best and represented a few guys on the Emperors, but right now, his annoyance was rubbing salt into the wound.

"I get it, Charlie. I'm not happy either. Staying in Espen was my goal, you know that. But this is out of our control."

"I'm not sure it is. As fucking shitty as taking a call like that about one of my players is, when they are already on the best team, I don't think it's a done deal yet."

The conversation I had with Tim seemed to be different than the one Charlie had, or were my emotions clouding my memory? "What do you mean?"

He blew out a breath on the other side of the line. "Tim made it sound like they haven't decided yet. They need a new second baseman at the end of this year when Gian retires. It's going to come down to how much it's going to cost to replace him versus the trade value you have to get them someone good."

My lip curled. "And they don't need a good catcher?"

"Oh, they do, and Pena's not bad. He's not as good as you but sounds like they could go with him if they have to and make sure second is covered."

"And where does that leave me?"

"It leaves you playing your ass off and pushing yourself from one of the best catchers in the league to the best. Hopefully, that will keep you on the Emperors, if not, it will give us a better say in where you go."

I scoffed. "Yep, sure I'll just jump on the field and play my ass off. All the questions in my head won't affect how I play."

"Well, if you can't stay with the Emperors and want to get on another team with the ability to win the World Series, *and* who will pay you what you deserve in the next contract, you need to show them that you are worth every penny."

I sighed. "You're right. I'm just frustrated as fuck."

"You know it's part of the business. I'll start making calls to see about places we may be able to get you to land. Places you want to be."

Even if I wanted the conversation to go differently, I knew being traded was the reality. And if Charlie could work his magic and get me on a team worth being a part of, I had to let him do his job and I'd do mine. I couldn't rest my hopes on Charlie being right about the team still making up their minds. The uncertainty would drive me mad. Kasper promised we'd be together, no matter where I ended up, and that was what I had to focus on.

Before I'd taken Charlie's call, I'd talked to my parents. Of course, they were disappointed for me. Mom had lots of questions about how that would affect mine and Kasper's relationship, many of which I still had myself. Dad wanted to know where I could end up. Not like I could answer that either. I'd used the excuse of calling Charlie back to get off the phone. It seemed like everyone had questions, but they were the same ones I'd been running over and over again in my head.

Frustrated, I grabbed my keys and left for the stadium. We had an early game today. All of the problems now on my plate would have to wait until later. If I were going to play at my best, and even a little better, I had to push all of it to the back of my mind. The game would be my only focus until the end of the ninth inning. Afterward, I could dwell on it all, hopefully in Kasper's arms while we talked about my latest life crisis.

I stepped through the door of the locker room and all heads turned in my direction. An array of sadness and concern crossed their faces. Looked like word spread pretty quickly. *Fucking Charlie.* Tim had only talked to Charlie this morning, which meant there hadn't been time for the information to get out to the reporters yet. Charlie could've called Callen or Jose, maybe even Dave Meller. All three were his clients.

Ignoring the stares, I went right to my locker and sat down. My bag still hung where I left it the night before. My chest tightened. Breathing in through my nose and out through my mouth, I started my normal routine to get ready for the game.

"Are you okay?" Callen's voice came from directly behind me.

I kept digging through my bag, pulling out my stuff. "Yeah. It's all good."

Callen grabbed the back of the chair and spun me around to face him. "Bullshit. There's no way you want to leave Espen."

"You're right, I don't. Hell, my relationship with Kasper just started. Leaving him will suck." I shrugged and turned my chair back around. "But we all know it's part of the business. Any of us can be traded at any time."

"Marcus—" Callen started, but I cut him off.

"Look, I appreciate everything, but can we not talk about this?" I looked over my shoulder, hoping he could see how much I didn't want to deal with it. At the moment, I had to have one focus: to play the game I loved. To do that, I couldn't think about leaving part of my heart behind when I had to go.

He nodded and walked back down toward his locker, stopping a few of the other guys who tried to make their way over. Out of the corner of my eye, I could see Micah Pena sitting in his chair, head down. He knew what the news possibly meant for him. Everyone gave him a wide berth and I appreciated their loyalty, but it wasn't what we needed as a team right now. It wasn't what I needed.

Dominic rolled his chair up next to mine, moving me to the side a bit. "Talk to me."

I glanced over at him without giving him any more attention. "Did you miss me telling Callen I didn't want to talk about it?"

"No, I just know this is completely fucked up."

"Yes, but this is part of playing a professional sport. There's no guarantee you'll stay with the same team. It's not the first time I've been down this road. It is what it is."

"Don't do that, Marcus. It's bullshit and you know it."

I set my bag down and turned to face him. "You want to help me?"

"You know that's why I'm over here."

I lifted my chin in the direction of Micah. "Then, stop ostracizing him. This is no more his fault than mine. Tim has to make whatever decisions are best for the team."

"No one's ignoring him."

I lifted a brow. "Then, why is he sitting alone with a five-foot circle of space around him? Just—" I sighed. "Do this for me. Right now, I need to worry about the game and not about the tension this is causing around me."

He opened his mouth to speak and I shook my head. Finally, Dominic got it and pushed his chair toward Micah. I closed my eyes and tilted my head back, praying for patience. Anything to keep me on the right track today.

After Dominic rolled away, the rest of the team let me get ready in peace. It didn't escape me that Micah was no longer sitting in the corner by himself. Other members of the team, besides Dominic, had walked over to talk to him. The locker room resembled what it had before last night's revelations. One less thing to take up space in my already overtaxed mind.

Somehow, in the midst of all the tension that had existed when I first walked into the locker room but had lessened slightly when we went into the dugout, I managed to play a damn good game. Stopped a couple of stolen bases and even got a homerun of my own. It helped that Ayden had been on fire tonight, letting only a handful of their batters reach base.

Showered and dressed, I glanced at the time and saw that Kasper would still be at the office. As much as I wanted to see him, I knew he had work to finish. I would have to be patient and find something to do with myself until he was done.

A hand clasped over my shoulder. "How about a drink before going home?"

I looked up to see Callen and Ayden standing at my side. I knew when Callen walked away earlier, we weren't done. There was no doubt in my mind at the time that he'd push the issue after the game. I appreciated him understanding that it had to be now and not before.

"Yeah. A drink sounds good." I pulled my bag onto my shoulder and followed them out to the parking lot.

We decided to hit Smitty's. The place wouldn't be too crowded this time of day, even after a game. When I arrived, Vander already had a table in the back and was waiting with beers for everyone.

"You move fast."

He pushed a bottle of IPA toward me. "I'm always fast, but even more so when my friends need me."

Ayden sat down next to me and grabbed his own bottle. "Dude, it fucking sucks what the team's doing to you."

"It does, but I know it's just business."

Callen shook his head. "It doesn't have to be. They have other options. Is it a done deal?"

I lifted the bottle to my lips, letting the alcohol burn away the bitter taste on my tongue from the conversation. "Not according to Charlie or Tim, which is why I need to play my ass off. But I'm not sure what choices they have. Gian retires at the end of this year. They need a second basemen and have two starting catchers."

"So trade Pena," Dominic cut in.

Vander shook his head. "Pena doesn't fetch the same price as Marcus. They got him for a steal off the free agent market."

"Vander's right," I agreed. "With negotiations coming up next year for a new contract, it will be cheaper to keep Pena, as much as I hate to admit it."

"It really does suck." Vander picked up his bottle of beer.

Ayden bumped my arm. "What did Kasper say?"

I twirled the bottle around in my hands. "That we'll figure it out."

"You will," Callen agreed.

Over the conversation, I steered it away from me and on to the rest of the guys. Having a few drinks with them was a good way to push it to the back of my mind, at least until I could bury myself deep in Kasper's body and forget about it until the sun came up and Kasper left for work. Over the next few hours, we ordered a few more rounds and signed a couple of autographs for fans who had been at the game.

When I saw it was time for Kasper to be heading home, I told the guys I'd see them the next day at the airport. We had an away series starting the day after tomorrow. Just another reason to leave and spend the night with Kasper. It would be ten days on the road before I'd see him again.

Kasper's car was in his spot when I pulled into the visitor space below his building and took the elevator up to his floor. I stepped off and knocked on his door. The anticipation of seeing him thrummed through me. The door opened wide. I didn't bother waiting until we were inside, I tugged on Kasper's suit jacket and pulled him into my arms. I crashed my mouth down on his and savored the moan that left his lips as they parted and I darted my tongue inside.

He pulled back, panting a few moments later. "Hello to you, too. Miss me?"

"Very much." I backed him into the foyer and kicked the door shut with my foot. "I wanted to see you all day."

"I wanted to see you, too." He took my hand and led me down the hallway, though the living room, and into the kitchen where he had two plates of food waiting on the high-top counter. He took his jacket off and laid it on the back of one of the chairs. "In fact, I even watched you play today. You were back on your game."

I sat down and inhaled. The chicken dish smelled delicious. "It felt good. After talking to my agent, Charlie, I know no matter what happens, the best outcome depends on me playing that way every game."

Kasper leaned over from his chair and placed a soft, sweet kiss on my lips. "You will." I didn't miss how that simple point of contact made tingles race through my body. Now that I had Kasper, I didn't think I'd ever get enough. Even sitting here trying to eat, it was hard not to notice the way his broad shoulders stretched out the fabric of his button-down shirt or how his bicep flexed every time he brought a bite to his mouth. My dick stirred in my pants. Who knew I would ever find that so attractive?

We talked more about my conversations with Charlie, my parents, and my teammates throughout dinner. Kasper had just finished washing our plates when I stepped up behind him and ran my lips across the back of his neck. Pressing my dick into the crease of his ass, encased in those fitted dress pants, Kasper bent his head, giving me better access.

"Fuck, Marc. I'm going to miss you next week. Don't stop touching me."

My chest ached at his words. This was only going to be a short period of time; I couldn't imagine how hard it would be for six months. Not wanting to think any more about that, I moved my lips over his neck and up to his ear. "Never. Now get your ass upstairs so I can strip you bare and touch you everywhere."

Kasper shivered. Neither of us wasted a second racing up to his bedroom so we could spend the night lost in one another.

Chapter 24

Kasper

This was what slow torture felt like. Marcus had been gone for three days. I was going out of my mind missing him. No, I'd never been like this before. It was different now that the fear of a trade loomed over him. A ten day stretch of him being gone would be nothing compared to if he were traded to another team far away.

Would I be like this for six months? A caged lion ready to rip the head off anyone who got near me? So full of pent-up frustration at having my partner away from me?

Paz knocked on my door then came in with a bag. "I've got lunch for you. Your sexy boyfriend texted me to make sure you're eating." He chuckled as I stopped pacing and stood near my desk. "If I didn't know you so well and how when you're stressed you tend to skip meals, I would think he's overbearing. He's absolutely right, though. Here." He sat the bag on my desk and pulled out two containers of food. "A Greek salad with grilled chicken for you and a Caesar salad for me."

"Thanks, Paz. I appreciate it. I'll be sure to send my thanks to Marcus as well."

I loved that he cared enough about me to text Paz, whose number I gave Marcus, just in case he couldn't get ahold of me. Of course, I'd texted Marcus as well to make sure he was taking care of his knee and that his mind was on the game and not the other things that could and would weigh him down. We were quite a pair. We took care of each other better than we took care of ourselves.

"You're welcome. Don't forget you're meeting with Gabe at one."

"I remember."

"I'll send him in when he gets here. That gives you thirty minutes to eat and I mean it. You need to eat because once you go home tonight, I'm not sure you're going to. At least this will get some protein in you."

"I don't deserve you."

"You say that all the time but the feeling is mutual. I don't deserve a boss as great as you."

I scoffed but smiled. "Flattery won't get you anywhere."

"Maybe not, but it did make you smile." With that, he turned and went out the door, closing it behind him, lunch in hand.

Opening my salad, I took the small containers of dressing out and poured them over top. Before taking a bite, I grabbed my phone and sent off a quick text to Marcus. He had a one o'clock game today, so he wouldn't read my text yet, but I wanted him to know I appreciated him.

The rest of my afternoon went smoothly. I met with Gabriel Kelone, who was the Jetties' general manager. He and I worked closely together and he never got tired of me being an overly involved owner. The man worked as hard as I did and had the nonexistent social life to prove it. In other words, he fit right in.

When I finally made my way home, I was able to push work aside and focus on Marcus. The longer he was away, the more restless I became. I knew I had to do something to get him to stay in Espen, but what? I had no pull over the Emperors. Sure, I knew Tim but I didn't run his team.

Then an idea occurred to me that had hope filling my chest. Could I really make it work?

***

The next day felt like it ticked by at a snail's pace. I felt every single minute until my three o'clock meeting. My nerves were shot. All night I kept going back and forth wondering if this were the right move.

I sat across from Tim Deary. His dark eyes assessed me, and if I wasn't mistaken, there was a little bit of hope in them. I called this meeting. Told him I had an answer for him regarding the deal he presented me about the Sandpipers and told him it was best we met in person.

"Don't keep me waiting, Kasper. Ever since you called, I've been curious what your answer would be. If I'm being honest, I thought it was going to be no, but a meeting in person gave me hope that maybe I'm wrong."

It was time for me to make a deal. One I hoped Tim would take me up on. "I have a proposition for you. If you agree, we both get something out of this."

"Go on. I'm listening."

"First, I'd like to stress that no part of this discussion is recorded in any way. I want no mention of it outside the two of us. There will be no formal contract for what I want. No record of our conversation. And you are to never tell anyone."

Tim leaned back in his seat and steepled his fingers. "Do you think I have something in here that records my conversations?"

"No, but I need to take the utmost caution with this."

"You have my word. Whatever is discussed stays between us and never documented. Proceed."

"I want you to extend Marcus's contract so he remains with the Emperors, and in return I'll go in as a fifty-percent owner of the Sandpipers with you."

I knew I was pushing things by presenting this to him. I was also walking a tight line of my relationship with Marcus. If he found out, I had no doubt he'd be furious. He wanted to play here because he loved his city, loved his team, and wanted to stay with me. But I was sure he didn't want his position secured this way.

What Marcus didn't know was how deep my feelings ran for him. I'd kept them close to me. Not uttering the words yet. I couldn't let him go, though. These days without him proved that.

It was a risky move, what I was doing. I just hoped it paid off in the end.

"You understand I don't want to trade him, right?" Tim asked. "It's a business decision, not personal. The money he'd free up would allow me to acquire a seasoned second baseman. We need that."

"You're telling me you'd feel confident with Marcus gone and Pena behind the plate? That he'd have the same skill and could handle the game the way Marcus does?"

"Pena is good. No, he's not Marcus, but you're not looking at this as a bigger picture."

"You're right. I'm not. I have one goal in mind and that's to keep the man I love with me." I would have thought the first time I spoke my words of love for Marcus it would be to him, but I needed Tim to understand just how deeply personal this was for me.

Tim sighed. "I want that team."

"I know you do. Don't forget you got Vander Devlin for a steal. I'm sure that left some money free you could use on a second baseman while keeping Marcus." I came into this meeting knowing I wasn't going to pull any punches.

The asking price for the Sandpipers was steep. I had the money to invest, though I never wanted it to be in another professional sports team. Fortunately for us, there was no longer a cross-ownership prohibition in the NFL. Meaning Tim and I could own the Sandpipers and our other sports teams in Espen.

"Going into this with you, the city will rally," Tim stated. "You and I are both established owners. We wouldn't move the Sandpipers away. The fans will appreciate us keeping them here."

I nodded. Tim wasn't a stupid man. "You're not only getting a co-owner with me; you want my name there. The security it provides for the city and their team." My name meant a lot. It was one people regarded with professionalism, passion for what I invested in, and the knowledge that I never did anything without my full heart in it.

Fans were the same. They were loyal to the teams they followed. I saw it with every sporting event, no matter what level the team was. Tim and me buying this team would give them comfort in knowing it wouldn't go to an outsider who didn't want to keep the Sandpipers in Espen.

"If Marcus finds out..." Tim left the sentence hanging.

"Tell me you want to trade him. Tell me it's an easy decision to make. That he wasn't playing to his full potential and you needed to get someone better in there."

"You know I can't do that."

"Me offering up this deal isn't like I'm asking you to keep a shit player on your team. I'm asking you to keep a man who has given everything he has to the sport he loves—the team he loves—and is really damn good at it. His heart is in Espen with his team."

Tim shook his head. "I'm worried about you, Kasper. What if he figures this out? I won't breathe a word of it; however, it's a possibility he'll put it together." He was voicing my biggest fear, but I couldn't sit back and do nothing. Not when I had the power and money to change things.

All my adult life, I worked my ass off. I built up a reputation and companies. I invested wisely. At the end of the day, my friends and family always came first. I would drop whatever I needed to for them. I would do anything in my power to make them happy.

Marcus could stay here. Play with the Emperors. And yes, there was the selfish side of me that wanted him by my side.

I wasn't able to forget the tears in Marcus's eyes. The way he clung to me after he received the news of a possible trade.

Maybe he would find out what I did and would hate me. At least, if everything went to hell, Marcus could still play here. He wouldn't have to move.

There was also the knowledge that Tim didn't want to trade Marcus. He didn't want to lose him, but he had tough decisions to make as the team's owner.

When I didn't answer Tim, he asked, "Are you sure about this?"

Marcus came first. Before me. Always. He wanted to stay here and I was going to make it happen.

I nodded. "I am. Do we have a deal?"

Tim smiled. "We do. Let's buy a football team and keep your man in the city."

Tim printed out the contract and together we looked it over. Tomorrow was the start of the NFL draft. We would need to put a clause in the contract that the current owner would handle the draft since we weren't in a place to do so. Neither Tim nor I were up to speed on who the prospects were.

There were lots of red lines on the contract. Places we wanted changes to be made.

Any changes we wanted to make regarding the team could be done once we took full ownership, which would be in roughly two weeks if everything was agreed upon.

We had looked it through. Tim called the owner of the team. Kyle Verano confessed he didn't want the team to leave Espen and that was why he went to Tim with the option to buy. Kyle was a lifelong resident of the city and was proud of it. The team might have sucked but they could always improve. He was relieved when Tim told him he wanted to buy the team, along with me.

With that squared away, both Tim and I had to get our lawyers involved so they could look over the contract once Kyle sent a revised version over. There would be a bit of back-and-forth until it was done. I was okay with that. We would execute it in the morning if possible.

Later that night, I sat on my couch with a whiskey in one hand and my phone in the other. I talked to Marcus. Just hearing his voice helped soothe my inner turmoil. I was scared of losing him.

If Marcus would have come to me and been happy about the trade, excited about moving to a new team, I would have supported him. I also would have never entertained the idea of this deal with Tim. However, that wasn't the case. Marcus didn't want to leave. Whether we ended up together in the long run or not, Marcus would get to the play the game in this city with the men who had become close to him.

And if something did happen between us, I would break. There was no doubt. Although, I would take comfort in the fact that I did something for someone I loved. I had good intentions. I just hoped if Marcus ever found out, he'd see it that way.

Chapter 25

Marcus

The crowd noise filtered into the sides of the dugout. Normally, a night off from catching would feel relaxing but not tonight. Tonight it felt like another nail in the coffin of my time in Espen.

Micah squatted behind home plate. His stance stiff and the mistakes were mounting. Many I'd made myself in the first few weeks of the season. The Espen fans seemed to be more forgiving then, or maybe it was just me. Only the top of the fourth and he'd already missed two pick-offs at second and a throw to home, which allowed an extra run to score.

The entire situation wasn't fair to him. He'd been thrown to the wolves and the Emperors' fans were making it clear they didn't want him here. There was no doubt that part of his poor performance tonight came from the stands. Chants for Warnes warmed my chest, yet it did nothing to dissuade the guilt that I somehow caused the fans to be hostile toward him. Word had gotten out through the league, and eventually the public, that I was on the market.

Charlie had been getting calls left and right, wanting to know what it would take to get me. We both knew it wasn't his decision or mine. Although, the deal had to come with a second baseman or there would be no reason to make the trade in the first place.

The entire time I was on the road and since coming back, I made sure to keep Kasper in the loop. It was only fair he knew where I might land in the next few months and how far away that would put us from one another. He never seemed dismissive, but I could tell he didn't want to talk about it. Neither did I. There just wasn't a choice for me. The reality was, as soon as Tim made the deal, I'd be packing up.

I still hadn't decided if I would keep my condo or sell it and buy a new place in the new city. I guessed in the back of my mind, even though it was early in our relationship, Kasper might ask me to stay with him for the six months I'd be in Espen. It would maximize the short time we would have together. No need to drive to each other's place.

By the bottom of the sixth, things hadn't gotten any better for Micah. Another mistake that cost a run and his bat hadn't connected with the ball the entire game. I glanced up when Joe called my name. He waved me over.

"What's up?"

"Grab your helmet. You're batting for Pena." Out of the corner of my eye, I could see the defeated look on Micah's face. Nothing I could do about it now, but I'd sit down and talk to him later. No one wanted to be pulled off the free agent market only to shit the bed on their first start with a new team.

I asked one of the other coaches to pull my gear then stepped out of the box into the on-deck circle. The cheers started low and grew louder and louder as more people realized that I'd been listed as the pinch hitter for Micah and would be behind home plate next inning. I used the momentum to power me through the rest of the game. My home run in the eighth helped to kick-start our comeback. The Emperors pulled out a win, even after we'd been down by three runs earlier in the game.

Stepping into the locker room, there was an exuberance in the air. It was nice to be needed to get the win. I let myself enjoy the mood instead of thinking about whether or not it would be my last time feeling this way.

All I wanted to do was shower and crawl between the sheets of Kasper's bed, with him wrapped tightly around me. When I stepped from the showers and Joe called my name, I had a feeling that wasn't in the cards anytime soon.

Joe's face was pinched. "Tim wants to see you upstairs, if you have a minute."

The air in the room cooled suddenly. No longer was everyone cheering and talking about the last three innings. Hell, my plan to talk to Micah had just gotten sideswept. All eyes were on me in some way, shape, or form as I headed to my locker to get dressed. When I looked around, I'd catch my teammates watching me, but they would immediately look away when they realized I saw them. Their gazes didn't always move fast enough for me to miss the sadness in some of their eyes.

I picked up my phone and for the briefest moment, I thought about texting Kasper and telling him I was meeting with Tim. Deciding to wait until I had all the information, I shoved my phone in my pocket and grabbed my bag before heading to the elevators. This time, I knew I wouldn't want to go anywhere near the locker room after my chat. I appreciated him keeping me in the loop and not dropping it on me the day before the trade like some teams would. That didn't stop my stomach from being a mass of nerves. If I didn't puke in the elevator on the way up, it would be a miracle.

The elevator ride seemed to take twice as long as normal. Ever since I was a kid, things I hated always seemed to take longer than things I loved. The ride to see Tim definitely wasn't on the love list. I noticed my pace slowed the closer I got to Tim's suite door, as if I could delay the inevitable. The reality was, I couldn't, so I lifted my hand to knock and waited for my fate.

Tim opened the door a second later and gestured for me to come inside. Once again, Jamie, who had watched the game with his brother, stood.

"Great game tonight." He smiled at me on the way past and turned back to face Tim. "Dinner tomorrow?"

Tim nodded. "Yeah. Does seven work?"

Their simple conversation about dinner, while the fate of my career hung in the balance, had me shifting from foot to foot. So on edge nothing could keep me still. Tim eyed me as I heard the door shut behind me.

"Marcus, come in." He gestured farther into the room and walked over to the couches we'd sat on the night he told me my time in Espen was coming to an end. "You had a great save tonight."

It took him a moment to realize that I hadn't followed him. My feet rooted to the floor. I stayed close to the door, ready to escape once I had my answer. "Where?"

Tim watched me closely for a minute. No doubt he could see the way my muscles were coiled tight, about to bolt at any minute. He sighed. "I know the last time I brought you here, I dropped news in your lap neither of us wanted to talk about. Please come sit and we can discuss the plan moving forward."

Not wanting to burn bridges, I forced myself to walk over and take a seat across from Tim. I knew with only one year after this on my contract, I would have the opportunity to become a free agent, giving me more of a say in where I went afterward. If the original trade were too far from Espen, I could always have Charlie work on teams closer to here to pick me up later.

I set my bag on the floor and sat on the edge of the seat, my knee bouncing up and down. When it became clear I wouldn't be very involved in this conversation, Tim ran a hand down his face. "I hate seeing my players—my family—so worked up. The decisions I have to make as a businessman and what I want to do as a person don't always align, which is what led to our conversation a few weeks ago. Micah is normally a decent catcher and we got him for a steal. What we couldn't find was a good second baseman we could afford with the current salaries we had."

I wanted to shout at him to get to the point. I gripped the edge of the couch to keep myself under control. All I needed was the name of the team, then Kasper and I could figure out how we handled it from there.

Tim had continued talking, but I'd zoned out trying to imagine who had actually picked me up from all the teams Charlie had mentioned over the last few weeks. I forced myself to pay attention and listen to what he was saying.

"I'm sorry to bring you up here again, but I didn't want to make you wait any longer. The perfect scenario fell in our lap and we decided—" I braced myself for the blow "—not to trade you."

"Okay, I can… Wait, what?" I couldn't have heard him right. The Emperors were keeping me?

"We're going to keep you here in Espen. I actually plan to call Charlie in the morning and start work on a long-term deal that will override your last option year."

I shook my head trying to clear it. I could hear Tim's words, but my mind was struggling to process them. "Wait." I held my hands up. I needed a moment for my brain to catch up to what was actually being said. "Are you saying I'm staying here?"

Tim smiled and it brightened his entire face. "That's right. All of this was about finding a second baseman. And like our luck with Vander, Joe found a shortstop in Triple A who actually plays second. The coach there is an idiot and, instead of finding the players he needs, he puts whoever he has on the field like it's Little League." He shook his head, his disgust for the coach evident.

"And this guy is good?" That was the golden question. They wanted a good player, someone of Vander's caliber, and I didn't want the rug to be ripped out from under me again.

"Very good. He's currently batting a .326 and has a knack for stealing bases, but to the team his defense sucks. That's only because he's playing the wrong position. He's actually not bad at shortstop and Joe and I have a feeling he will kill it at second. The trade was completed this morning, and I didn't want to make you wait any longer."

My heart started to race in my chest, excitement pouring through me. "Wow... Just wow. I expected to come up here and find out where I was heading off to. I'd planned to go home and figure it out with Kasper. This changes everything. I think we'll need to celebrate."

"Go home and have fun with your man. I look forward to meeting with you and Charlie to plan a long future with the Emperors."

"Thank you." I stood and lifted my bag onto my shoulder. "Thank you for believing in me."

Tim stood and held a hand out to me. "We always believed in you, Marcus. That's what made the thought of possibly trading you so hard and why we looked for a solution that would keep us from having to do it."

I took Tim's hand and shook it. The heaviness in my heart lifted and I couldn't wait to get home to Kasper. As soon as I could leave without offending Tim, I raced to my car and floored it to Kasper's place. He was the first person I wanted to tell. More than that, I wanted to celebrate and I knew exactly how.

I left my bag in the car and went straight for the elevator. The numbers ticked by on the way to the top floor while I pulled out the condom and a small lube packet I'd begun caring around with me and shoved them into my front pocket. After the first time I slid inside Kasper, it was obvious that I would never get enough.

The chime on the elevator sounded and I walked with purpose to Kasper's door, ringing the bell and waiting. The door opened and Kasper's concerned gaze settled on me. I'd gotten to his place later than I planned and considering what happened the last time I'd done that, he had every right to be worried.

"Is everything o—" I didn't give him a chance to finish his sentence, backing him up and kicking the door shut.

I slammed my mouth down on his in a demanding kiss. Slipping my tongue between his lips. I let my body lead as it surged with lust. I wanted to celebrate all right, balls deep in the sexy man before me.

"Fuck, Marc," Kasper groaned when I started kissing down his neck, sucking on the skin where it met his shoulder.

I reached for the button of his jeans and zipper, undoing them in seconds. "Face the wall," I whispered in his ear before nibbling on the lobe.

His entire body shivered as he turned and faced the wall, hands braced against it. Kasper loved to be commanded in bed and tonight I would give him that and more. I tugged his pants and briefs down just enough to expose that sexy, round ass of his.

"Please," he begged. All concern for why I was late was gone in the face of his desire.

"I love when you beg." I ran my finger down his crease, enjoying the way his puckered hole reacted to my touch.

My dick surged and I knew I needed to get inside him before I came in my pants. I tugged the packets out of my own pocket and undid my pants, letting them and my boxers fall to the floor. Every inch of me burned to sink deep inside him and quickly. I tore open the condom and rolled it down my length.

Kasper's deep, rumbling moan at the sound had me gripping the base of my dick and hoping I had enough patience to prep him first. I'd learned a lot since that first night and knew exactly what my man needed. The lube packet opened easily and I squirted it onto my fingers, coating both my dick and Kasper's hole before slipping a finger inside him.

His hips bucked backed onto my finger. I quickly added another, scissoring them to stretch him for me.

"Fuck, I'm ready. I'm so ready." Kasper's voice full of need just about pushed me over the edge.

I let my fingers slip from his body and lined up my cock, pushing past his barrier in one long thrust.

"Holy shit." His warm body tightened around me. "You feel amazing. I will never get enough of you."

"I'm yours," he said on a moan. "Take me."

I reached up, laced my fingers through his against the wall, and set a pounding rhythm. Sinking into his body and retreating, right there against the wall in the foyer. Our cries echoed in the empty space as we both reached the edge.

"Marc!" Kasper called out as his body clamped down on mine and came all over the wall, without me even touching his dick.

That thought alone triggered my own orgasm as I thrust one last time and let go deep inside Kasper's body.

Neither of us moved as we leaned against the wall panting. Eventually, I had enough strength to move my lips to his ear.

Catcher Interference

"No trade. I'm staying."

Kasper

To say I'd been flying high since Marcus showed up, fucked me into oblivion, then told me he was staying in the city was an understatement. That was a week and a half ago. Everything since then had been better and more wonderful than I could have ever hoped.

It was Friday and Marcus had a game tonight. Luckily, he was home and would be until Monday morning when they left for away games.

As I was driving home from the office, a text from Paz came through, letting me know the deal with Tim and me buying the Sandpipers had been announced. A press release went out and it was making its way through the media outlets.

I ignored the texts and calls coming into my phone. I knew this would happen. The deal was kept very quiet. I hadn't told anyone unless they needed to know. By the time I pulled into my parking spot, I had multiple texts and voicemails. There was only one I wanted to call back, though—my brother.

Stockton picked up on the first ring. "Why didn't you tell me?" His voice wasn't hurt but happy.

"I didn't want to say anything until it was announced. You know how fast shit spreads."

"Yeah, but I'm your brother."

"Uh huh, and by the sounds of it you have a team of people around you who can possibly hear our conversation." Stock was on set in Australia filming for his next role. It was an action movie, of course. I didn't ask for details. I preferred to see it on the big screen at the premier. Stock always invited me along. I was hoping for the next one so I could bring Marcus.

"You have a point. Anyway, congrats! I'm really happy for you. I'd also like to attend some games once you whip that team into shape."

I was in the elevator on my way upstairs and scrubbed a hand over my face. "We have our work cut out for us but we got some new talent in the draft."

"If anyone can do it, it's you." Someone called his name in the background. "Listen, I have to go. We'll catch up soon. Congrats again, Kas. I'm so proud of you."

I smiled. "Thanks, Stock."

We hung up as the elevator doors opened. I went to my door and unlocked it. Inside, I pushed it shut and dropped my keys, wallet, and phone on the kitchen counter. As I got changed into a pair of sweats and a T-shirt, Stockton's words of him being proud of me ran through my head. Would he be proud if he knew why I bought the team with Tim? Would he yell at me for doing something foolish? I wasn't sure.

After heating up dinner, I sat on the couch and watched the Emperors game. Marcus was off tonight. He threw wide a couple times. He struck out twice.

Could it have been more than a bad night? Could he have heard about the team purchase and figured out what I did?

Yes, I'd been living high with Marcus but that didn't stop me from waiting for it all to come crashing down. I knew, once the news hit the media, there would be questions as to why I would buy another team, and with Tim Deary since we'd never done business together before. People loved to speculate and start rumors. Now that I was publicly dating a player on the Emperors, I was sure the gossip would be packed full of questions.

I groaned and leaned my hand against the couch as the game ended. The Emperors lost by two. Marcus would blame himself. He didn't play his best. But that also meant he'd be in a shit mood when he got here. I couldn't blame him. I had my ways of making him feel better after losing a game, however.

Time ticked by until there was a knock on my door. Just one. A loud bang of a fist. My nerves were shot wondering what was about to happen.

I got up slowly and walked even slower to the door. I had a bad feeling in the pit of my stomach. Even if shit went downhill, I had to remember I did it for Marcus. He loved his team and wanted to stay in Espen. What I did was for him.

I opened the door and revealed Marcus, angry like I'd never seen him before. He stepped in and I stepped back, keeping a distance between us. He kicked the door shut as his hands tightened into fists at his side.

"What did you do?" he asked in a deadly even tone.

I couldn't lie. Not to him. But I could omit pieces unless he brought it up and specifically asked me. "I bought a football team."

"I heard. Only you didn't tell me. You talk to me about other parts of your businesses, yet this I had to hear from the media." He was too calm. His voice betrayed the tension that lined every inch of his body. "Which makes me think you didn't want to tell me. So, do you want to tell me now why you bought the team?"

Shit. He was right. I didn't think about that. "I only told Paz and my lawyer before today. I didn't even tell my brother. We kept it quiet until the press release went out. Tim came to me saying he got a call from Kyle Verano, the Sandpipers' owner. Kyle wanted to see if Tim was interested in buying the team before it went to the market for anyone to make a bid on. Tim came to me because he couldn't foot the bill alone." That was the truth.

"And did Tim offer you any incentives to go in on this deal with him?" His gaze burned into mine, as if he were peering right into my soul and could see what I'd done. Could see the length I went to so he could stay in Espen. "Don't you dare lie to me."

"No, Tim didn't offer any incentives. But I..." The words stuck in my throat. Once they were out, everything would change. Hell, it already had. Marcus had put two and two together. He knew something was up.

"But I, what? Say it."

My shoulders slumped and I dropped my gaze to the floor. "I told him I'd go in on the team with him if he kept you on the Emperors."

"For fuck's sake, Kasper!" Marcus roared. I was grateful no one else lived on this floor and the soundproofing was solid so the people below me wouldn't hear anything. "How could you do that?"

I wanted to yell back. I wanted to match his level of intensity, but it wouldn't get me anywhere. So I stayed calm when I spoke. "You didn't want to leave. You wanted to stay and play with the Emperors."

"Of course, I did! They're like family to me and you're here! But you went and bought my way to stay on the team!"

"Tim didn't want to trade you. He knows how good you are, but it was the money that was the issue. The budget for new players and he needed a second baseman. Vander was cheaper than he hoped when he acquired him, so he had money left over. We talked. I made him see the positives and how it could work. Then he found this guy in the minors who was also cheap. It worked out. You got to stay and he gets a second baseman who isn't complete shit. He and I got a football team, which will mean it stays in Espen instead of a different owner moving it out."

A vein throbbed at Marcus's temple. "You fucking bought me, Kasper. What did I cost?" He sneered. "I think the press release said the team you bought was two billion. So what, I'm worth a solid billion to you?"

"I didn't buy you. I made a business deal. Much like Tim has to run his, I have my own investments. He presented me the opportunity and I made sure I got something out of it as well. Or rather, you did."

"You think because you have all this goddamn money you can get people to do whatever you want." He shoved his finger into my chest. "That you can drop cash on an issue and it just goes away."

Marcus was an athlete. He didn't manage the team or any other business. He didn't know how things worked, but I did. Not everything was done with rainbows and sunshine. Sometimes you had to bargain, even when you didn't want to. Plus, I had age on my side. I'd experienced a lot. Knew how things worked. We worked on two different ends of the teams we were part of. And yes, with enough money, I could handle a shit ton of issues. But I didn't say that.

"I can't believe you fucking did this," he snarled.

I was close enough to smell his freshly showered skin but he felt like he was miles away. "You didn't want to leave. You can't tell me you did. Tim didn't want to lose you. I made it so everyone got what they wanted."

His cold, hard gaze zeroed in on me. "Is this how our relationship works? You solve everything with money? You don't talk to me? You don't ask me how it feels to have the media running rampant about how my *boyfriend* bought a football team to save my career?"

I clenched my jaw. It was bound to happen that they'd look at that angle. Marcus's position with the team was up in the air. The media knew it. Then I bought a football team with Tim that gets announced after Espen secures Marcus long term.

"Got nothing to say?" he asked harshly. "How did you think this was going to go? I would find out what you did and fall into your arms like you're some white knight who came to my rescue? I would be grateful for what you did for me? I'm a grown-ass man. I don't need anyone to save me. I got this far on my own and I'll go farther doing the same."

"I never doubted your talent, Marcus, and neither did Tim."

"Don't bring him into this. I'm pissed at him, too, but since the contract has been offered and he pays me, I'll keep my mouth shut where he's concerned. This, right here," he motioned between the two of us, "is about you and me and how you crossed a line so big it's the size of the fucking Grand Canyon."

I opened my mouth to speak but Marcus wasn't done.

"Maybe this was why Hunter cheated on you. He saw you for who you really are. Someone who only thinks about himself. About what *you* want. How *you* feel. Not about the person on the other side of the relationship."

His words hit me like a physical blow right to the chest. I gasped for air as my hand clutched over my heart.

"You destroyed everything, Kasper. I know better than to think the media will get any confirmation about this deal because I'm sure it doesn't exist on any piece of paper. They have nothing solid. But I'll know. I'll always wonder if I'm good enough. Because that contract was given to me with a price tag attached to it and not the one that will pad my bank account. No, it came with the end of our relationship." He turned toward the door.

"What?" I gasped again. "No, please. I don't want to lose you. I hated seeing you hurt at the thought of being traded. I had to do something. I couldn't lose you." I saw this coming. Knew it was going to happen if he figured it out. And yet, the pain from it was worse than I could ever have imagined.

He glanced over his shoulder, his eyes narrowed to slits. "You told me we would figure it out. Instead, you get to sit on your throne throwing money at life's problems while I get to deal with the speculation about my place on the team. I know the truth."

"I couldn't lie to you."

"You already did that when you told me we'd make it work." His voice no longer carried through the entire room but became low and deadly. "Stay away from me." He twisted the knob and opened the door. "And definitely don't do me anymore favors. But don't worry, I won't tell the media about our breakup. That will only fuel this fire and I've already been burned badly enough by the flames." With that, he stepped out and slammed it shut behind him.

I dropped to my knees. The hardwood floor giving no mercy when I landed. Tears built in my eyes as I kept them trained on the door. He left and took my heart with him. He wasn't coming back. There was nothing left inside me, except a big gaping wound. The pain was far greater than when things ended with Hunter. That was nothing compared to this. And I brought it on myself.

I wasn't sure how long I stayed on the floor before standing on shaky legs and dragging myself to the couch. Highlights of the baseball games played today were running on the screen. One blurred into the next.

Marcus didn't have to leave the Emperors. He was signed on. Then his words hit me again.

I'll always wonder if I'm good enough.

Marcus was good enough. He was an amazing catcher, but he was right, I tainted things for him. I thought I was doing something good, and in the end destroyed not only me but hurt him, too. He would never forgive me, not that I blamed him. No, this was on me. All of it.

What was done was done. There was no going back. I had to find a way to move forward. Without Marcus. Without his warmth and his touches. Without his kisses and the way he made me feel like I was everything he'd ever wanted.

I destroyed us. I poured the gasoline, lit the match, and burned us to the ground. All I had left were the ashes. Dust that slipped easily through my fingers, unable to hold on to. Much like Marcus.

He was the bright, shining light in my life. The one I never thought I'd have and then did. Until I ruined us.

No one would ever compare to Marcus and I never wanted anyone to take his place. He was it for me and now we were nothing.

Chapter 27

Marcus

The key card slid off the table onto the floor where I'd thrown it. A bunch of the guys from the team had gone out to dinner in town, but I declined again. Like I'd done every time someone asked me to do something since my breakup with Kasper. I wasn't in the mood to do anything.

When I was out on the field, I busted my ass to prove I deserved to still be in Espen. The naysayers and sports critics continued to question how I'd gotten the contract offer in the first place, and I refused to let them believe I wasn't worth it, even as I questioned it myself.

The contract had been tendered, but that still left us negotiating salary and terms. After the shit I'd had to deal with because of Tim's and Kasper's meddling asses, I was going to get the best deal possible. But I couldn't let my anger at them affect the team. They deserved me at my best, so I'd be the best. I'd managed to build a little box for my anger in the back of my mind. Once the game started, I locked the box and wouldn't let it open until after the ninth inning.

The moment I stepped into the locker room, I felt the rage flood my system again. It was no longer the kind that made me want to strike out at everyone, but it simmered just below the surface. So when the guys offered to grab something to eat, I went back to the hotel alone.

I changed into a set of gym shorts and tank top and took the elevator down to the workout room. The hotel gyms did not offer the same options as my home gym, but it would still do the trick.

The night I left Kasper, my hands shook the entire way up to my condo. I couldn't purge the rage that coursed through me. I'd almost punched the wall when I realized that would only result in a broken hand. Trying to find an outlet, I'd gone into my building's gym and spent the next few hours blowing off steam. By the time I practically crawled back to my place, I had enough energy to shower and get in bed. And I'd done the same thing every night for the last ten days.

It didn't matter if I played a game or not, I still found myself working out to exhaustion. At first, it had been a great way to calm down before bed, but the last few nights my traitorous dick and body missed climbing into bed with Kasper. Since that was never fucking happening again, and my right hand didn't seem to do the trick, I pushed myself until I was too worn out to try and get it up.

And even though I wouldn't admit it to myself, my heart missed Kasper, too. It didn't seem to understand what my brain did—Kasper betrayed us. Betrayed our trust. Our love.

Love? Fuck. No way would I let my mind worry about that. I shoved that thought down as quickly as it had appeared.

A little over an hour later, I found myself on the elevator heading back up to my room. My muscles were sore and my lids were heavy. All I wanted was a shower, food, then sleep. We still had two more games in this series before we'd be on our way home for three more series.

After months of excitement in my life, it seemed weird to only measure time in games away and games home. And that's exactly what I did. I kept my focus on the next game, the next team. It left me very little time to think about what Kasper had done. It also kept me from wondering if I really belonged in Espen.

I'd considered asking Charlie to withdraw from negotiations. With the contract tendered, meaning they offered it, not all the details had been worked out. The entire deal felt tarnished anyway. I wondered if it had come time for me to move on to another team. Start over in another city. Then my dad called.

He knew about the team and the gossip surrounding the new contract. Hell, I'd told them the whole story the next morning when I'd calmed down enough to talk to them. He told me I'd be stupid to turn down the deal. If I left, I wouldn't be able to prove I was worth it. If I stayed, the reporters who wanted to question whether or not I would still be in Espen without Kasper would have to eat their words when I killed it every game.

And that was exactly what I'd done. The reports were starting to die down. But there were still a few holding on to that rope with both hands. The press did notice that Kasper and I hadn't been seen together in a while. Like I'd told him before I left his place for the last time, I wouldn't confirm or deny to the media whether we were together or not. It would only add fuel to the fire. There was enough of that in the first place.

When I got back to the room, I ordered something from room service and went right for the shower. By the time I finished, my food would be here. I could watch TV while I ate and hopefully drop from exhaustion after that.

I'd just pulled on a pair of sweatpants and an Emperors T-shirt when I heard a knock on the door. My stomach growled, so I answered it without checking. As soon as I saw who was on the other side, I wanted to slam it in their faces.

"Waiting for something?" Callen held the tray from room service with Ayden standing next to him.

I scrubbed a hand over my face, trying to think of a way to get rid of them. "Thought you guys went out to dinner."

Ayden stepped forward, forcing me back into the room. At six foot two inches, I was tall, but Ayden's six-foot-four-inch frame stood over me and Callen. "We did, but at dinner we decided to come back and keep you company."

"I don't need company. I need food and sleep, in that order." I reached for the tray, but Callen held it out of my reach, insisting instead he needed to come in and set the tray down.

I knew he was full of shit, but if playing his game for a minute got him out of my space, then I was in. It wasn't often I closed myself off from my friends. This time I needed to do it for their sake and mine.

Callen set the tray on the table then took a seat on the couch like he was settling in for a long night of hanging out. Ayden pulled the desk chair out and straddled it, leaning his arms on the top of the backrest.

"Did you miss the part where I said I didn't need company?"

Callen shook his head. "Nope, I just ignored it."

Anger I thought I worked out of my system sizzled right below the surface of my skin. "Then, you can unignore it and drag your ass back to your own room to hang out."

This time it was Ayden who spoke up. "We're staying here. You can't keep going on like this. None of this is doing you any good. We're your friends. Talk to us."

This hadn't been the first time one of my friends had tried to talk to me after that night. The next game, I'd walked into the locker room with everyone's eyes on me, like they had after the trade rumors hit. At least then it had been pity for me being put on a new team. Then, there was no doubt if they wondered how things had changed so rapidly after news of Kasper buying the Sandpipers with Tim came to light.

Did they think I was worth being an Emperor? Would they blame me if the next second baseman didn't live up to their expectations? It had been too much, so on top of my temper, I'd avoided them.

"You can't keep hiding until the end of time," Callen said.

"We're your teammates, but more than that, we're your friends. We know shit went down between you and Kasper but not the details." Ayden sighed. "I know I bitch out relationships since the divorce, but that doesn't mean I want to see my friends suffer."

"There's nothing to talk about. Kasper and I aren't together. End of story."

"Bullshit," Callen snapped. "It's not the end of the story. We each have our ways of coping with things we can't control. I lash out and get thrown out of games, Ayden goes out with Dominic and gets his ass shit-faced drunk, you spend hours in the gym, even after playing a full nine inning game." I froze in my seat. Callen must have seen it. "Yeah, don't think I didn't notice you coming back from the hotel gym every night for this entire away series. I have no doubt it's the same at home."

I shrugged like it was no big deal and it wasn't. I was blowing off steam.

"What happened with Kasper? Spencer says you left him, but I don't understand why. You seemed happier than I'd seen you in a long time."

The reminder that what I had with Kasper had been everything I'd been looking for made the rein I had on my anger snap. I was out of my seat in seconds, pacing the floor.

"You want to know what he did? I'm sure you've figured it out by now, almost everyone else has."

"Does this have something to do with the Sandpipers?" Ayden asked.

"Something? It has everything to do with that goddamn football team." I stopped mid-pace and whirled around to face them both. "You want to know why I left Kasper? Why I can't trust him anymore? He bought the fucking football team as a deal to get Tim to keep me on the Emperors."

Callen dropped his eyes and blew out a breath. "I had a feeling it was something like that."

"Everyone fucking knows it. It's all over the goddamn media and you had a feeling? Bullshit! Now I have to spend every day of my fucking career wondering if the Emperors could have done better if they'd gotten a seasoned second baseman with Micah instead of a Triple A rookie with me behind the plate."

"Of course, we're going to do better with you behind the plate. We—"

I cut Ayden off before he could continue. "And how do you know? The answer is, you don't. Tim didn't make the decision based on what was best for the team. He made it with what was best for him and Kasper."

Callen stood and walked over in front of me, placing his hands on my shoulders. "Did you ever wonder why Kasper did it? Maybe ask him?"

"It was pretty clear it was all about him. He told me we'd figure out me being gone for sixth months of the year. Apparently, that wasn't good enough for him, so he decided to throw some money at it."

"Maybe." Callen shrugged. "Or maybe he did it because he loves you and he didn't want to see you lose what you love."

That was the second time tonight the thought of love creeped into my mind. I pushed it down. Buying someone wasn't love under any circumstances.

I crossed my arms over my chest. "If he loved me, he would have left my career alone. He would have trusted me to be in a different city. He would keep his promises. But no. He just filled our relationship with lies."

Ayden stood up and came over to join us. "Marcus."

I shook off Callen's arms and pushed around him to head to the couch and my dinner. "You both know where the door is."

I noticed them glance at each other before walking to the door. Callen opened it and stepped out into the hall.

Ayden stopped and looked at me for a moment. "Try to put yourself in Kasper's shoes, then see how you feel about what he did. And for the record, you are absolutely worth it." Ayden shut the door behind them.

I reached forward to the table and lifted the lid on the tray. The scent of the warm burger filled my senses and made my stomach churn. I wasn't hungry anymore.

I dropped the lid back on the tray and wandered over to the bed. Climbing onto the mattress, I tried to stop the trembling of my hands. The fury I held on to the last week or so leaked from me, hurt taking its place.

How could Kasper do this to me?

I fell asleep frustrated, back to having more questions than answers.

Chapter 28

Kasper

The door to my office flew open. I was sitting at my desk with nothing more than the task light on to illuminate the area. I had the other lights turned off. I preferred to work in the dark these days. Plus, people thought I wasn't here if they didn't see a bright light from under my door at night.

Evan stood in the doorway with his arms crossed. Spencer was just behind him and Paz took up the rear of their little parade.

"Get up," Evan demanded as he stalked over to me.

"Go home, Ev."

"No can do. It's Saturday night. You're sitting in your office like it's some sort of cave of despair, and we're not having it."

I glared past Evan and Spencer to the one I knew was guilty for this intervention—Pascal. He immediately put his hands up like he had nothing to do with it. I knew better. And as pissed as I was that he called in reinforcements, I would never do something drastic like fire him for it. Paz was stuck with me for the long haul, no matter how much of this shit he pulled.

"So help me, Kasper Wilder, if you don't get up from behind that desk and shut that computer off, I'm going to drag your ass out of here," Evan stated.

"You couldn't do any such thing." Actually, he might be able to. Evan was shorter than me and slender with lean muscles. He wasn't weak. Add in Spencer and Paz, they could get me out of here.

Evan cocked an eyebrow. "Is that a challenge because I'm up for it?" He planted his hands on my desk and leveled me with his hard glare. "You're working seven days a week. Only going home to sleep. You have dark shadows under your eyes and I swear you've lost ten pounds. At least your suit looks good, even if it is hanging on you a little. This has to stop and since you don't want to seem to do anything about it, the three of us are."

I leaned back in the chair and studied my best friend. Evan was only going to let me wallow for so long. I was surprised it took him this long to storm in here.

His features softened. "When the shit hit the fan with Vander and me, you were there. You and Spence. Now, we're here for you. What you're doing isn't healthy. So get up and let us get you home. I already have Sylvia setting the table for us. She cooked a great meal and you don't want to ruin it by not showing up."

Dammit. He was right. I never wanted to do anything to upset my housekeeper. She took good care of my place and me. Always made me dinners. In fact, since everything went downhill with Marcus, her meals were the only ones I was eating. The rest of the day I survived on coffee and air. If she hadn't been making me dinner, I probably wouldn't have eaten at all.

"Fine," I grumbled and powered down my laptop. I didn't bother trying to take it with me. Evan wouldn't let that fly. Also, I had another at home, so if something did come up, I could easily log on there. Not that I thought it would on a Saturday night.

"Good." Evan nodded.

He waited for me to grab my suit jacket and followed me out of the office. All three of them did.

Downstairs, I got into my car and Evan slid in the passenger side. "Spence is driving himself over to your place," he said. "Paz has a date, so his work is done for the evening."

"I didn't even want him in the office today."

"I know but Paz goes where you do."

He did. Every day since Marcus left me, Paz had been in the office with me, only leaving when I did. I tried to get him to go. Bribed him even. He wouldn't budge. I was glad he was going out tonight. He needed a break.

When I unlocked the door to my place, everything looked the same as it always did. It was immaculate. There was a rich scent in the air from dinner. But I saw what others didn't. I had the memories to prove Marcus had been here. All over my space. Where he kissed me breathless. Where he held me close. Where he slept in my bed. Each memory was like a knife to my heart. Every time I opened the door, they assaulted me.

It was another reason I was working so much. Not only to keep my mind busy and off the man I loved and lost, but to stay the hell out of my home where I couldn't escape thoughts of him.

My eyes strayed to the television. I tortured myself with the Emperors games. When I missed them, I caught the highlights. Marcus had been playing amazingly. While most wouldn't have noticed the way he held himself, how tense he appeared at times, I did. I caught every single one of his moods while playing. I knew I was the cause of it.

Evan nudged me forward until we were standing near the dining table. Sylvia was plating the last of the food. She was in her sixties and had been with me for years. Her brown hair was cut short. She always kept herself looking nice. I never asked her to, but she told me like everyone else on my team, she represented me and wanted to look her best every time she came here.

I stepped forward until she was able to place her hand on my cheek. She was a solid nine inches shorter than me. "I made you your favorite," she said. "My mom's beef stew. There are also freshly made rolls on the table and dessert is in the refrigerator. Let your friends take care of you. And do yourself a favor. No going into the office tomorrow. I'll be here in the morning to feed you breakfast and again for dinner."

"You don't have to do that. Enjoy the day with your family." Sylvia lived with her husband. Their daughter, her husband, and their three other kids lived just down the street from Sylvia. They always had big Sunday dinners together.

"When are you going to realize you're my family, too, hmmm? I care for the ones I love. I'll make an extra big dinner tomorrow and bring you some before we sit down to eat. I'd invite you, like I've done a thousand times before, but I know better than to expect you to come."

"Maybe one day." I never wanted to interrupt her time with her family.

"Maybe."

Sylvia did one last check of the table, making sure everything was set and in place, then grabbed her things and left without another word.

The guys dragged me to the stairs and sent me up to get changed. I did so on autopilot. I grabbed a pair of worn, comfortable jeans and a T-shirt before padding barefoot back downstairs. It was hot outside, but the air-conditioning kept my place cool.

Spencer was waiting for me at the bottom of the steps.

"I can find my way to the table," I told him.

"Yeah, and you know how to feed yourself, too, yet you've been doing a piss-poor job of it lately." I deserved the bite of anger in his voice.

Spencer and Evan cared about me. Would they once they knew what I did? I hadn't told them the reason for my breakup with Marcus. They just knew it happened. Once Callen and Vander spilled that Marcus had been moody as hell, they figured out something happened. I'd put them off until tonight. I told them I was okay and not to worry about me. Pascal saw me every day, however. He knew something was wrong without asking me.

The three of us sat down at the table. Conversation was kept light but I barely participated. Spencer and Evan did most of the talking. They seemed fine doing it until the dishes were loaded in the dishwasher and we moved to the living room. I was sandwiched between them on the couch.

"Spill," Evan said.

I didn't want to but had no choice. They were my closest friends. They should know what I did. "What if, after I tell you, you think I'm a horrible person?"

"Never going to happen. Right, Spence?"

"Nope," he confirmed. We would see about that.

Then I laid it out there. Every single bit of information. I wanted them to have the whole picture. Well, except for the intimate details of mine and Marcus's relationship. Some things even my best friends didn't need to know. As far as the deal with Tim and the blowup with Marcus, they got the gritty details.

By the time I was done talking, I had tears running down my face I didn't bother to wipe away. I deserved the hurt. Deserved to feel that pain slicing into me over and over again.

First, Evan's arms went around me, then Spencer's. They both held me tight while I cried. The only other time I shed tears over Marcus was the night he walked out of my life. Since then, I kept it bottled up and pushed down deep.

The tears didn't make me feel better. There was nothing cathartic about them. Instead, they made me feel worse. On top of reliving the night Marcus left, I was drained to the point of barely holding myself up. The weeks of busting my ass at work and not eating enough finally caught up with me.

The guys pulled back. Evan took my hand in his. "What I'm going to say is the truth. I'm not going to sugarcoat it because that won't get us anywhere. Kas, what you did, I can understand Marcus being upset."

"Evan," Spencer warned low.

"No, let me finish. But that doesn't mean what he did was right. He should have sat down and talked to you. Instead, he reacted and flew off the deep end. He also doesn't know you as well as you thought he did. As all of us do. Because had he known you better, he wouldn't have been surprised by this. You love with your whole heart. Everything you do for others comes from a place of deep caring for them. Of course you were going to do what you had to so Marcus could continue to play in Espen. And yes, I'm sure there was a part of you that wanted him here for yourself, too, but that wasn't the main reason."

"He's right," Spencer added. "You'll put any one of your friends or family ahead of yourself. You've done it since I met you. You'll go to whatever lengths you have to so those you love are happy."

"I crossed a line this time," I muttered.

Evan shrugged. "And? When you're in a relationship, there are no lines. There never should be. No rules either. All that matters is love. And while you haven't said you loved him, not to us or him, I can see it plain as day when you talk about him. What you did wasn't to try to strong-arm him into staying in Espen. He wanted to stay here. It was because you love him and wanted him happy that you arranged for him to remain on the Emperors."

I leaned my head back against the couch and closed my eyes. I did love Marcus with everything in me. Evan and Spencer were right. I would do anything for those I cared about. I went too far this time. I would never forgive myself for driving him out of my life. If Marcus would have been traded, we still would have made it work. It wouldn't have been easy, but we could have done it. In the end, it was my fault our relationship ended.

Turning, I looked at Spencer. His dirty blond hair was cut close on the sides and back, longer on top. Those blue eyes of his were full of compassion I wasn't sure I deserved. "You don't hate me?" I asked. "What I did... It wasn't right." I didn't need to ask Evan. It would take a whole hell of a lot more for Evan to hate me. Spencer, though, he was different. He looked at things in a way Evan didn't.

Spencer put his hand on my forearm. "I couldn't hate you, Kas. It wasn't like you did this to harm someone. You did it to make Marcus happy. There's no reason for me to be mad or hate you for it."

"I'm pissed at Marcus," Evan cut in.

"Don't," I said. Marcus didn't deserve his ire.

"You don't get to tell me who I can and cannot be mad at, Kasper Wilder. He's been stewing long enough. He needs to come to his senses and realize what you did for him. The lengths you went to. Hell, if it got out what you did, I don't even want to think about what would happen to your reputation. You put yourself on the line for him."

"I shouldn't have taken the risk."

"Don't you dare wish you could take back what you did. Even if Marcus never pulls his head out of his ass and comes back to you, he still gets to stay in Espen and play for the Emperors. You did that for him. You helped make it happen. Now it's up to him to continue to work his ass off for the team he loves, just like the other guys do every game. Not everyone gets to where they are in life by climbing up the ranks, putting their time in, and suffering before they get to the top. There's luck. A whole lot of it. Some people get really fucking lucky. Others know someone who can give them a helping hand. That's what you did."

"I should have talked to him before I did it." I wish I had. Maybe everything would have turned out differently.

Evan shook his head. "He would have forbidden you from doing it and currently be trying to figure out if he should buy or rent in the new city he was moving to. He still would have been pissed that you even thought to do it for him."

"But it would have been his choice."

"And I would like to wake up with Vander worshipping my dick while his fingers are in my ass on a daily basis, but we don't always get what we want."

Spencer groaned on the other side of me. "Really, Ev?"

He waved him off. "Whatever, you get my point. Shit happens. Decisions are made. Blah, blah, blah. It's over and done with. You did what you did out of love, Kas. Now it's up to Marcus to realize how much you care about him before it's too late."

It would never be too late. I'd always want Marcus in my life. No matter how much time went by, if he showed up at my door, I'd welcome him in. But he wouldn't come here and I couldn't blame him. I hurt him too much. I destroyed us. There was no going back.

I had to learn to live without Marcus in my life. To love him from afar. To cheer him on, even though he didn't know I was doing it.

I would always be in his corner. Always have his back. No matter what he said to me in the past or did. His words hurt but I deserved them. I fucked up. Losing him was my penance.

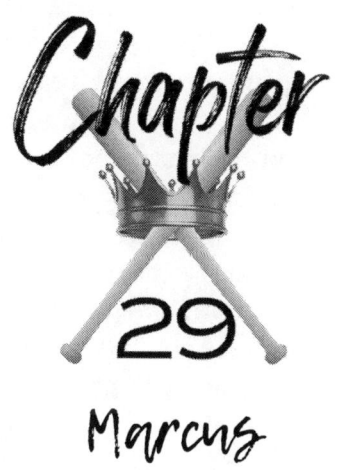

Marcus

All eyes were on me as I lowered the pen to the paper with a shaky hand. I stared at the figure, a dollar amount it had taken more than a month to agree upon, with Charlie and Tim having the conversations without me. Charlie kept me in the loop on what the Emperors were offering. But now, faced with the reality of signing the papers, of putting my name on a giant lie, I couldn't bring myself to do it. Not when I knew where this contract came from, and it didn't have shit to do with my playing ability.

I set the pen down, leaving the signature line blank and stood, walking over to the windows on the far side of the office.

"Marcus, you didn't sign." Charlie's voice carried above the other murmurs filling the space. There would probably be questions about whether the figure on the contract made me happy. It sure as hell did. That number would make me one of the highest paid catchers in the majors. The problem was whether or not I was actually worth it.

"Do you think everyone could give us a few minutes? Caroline will take everyone down to the reception room," Tim said, but I continued to look at the city spread out before me.

"Follow me," Caroline called out. Charlie began to argue, but something stopped him and his voice disappeared. The murmurs grew softer until finally the door closed and for the first time since he told me I was staying in Espen, I was alone in the room with Tim.

"Is everything okay, Marcus?" I turned around and found Tim standing with his hands in his pockets, watching me.

I shook my head. "I can't sign that. I didn't earn it."

"Let's sit." He walked back over to the table and pulled out a chair, taking a seat and waiting for me to do the same. Tim didn't speak again until I sat down. "Does this have something to do with Kasper?"

I scoffed, suddenly no longer worried about what my boss would think. "Of course it does. I'm only here because Kasper offered to buy the Sandpipers with you."

Tim leaned back in his chair and steepled his hands in front of his face. "Do you really believe that I would keep you in Espen if I didn't want you?"

"Isn't that exactly what happened? You were set to trade me until Kasper came to you with his deal then suddenly I'm staying in Espen with a long-term contract and a no trade clause." The anger I thought had died in my hotel room the night Callen and Ayden came to see me rose to the surface once again. This time it wasn't the full-blown rage I'd been feeling but a deep frustration with the entire situation.

Tim sighed. "Marcus, I don't want you to think you don't belong here. Kasper might have given me the opportunity to buy the team with him, but I can guarantee I never would have taken the deal if I really didn't want to keep you as part of the Emperors. I'm a businessman, not one desperate enough to own a football team that I'd damage my successful baseball team. I told you from the beginning that the trade was a possibility, not a guarantee."

His words were starting to break through the belief I had that I wasn't good enough, but something else kept coming back to me. "So you just happened to find a second baseman on a Triple A team?"

"No, you're right about that." The corner of his lip curved up in a half smile. "I didn't start looking at Triple A until Kasper suggested it. I thought our best chance would be to get someone already established, but he was right. You have to trust that contract wouldn't be in front of you if I didn't think keeping you was the right move for the team. I even told Kasper I had to find someone of Emperors' caliber before I could offer you anything." He sat forward, resting his arms on the table. "Which is why it took almost two weeks after my meeting with Kasper to tender you the contract in the first place."

Tim's words settled into me. I was worth it. I belonged with my team. There was no reason for me to feel like I was here because my *ex*-boyfriend bought my way in. The word ex rattled through my brain and Callen's words came rushing back.

Maybe he did it because he loves you and he didn't want to see you lose what you love.

I tried to push those thoughts to the side for now. There would be time to focus on them later when there wasn't a roomful of people waiting for me to put my name on a deal that would keep me with the Emperors until I retired.

Tim must have noticed the change in my posture. He stood. "I think you're ready to sign now." He walked over to the desk and pushed the intercom, asking Caroline to bring everyone back into the room. Tim moved the folder full of papers in front of me. "You're worth every penny in that document."

Before I could say anything, the door opened and the room filled. In seconds, flashes went off as I picked up the pen and did what I couldn't do earlier. I signed my name, agreeing to stay with the Emperors long term.

After handshakes, photos, and congratulations, we made our way to the small reception Tim had set up.

I'd managed to push Callen's words out of my head, only to have Kasper's take their place.

No, please. I don't want to lose you. I hated seeing you hurt at the thought of being traded. I had to do something. I couldn't lose you.

Forcing the smile to stay on my face, I made my excuses to Charlie and Tim.

"We've got this," Tim said. "Go take care of things."

It was like he could read my mind. The silence of the car on the way back to my condo did nothing to help my state of mind. The night I walked out of Kasper's place kept replaying over and over again in my head. By the time I pulled into my parking space, I couldn't breathe.

My heart raced in my chest and I wasn't sure I'd make it up to my condo without throwing up. All the voices in my head. The puzzle pieces falling into place.

Why hadn't I seen it?

I stumbled through my door, barely staying on my feet. I slammed it closed and slid down until my ass hit the floor. Drawing my knees to my chest, I rested my head on them. Kasper loved me. He hadn't said the words, but it would be the only reason he'd risk everything to keep me in Espen. He didn't want another sports team. His fear had been there since the beginning. I'd just been too caught up in my own feelings to see it.

He hadn't wanted to date an athlete but took the risk with me. Then he would worry I'd be mad about little things like missing a home game. He stressed about me outing myself so publicly.

Yet, I still hadn't seen it.

I lowered my leg and tugged my phone out of my pocket. There was only one person who would understand. I dialed and waited for her to answer.

"Hey! Congrats. Just saw your signing pictures online." Sienna's tone was cheerful, unknowing the inner turmoil I was about to heap in her lap.

"He loves me." My voice trembled. Could I have lost everything?

"I know he does."

"What do you mean you know?"

Sienna sighed. "You figured it out, didn't you? He told you he went into business with Tim to keep you in Espen. You were just too pissed it happened behind your back for you to see why he really did it."

"Why didn't you say something before?" Sienna knew me better than anyone, except Kasper.

"Because you needed to figure it out on your own. You don't get that pissed often, but when you do, words aren't what you need. It's time. Time to realize on your own that you're not seeing the entire picture."

Even though it made my chest ache more, I knew she was right. She could've told me everything and I wouldn't have believed her.

"He was afraid to lose me and he did anyway."

"Did he really?"

I knew the answer to that question without thinking about it. He'd never lost me. Even through all my anger, all the hurt, my heart still screamed for him. I couldn't sleep without wearing myself down to the point of exhaustion. Then I'd dream about him.

"No, but I may have lost him."

"I don't think that's true either. What I do think is that you're afraid, too. You put on this front, big brother, that you have everything under control. That you know what you're doing. It's why you jump in with both feet and don't check if there's water first. But here's a secret." Her voice lowered, like when we'd tell secrets to each other as kids. We were in two different states, but it was like she was sitting next to me on the swing set in the backyard. It settled me. "There was water in the pool, but Kasper wanted to catch you to keep you from getting wet."

I closed my eyes and rested my head back against the door. "What does that even mean, brat?"

"Ah, there's my Marcus." Even she noticed I hadn't called her brat when she picked up, which meant things were really bad. "It means he wanted to protect you because even you didn't realize you were scared."

I'd thought about the heartache that would come from being away from Kasper for six months of the year if I'd gotten traded, but I never thought about why. Deep down it had always been there. The fear that being with an athlete moving from team to team would be too much for him. And after I'd put my heart out there, found a partner, someone to come home to at night, I didn't want to let it go. I was deathly afraid of losing it. Instead, I'd thrown it away.

I sucked in a breath. "Oh god."

"Breathe, Marcus. I don't think it's too late to fix. Do you?"

I hoped like hell it wasn't. "How do I fix it?"

"You have to apologize and you need to prove that you're not afraid. That you're in it as much as he is."

My mind raced, dismissing idea after idea. Until one settled firmly in place. One that could end both our fears and prove I wanted to be with him for the long haul. "I know what I need to do. I gotta go. I have a stop to make on my way to Kasper's."

I glanced at my watch. He should be home from work by the time I got there.

"I'm proud of you, big brother. Once you get your man back, do you think we could finally meet him in person?"

"*If* I get him back, I'll make sure that happens." I hung up with Sienna and bolted out the door.

Thank fuck I still had his elevator key card. I didn't want to give him the chance to turn me away in the lobby of his building. I needed to see him. The elevator ride up seemed to take forever. I'd counted the number of times I wiped my clammy hands on my jeans. Each deep breath I tried to pull in made my stomach churn. What would I do if he slammed the door in my face? Told me to leave?

Finally, the elevator opened, and I was standing in front of his door. It was now or never. Risk it all to have it all. I'd taken plenty of chances on my way to the majors but nothing like this. For Kasper, I was willing to climb any mountain I needed to have him in my arms again.

Sucking in a breath, I knocked on Kasper's door and waited. It took a few minutes for him to answer. My heart ached at the sight of him. Dark circles lined his eyes and I could see he'd lost weight in the last month. Hopefully, this would be enough to start to rebuild the man I loved.

His brows drew together. "Marcus?"

I lowered myself to one knee and pulled out the box I'd picked up on the way here. Kasper sucked in a breath and before he could stop me or say anything, I started talking.

"Kasper, I love you. I know I've made mistakes. I should have listened to you that night. Should have let you explain. I understand you only did it because you love me. You didn't want to lose me if I went to another team. That fear has always been there. You've been hurt before and you've been waiting for it to happen again. Looking back on our relationship, that fear has existed from the beginning. Yet, you were still willing to let me go as long as I had what made me happy. I made a mistake walking away that night. I was so angry I couldn't stop to see the whys. I'm sorry it took me so long to get here. But I was afraid, too. Afraid that I wouldn't be enough. That being with an athlete would be too much for you."

The words were pouring out of my mouth and I couldn't stop them. It was my turn to be afraid. Afraid it was too late and Kasper would slam the door in my face. "But I don't want you to fear losing me anymore and I don't want to fear losing you, because I'm not going anywhere. This is the only way I know how to prove to you I'm here for the long haul and I always will be. Kasper Wilder, will you marry me?"

Chapter 30

Kasper

Bone-deep exhaustion had settled in long ago. I was going home at a reasonable hour every night since the talk with Evan and Spencer. Paz made sure I got out the door on time. That didn't mean I was resting when I got home. I would work until my eyes couldn't stay open any longer, then, I would crawl into bed or onto the couch and fall into a restless sleep, only to do it all again the next day.

Evan and Spencer tried to get me to do fun stuff with them over the weekend but my heart wasn't in it. I was still mourning the loss of Marcus in my life. At least my work wasn't suffering because of it, just my body.

My eyes resembled a raccoon's and I'd lost even more weight. I wasn't exercising since I didn't have the energy. I was still muscular. It would take longer than a month to get rid of years of hard work, eating right, and staying in shape.

Someone knocked on my door. I debated ignoring it. Whoever was on the other side couldn't hear my TV on, so they wouldn't know if I were awake. It was early, though.

I sighed, shut the TV off, and eventually stood. I'd smile and put on a nice front so they'd leave. Lie and tell them I was doing better. Not that they'd believe me.

Opening the door, I couldn't believe who was on the other side, but I wasn't foolish enough to hope it was because he wanted me back. "Marcus?"

Then he dropped to one knee and opened a box in his hand. My world tilted on its axis. Everything blurred as tears built in my eyes. Every word he said, every emotion I saw on his face, in his eyes… This wasn't really happening, was it?

He stopped talking and stared at me expectantly. I was frozen in place. Unable to tell if this was a dream or reality. Did he just ask me to marry him?

"Kasper?" he asked but never took his hopeful, gray eyes off mine. I noticed the box in his hand started to shake. It was an elegant ring yet masculine. Brushed platinum. Marcus had good taste.

I focused on his face again. "You're serious?"

He blew out a breath and dropped his head in defeat. The lid on the ring box snapped loudly in the quiet space when he shut it.

I didn't like that look on his face, so I sank to my knees in front of him and tipped his chin up. I needed to see his eyes. "I'm sorry, but you have to give me a minute to get over the shock of this situation. I haven't seen or heard from you in weeks. Not a call or a text. Then you show up and ask me to marry you."

"I couldn't stay away any longer. I needed you to know I want this with you. Only you."

Releasing his chin, I stood and held out my hand for his. He took it and I helped him stand, even though he didn't need it. "Come inside."

He followed me in, pocketing the ring he bought me. I tugged him until we were in the living room and could sit on the couch together.

Did I want to marry him? Fuck. Yes. But him showing up with a ring and a proposal didn't mean our issues and the reason for our breakup disappeared.

I watched him for a moment. He looked everywhere but at me. "Marcus." I said his name firmly so he'd know I needed his attention. His gaze snapped to mine. "What happened?"

"I signed the contract with the Emperors."

"Yes, I know, but what else caused you to show up here tonight? Something had to have changed."

He parted his lips then closed them. He did it again before asking, "You knew about my deal?"

"Yes. I still follow your career. Just because we broke up doesn't mean I stopped caring about you. Stopped..." I couldn't bring myself to say loving you. Not yet.

"I can't believe you kept up with me."

I shrugged. When he said it like that, I sounded pathetic, following a man who didn't want anything to do with me. Well, not stalking him but keeping up with his career. I never did that with Hunter. Once he was out of my life, that door shut and I bolted the bitch closed with fifty locks. Every key got tossed into the Bermuda Triangle.

"God, Kasper. I was with Tim and the others as they waited for me to sign the contract, and I couldn't help but think I didn't earn my place there. Then Tim asked everyone to leave the room and we talked. I told him I knew about the deal you made and he assured me he wanted me on the team. It was the same thing you said, but hearing it from him—listening to the sincerity in his words—it made me realize I was foolish to think you paid my way in. Tim wouldn't have kept me if I were a shitty player, no matter how much money and what deal you two went in on."

"He wouldn't have. You're right. At the end of the day, he has a business to run. He has to make the right decisions to earn a profitable return."

"It wasn't just him, though. I talked to Callen and Ayden while we were on the road. They told me that maybe you did what you did because you love me. Because you wanted me to be happy and play the sport I love in the city I love as well."

I nodded. "All true." Just like that I confessed to Marcus I loved him without saying those exact words. I couldn't have him go on thinking I didn't.

His eyes widened. "So you do? Love me?"

I cupped his cheek and brushed my thumb over the scruff there, enjoying the prickly feel of it. I was afraid I'd never get to touch him again. "I do. I love you so fucking much."

"Thank god."

Marcus closed the distance between us and kissed the hell out of me. It was raw and needy. Full of so much want and spoke of our time apart. The days we went without being in each other's arms.

I didn't fight for dominance as his tongue pushed into my mouth and fucked me like I wished the rest of his body would. I let him do whatever he wanted.

My hands were on his hips as he leveled me back on the couch so he was over me. He dipped his hips down to rub his length along mine.

Marcus pulled back and moaned on contact. "Fuck, I missed this." His eyes pierced mine. "I missed you."

He was starting to blur on me again as tears built in my eyes. "You forgive me?"

"I love you. Of course, I forgive you. But don't ever pull that shit again. We need to talk. Everything on the table. No more doing deals behind my back, especially ones that involve me."

"I promise."

He leaned all the way back and stood. This time it was him holding out his hand to me. "Let's go upstairs. I want to get inside you then fall asleep with you in my arms. This couch is too small for that."

I didn't hesitate putting my palm in his. Marcus pulled me up. Before I knew it, we were kissing again. Gripping one another wherever we could reach. We kept it going the whole way up the stairs and into my bedroom, only tripping once, laughing as we did so.

The mood changed inside my bedroom. "Strip, Kas. I want you naked and on the bed."

His words sent a delicious shiver through my body. I didn't think I'd hear his commanding words in this room again or see the heat in his eyes as I shed my clothes and moved onto the bed. I soaked him in as he did the same then crawled over top of me.

Marcus was a chiseled work of art. His muscles were a little bigger and more defined, like he'd been working out nonstop. I grazed my fingers over the ridges on his chest and stomach.

"You're beautiful," I murmured, appreciating his body.

"I had a lot of anger to work out in the gym."

I peered up at him. "I'm so sorry."

"Kas, stop. It's over. Done with. We're back where we're meant to be." He glanced down at my body, his eyes raking me over, then he slid his hand up over my hip, stomach, and chest until it rested on the side of my neck. "You've lost weight."

"You worked out and I stopped eating breakfast and lunch."

"Fuck," he growled. "That ends now. No more skipping meals. I want your body back to where it was. I need to know you can keep up with me in bed. I'll feed you myself if I have to."

"Whatever you want." He could ask anything of me in this moment and I'd give it to him. Every part of me, my heart, mind, body, and soul belonged to Marcus.

"No, not whatever I want. I need you to want it, too. You have to stay healthy, Kas."

I nodded. "I will. Now will you fuck me?"

He grinned and dipped his head to brush his lips over mine. "No, but I'll make love to you," he whispered.

I arched up at his words, needing his hands on my body. Needing him to take care of me here. To put the pieces of my heart back together and make me whole again.

We were skin to skin, dick to dick, as we started a sensuous glide of our bodies. He rubbed his hard length against mine. I was so close to coming from that it wasn't even funny. Not once had I gotten myself off while he was gone. I couldn't. My mind was too sad, too broken, without him. I didn't want anyone, including myself, touching me that way except him.

With one hand on his waist and my lips on his as he kept rubbing against me, I reached out without looking for my nightstand drawer so I could find what we needed. I grabbed the lube and tossed it on the bed, but the condoms weren't there. They must have been in the other drawer.

"Shit," I muttered and tried to move to the other side.

"What are you doing?"

"Condoms."

"Do we need them?"

I froze. "You want to go bare?"

"I'm clean. I get tested regularly."

"Same."

"No more barriers, Kas."

I swallowed, unable to trust my voice, and nodded in agreement.

Marcus rolled to my side and grabbed the lube. "Lift your legs and open yourself for me."

I did so without reservation. I was vulnerable to him.

After slicking his fingers, Marcus dipped one slowly inside me. He moved it in and out, coating me with lube while carefully stretching me.

"More," I pleaded. "I need you."

He pushed a second in. The burn was there. The bite of pain at having nothing in me for weeks. As soon as my body adjusted and I relaxed slightly, he pushed another finger in, continuing to stretch me while his other hand, slick with lube, started stroking my dick, bringing it back to life.

His talented fingers found my prostate. I arched off the bed, my dick hardening quickly.

"Goddammit, Marcus. Get in me."

Releasing my dick, he slowly pulled his fingers out then gripped his length and coated himself. His eyes bored into mine as he dripped more lube into my crease. "You're not in charge here. I am. Your job is to feel. To let go and let me take care of your needs. Can you do that for me?"

"Yes."

"Good."

Marcus looked down between us as he entered me for the first time without a condom on. I watched, too. Mesmerized by the sight. When he bottomed out, I threw my head back and squeezed my eyes shut. It had been too long without him. Too many feelings were rushing through me.

He started with slow, easy glides so I could adjust to him. By the time my body was fully relaxed, he kissed me hard and started pounding into me. I held on to his shoulders and pulled my lips away to bring more desperately needed air into my lungs. Marcus kissed down my neck until he reached the spot where my shoulder met it and bit there.

"Mark me! Fuck, yes!" I wanted the world to know I was his. I didn't care what anyone would say. This man was back in my bed where he belonged and I was deliriously happy about it.

He was fucking me so hard, so good. And I was right on the edge.

Marcus reached between us and gripped my dick in his hand. Two strokes later and my muscles tightened as my orgasm tore through me and I came all over his hand and my stomach and chest.

Not letting up, Marcus drove into me until he was calling out my name and emptying inside of me, claiming me, marking me as his from the inside.

His movements slowed, wringing out every last drop of his climax. "Fuck, you're perfect, Kas." He dropped down on top of me, not caring about the mess between us, and rolled us to our sides. Gentle fingers brushed my sweaty hair off my forehead. Kind, caring eyes met mine. "I love you, Kasper. Never again do I want to be away from you."

"Ask me again," I told him. I needed to hear his question one more time. I was so stunned when he first asked. Now I was ready.

A slow smile spread over his lips. He clasped the back of my neck and brought us together until our foreheads were touching and our eyes locked. "Kasper Wilder, will you marry me?"

I grinned. "Yes."

Marcus

The moment the 'yes' left his lips, I let go of him and climbed from the bed.

"Where are you going?" Kasper leaned up on his elbow, and I noticed the way his eyes wandered down to my ass.

I reached for my discarded jeans and tugged out the box I'd held out to Kasper earlier. After his silence at my original proposal, I wasn't sure if he was ready to say yes to me. But hearing him tell me to ask again made my heart race in my chest, even though I knew what the answer would be.

His eyes tracked me as I sauntered back to the bed. I opened the lid, taking the ring out, and tossed the box toward the table. Didn't matter where it landed, the only thing that did was slipping my ring on Kasper's finger.

"If I had more time, I could have something custom made, but I didn't—" Kasper covered my lips with his fingers.

"It's perfect."

I took Kasper's hand from my mouth and slid it down his finger. The brushed platinum glinted in the light. A sense of calm and awe settled over me seeing the ring on his finger. I laid down on my back and let Kasper curl his body around mine. His hand settled on my chest and I couldn't stop myself from covering it with my own, rubbing my thumb back and forth over the metal that would someday make Kasper mine forever.

The silence that filled the space was like a warm blanket. Comfortable and contented. I relived every moment from the time I showed up at Kasper's, thanking my lucky stars he was in my arms.

My fiancé.

That would take some getting used to, but I loved the way it sounded.

"I talked to my sister earlier today."

"Yeah? What did she say?" His warm breath ghosted over my chest, making me shiver.

"That she knew all along why you made the deal with Tim, and she was happy I finally figured it out on my own. She told me I wouldn't have listened to her if she tried to tell me before."

He chuckled. "She sounds like a smart woman. I can't wait to meet her one day."

"Well, speaking of that. She actually made me promise she'd get to meet you in person soon. What do you think?"

"We can meet for the wedding."

I glanced down at the top of his head, very confused. "Are you saying you want to wait until we get married to meet my family? Who knows when that will be?"

Kasper moved to rest his chin on my chest. "No, I'm saying that the All-Star break is in a month. I think we should get married then. Why wait? I can fly your family in for the entire two weeks before if they can get time off work."

My eyes widened. "You want to get married in a month? Kas, I love you with all of my heart, but it's the middle of the season, I don't have time to plan the wedding."

"That's what you have me for. I've spent my entire life waiting for you. We've spent enough time apart, don't you think?"

I knew exactly what he was saying. Deep down, I didn't want to wait any longer either. Kasper was my world and I wanted to call him my husband.

"Okay. Let's do it." I ran my hand down his side. With my lust and nerves firmly under control, I once again noticed how much weight he'd lost in the last month. "Did you eat dinner tonight?"

"Sylvia left it warming in the kitchen, but I didn't feel like eating yet."

I tapped lightly on his ass. "Come on, get up. We can talk about the wedding while you work on putting some of the weight you lost back on." Kasper slowly climbed out of bed. "I don't have to be at the field until three tomorrow, and you bet your ass we're having a big breakfast in the morning." I picked up my jeans and tugged them on commando.

Kasper watched me. "We're putting on clothes?"

I took hold of his shoulders and turned him toward the dresser. "Yes. Grab a pair of shorts unless you want me to fuck you bent over the dining room table." Heat flashed in his eyes and I shook my head. "Not happening. You're going to eat at that table. But I promise to bring you back up here and fuck you nice and hard afterward," I whispered in his ear before taking a light nip of the lobe.

He groaned but got a pair of gym shorts out and tugged them on. I followed him down to the kitchen where he grabbed two plates from the cabinet.

"Don't even think about splitting your dinner with me. You need to eat. I've at least been eating all my meals."

He started dishing out the food. "She's been making double the portions, hoping I'd eat more."

I glanced at his plate to make sure there was a reasonable amount of food on it before I took the one he handed me. We carried them into the dining room and sat down, him at the head of the table and me to his left. The other end of the table seemed too far away at the moment.

"So, our wedding?" Kasper asked, but I pointed at his plate.

I needed to see him eat. Needed to know we could fix some of the damage I caused. He put a forkful in his mouth and I felt like I could breathe. Later, I'd fuck him into exhaustion to work on the dark circles under his eyes.

"What are you thinking?" I lifted my fork to my lips.

"Something small. Just our close friends and family."

"Agreed." I didn't want some large affair where half the people were only there to get a picture of the two of us. "Are you sure we can do it in a month, though?"

"Paz will help me move heaven and earth if we have to."

I set my fork down. "I don't want you working yourself to the bone. You've done enough of that lately."

He reached over and took my hand in his. The edges of the ring hitting my hand sent a shiver down my spine. "I promise not to push too hard. I'll be home whenever you are, but we can make this happen. People will be jumping at the chance to help."

"Okay, but you better promise to let me know if it gets to be too much. I'm a simple man who only needs you standing next to me, promising me forever."

Kasper tightened his hand on mine. "Forever."

I leaned forward and pressed my lips to his. The kiss was simple, not the blazing inferno of earlier, but it held so much promise of things to come. When I pulled back, the smile I'd missed so much in the last month reappeared.

"I love you," he whispered against my lips.

"I love you, too." I tilted my head toward his plate. "Finish eating and we'll figure out the rest."

"Like where we're going to live?"

My head snapped up. Of all the things I thought about on the way here, like would he slam the door in my face, what I could do to make him say yes, living arrangements didn't even cross my mind. "I have to be honest. I didn't think about that part when I decided this was what I wanted."

He finished off the last bite of food and wiped his mouth on the napkin. "Let's clean this up and we'll go back upstairs to talk about it."

Dishes in the dishwasher and the leftovers in the fridge, hand in hand, we climbed the stairs. Kasper stopped at the doorway and turned me to face him. "I want this to be our bedroom. To be our home. I know you have the condo, but here we have room for a family."

I took a step toward Kasper until our chests were touching. "I'd love to make this our home. The condo is a place to sleep. Home is wherever you are." I caressed down the side of his face. "And let's be honest, anyone would be crazy not to want to live here."

I smacked him on the ass again and dashed past him into the bedroom. We ditched our clothes and made ourselves comfortable on the bed, sitting back against the headboard, Kasper's hand in mine. No matter how hard I tried, I couldn't stop touching him. It helped me remember that this was real. It wasn't a dream and Kasper was mine.

We talked about what we wanted for our wedding and reception and thought about a honeymoon in November, long after the baseball season, in case the Emperors made it to the World Series again.

I linked my fingers through his. "There's one more thing we need to talk about."

"When we're moving your belongings here?"

I smirked. "Okay, two. But let's come back to that. We need to talk about money."

"Okay." His eyebrows furrowed.

I twirled the ring around his finger. I couldn't stop myself from touching it. "I'm sure you know what I signed my contract for and I know it's nothing compared to what you're worth. I just want you to know I'd be happy to sign a prenup—"

"Absolutely not." He lifted our hands to his lips and pressed a kiss to the back of mine. "I'm in this with you forever. If shit hits the fan at some point, we'll work through it. And if for some godforsaken reason we don't work out, you can have whatever you want of mine because I can guarantee you none of it will matter to me without you in my life. This place, my business, whatever, what I have is yours."

"And whatever I have is yours."

"Good, now let's go back to moving you in here. The only nights I want to spend without you are the ones when you're on the road. I can have a moving truck there this weekend. I'll even have them pack for you."

"We have a three game series this weekend. How about this? It's not like we need any of the furniture in my place."

"You can bring anything you want here. I want this to be your home, too."

"I know you do, but I have no attachment to my furniture. I have other things I want to bring, like my awards and clothes."

"We can set up a place in the living room to display your awards."

I moved closer, resting my head on Kasper's shoulder. "I like that. Why don't I start by packing my clothes over the next few days and on our next day off I'll bring them over. Then we'll work on everything else. The furniture can go into storage until after the season and there's more time to deal with it. Then I'll hire a realtor to sell the condo."

"Perfect. Until then, I expect you to have an overnight bag with you every time you show up. You're sleeping here with me in this bed."

My eyes lingered on his lips and I knew we were done talking for the night. There were many more decisions to make, but I couldn't resist the taste of his lips as I lowered him to the bed and covered his body with mine.

This morning, I woke up angry and alone. Tonight, I was going to bed happy and engaged to the love of my life. Many people would see me as lucky for signing the contract with the Emperors earlier, something that may not have happened without a little interference from Kasper. But that didn't make me lucky.

Lucky was holding tight to the man below me as I sank inside his warm body. A place that would be mine forever. Like I told Kasper, home was with him.

And finally, I was home.

Kasper

This life I was leading still felt like a dream.

Today, I was getting married to Marcus, the love of my life.

One month after he proposed to me. One day after he flew back from the All-Star Game. His very first one.

He was so excited to go. And even though the National League lost, which I hated for Marcus, it was still a memorable moment for him. The Emperors were playing damn well this year. They were setting up for another World Series run.

For the past couple of weeks, I'd been using my aviation company to fly family and friends in for the wedding. We weren't having a big one but given everyone was spread out across the country and world, we had a lot of flights to deal with.

Marcus's sister had been here for two weeks now. Since she worked freelance, her schedule was more flexible. His parents, my sister-in-law, nephews, and most others for a week. Stockton flew in two days ago since he'd been on set. It was harder for him to leave. He'd fly out again tomorrow, but his family was staying for a bit longer.

Those who had to be away at the All-Star Game got to either fly home last night after the game or this morning. Marcus came home last night. He was only gone for two days. He crawled into bed with me late, when I was already asleep.

Having my own planes was a hell of a perk in a time like this.

Our wedding was going to be small and intimate, which we both wanted. No need to have one with five hundred guests. We would clock in at around seventy-five people.

It hadn't been easy getting a wedding put together in such a short amount of time. This was a case of it mattered who I knew and how much money I had.

The wedding was going to be held on a rooftop terrace in the open air of the building Reese's was in. Reese was close with the building's owner and connected us. He kept the top few stories to himself and, with a hefty check, allowed us to use it this afternoon.

The reception was going to be held in Reese's. She closed it down for the day. She also was going to keep the windows covered to make sure no reporters or photographers saw us.

We kept our engagement quiet and our wedding plans even quieter. If the media got ahold of the news that Marcus and I were getting married, all hell would break loose. I didn't want that prior to the wedding. I'd been one of the most eligible bachelors for too long. They were going to have a field day once they found out I got married.

Marcus, me, and our wedding party were getting ready on the floor I rented in the building we were getting married in. Evan insisted on Marcus and me changing in different rooms then meeting up prior to our vows. It was ridiculous, considering we didn't do anything else traditionally. There was no way we were spending the night before our wedding apart. We were apart from each other enough when he went to away games and I had to fly out for business, which admittedly had been less since Marcus and I started dating. I did as much as I could from Espen.

"Show me your ass," Evan demanded from behind me.

"Would you knock it off?" I huffed and turned to face him.

His arms were crossed over the chest of his tailored suit. He was gorgeous. Hair perfectly done. Shoes shined, not a scuff on them. "I bought you a great wedding present. I want to see if you're wearing it."

"He's not going to stop until you show him," Spencer said from the other side of the room where he was staring out over the city. "The views here are stunning." They were. Another reason we chose this location.

"For fuck's sake." I relented and dragged my slacks down to show Evan what I had on underneath.

"Yes! I knew you'd look good in those. I'm going to get a picture."

"What? No!" I quickly dragged my slacks back up and tucked my white button-down shirt in. "You're not taking a picture of my ass to post on social media." Because that was exactly what he'd do with it.

One of my wedding presents from Evan was a pair of fuchsia briefs that hugged my body tightly and perfectly, with *Big Daddy Kas* emblazoned on the ass in bold, white letters. He told me he got Marcus a matching pair that said *Property of Big Daddy Kas* on them.

He stuck out his bottom lip in a pout. "But it's a great gift."

"You can take a photo of us once I get my hair perfect. Clothed."

"Fine, but I'm picking the hashtags tomorrow."

"I figured you would."

There was a social media post ban on everything to do with the wedding and engagement until tomorrow morning. Then I knew Evan would unleash tons of photos on the world as well as Katie, who handled PR for the Jetties, and Lali, who did the same for the Sandpipers.

Stockton came out of the bathroom chuckling, obviously having heard the conversation. "I'd let you take a picture of my ass if you bought me underwear." He winked at Evan, whose eyes went wide and a wicked gleam formed in them.

"Now you did it," Spencer cut in. "Next time you come out here, Stock, make sure your ass is on point because he'll have his phone ready and a thong for you."

Stock smacked his left ass cheek. "This bad boy is always delicious looking."

"I'm amazed all of our egos can fit in one room," I deadpanned.

"Don't bring me into this," Spencer stated. "I'm not nearly as bad as the rest of you. I'm just an average, every day physical therapist. No one wants to see my ass and I'm fucking grateful for it."

"I think Callen would disagree," Evan replied.

A knock on the door interrupted our conversation. "Five minutes!" Pascal called from the other side. He easily and happily took on the task of wedding coordinator. Thankfully, his assistant at the office had been amazing and was doing more work. It was easy for Paz to help me with the wedding.

Evan clapped his hands together. "Picture time! Get close to each other so I can squeeze us all into the picture. Stock, your arms are the longest, you do the honor."

Evan passed over his phone and the four of us pressed together so Stock could take a few photos. One had Evan pressing a kiss to my cheek, another he was licking Stock's, causing us to laugh.

We did have a professional photographer for the wedding and reception. One we used for the Jetties, but these pictures just now were more casual. More for us and for fun. The photos we'd store in albums and frames to hang on our walls would come from the photographer.

We talked for a few minutes more before there was another knock on the door. Evan opened it. "Hello, handsome. Don't you look stunning." I thought he was talking to Vander since he was getting ready with Callen.

Then a voice I'd know anywhere responded, "Why, thank you. You don't look so bad yourself."

Turning, I got my first look at my future husband in his suit. Navy blue. Custom-made. Cut in at the right places to showcase his body. Crisp white button-down. Marcus was fucking stunning.

I crossed the room to him like he was a magnet and I was unable to resist the pull. I didn't stop until my hand was on the nape of his neck and I was kissing him hard.

Marcus's hands found my waist as he brought our lower halves together. It was a full-on make-out session until Evan somehow wedged his body between ours to pry us apart.

"No fucking before the wedding," he chastised. "You've bucked every other tradition. Lips off each other."

"I can't believe he just put himself between you two," Stock observed with a chuckle.

Evan peered around me to stare at my brother. "They're keeping their dicks to themselves. I'm in a room of hot men. If Vander were in here, I'd never leave." He turned and checked Marcus over from head to toe. He straightened his navy tie that perfectly matched his suit then used his fingers to fix his hair where I had messed it up. "Perfect."

It took about a week of Vander and me talking to Evan before he gave in and forgave Marcus for what happened between us. Evan was fierce and extremely loyal. Once he saw how happy I was and Vander had threatened him with withholding sex, Evan finally caved and had a heart-to-heart with Marcus. From what Marcus had said, there were lots of things said that Evan promised he'd follow through on if Marcus hurt me again. I was just happy Evan let the past stay in the past.

When Evan turned to inspect me, he straightened my suit jacket and tie. I was wearing the exact same color as Marcus, while everyone in our wedding party wore a deep shade of gray.

"You're perfect, too," Evan brokenly whispered. There were tears in his eyes as he peered up at me.

I pulled him in for a hug, not caring that he'd have to fix me again. I didn't need to tell Evan I loved him or any of the guys in the room. They all knew. They were here for a reason. This special day was for Marcus and me, where only those closest to us were invited, but the men in this room were everything to me.

"Oh my god, you all look amazing!" Sienna examined as she walked into the room.

Evan and I both wiped tears from our eyes. She was breathtaking in a strapless gray dress. The material was fitted on her chest, cinched at her waist, and the dress flowed loosely down from there to her feet. It perfectly matched the suits the guys were wearing.

Sienna was Marcus's best woman. Dominic and Ayden would also be standing up there with him when we said our vows. Stock was my best man and Evan and Spencer were going to be with me as well.

"Come on," Sienna said. "They're waiting for us."

We filed out of the room and met Dominic and Ayden in the hallway. Together we went up to the rooftop terrace. Marcus's warm hand was in mine. We were both smiling like fools and I loved it. If only we got to leave for our honeymoon after this, but we put it off until November when baseball season was over.

Since I took care of the wedding, Marcus said he wanted to handle the honeymoon. I still didn't know where were going, just that Marcus cleared two weeks on my schedule with Paz and the two of them worked together to arrange everything. In all honesty, I didn't care where we went as long as I had Marcus with me. We could stay in our bed, wrapped up in each other, for those two weeks and I'd be blissfully happy.

Marcus and I stopped at the entry to the terrace to let those in our wedding party walk down the aisle first. And there was an aisle. It was white and the chairs on either side of it were white as well. Lilac colored flowers adorned the ones along the aisle but they were simple and not overdone. At the end of the aisle stood no archway or anything fancy. There was a glass wall around the terrace to keep people safe when they were up here without obstructing views of the city. And that would be the backdrop to us vowing our lives to each other—the city we both loved and lived in. It was simple and tasteful. Just what we wanted.

When it was our turn to walk down the aisle, there was no one giving either of us away. We were entering our ceremony like we were our lives—together.

Hand in hand, we walked, with our families and friends standing from their chairs on either side of us. Some had tears in their eyes and others wore big smiles. My heart warmed seeing the ones we loved here for us.

There was an ache in my chest when I thought about my parents missing this moment. They loved Stock and me with all their hearts. They would have been proud of the men we'd grown into. The men they instilled their love and values into. They would have loved to know we were still as close as ever, even if our jobs kept us apart a lot of the time. Most of all, they would have adored Marcus.

But today wasn't about the things that made me sad. Today was about Marcus and me. Everything right in my life.

At the end of the aisle, we stopped in front of Pascal. He was officiating the wedding for us. He told me in no uncertain terms that no one was good enough to marry us. No matter how much he searched, he didn't like anyone, so he got himself ordained online.

Marcus and I stood facing each other, holding hands while Paz started to talk. "I promised myself I wasn't going to cry," he said as he sniffled. "You see, Kasper isn't just my boss. He was the first person to give me a real chance. He saw something in me I didn't see in myself. I wouldn't be where I am today without him. It doesn't matter where he goes or what job he does, I will always be there for him. And today, I'm here to perform his wedding ceremony to this wonderful man."

Tears built in my eyes. Paz was perfect to do this. He was right. No one could have done it like he did.

"Okay, so I am crying." Paz laughed. "Apparently, I'll do this through the entire thing. Get used to it." He swiped away tears and had Marcus and I grinning. "I had this whole speech printed out of what I was going to say, but the hell with it. I'm saying this one from the heart."

He took the paper he had and stuffed it into his pocket. He had on a black suit and a lilac tie, looking handsome as always. I focused on Marcus while Paz spoke. "Love is something we search for and hope to find. Not everyone does. Those lucky enough to do so and choose to hold on to it for all its worth, they know they've found something special. I've never seen Kasper like I have when he's with Marcus. He smiles wider. He laughs more. He deserves this kind of forever love more than anyone I know."

"Marcus, you are the perfect match for him. You challenge him and push him. You care for him in a way no one ever has. It comes across in everything you do. In return, Kas looks at you like you hung the moon. Together, you two are what I strive for. I want the kind of love you have. The forever love that will never dim and fade away. If soul mates do exist, you two are it."

My eyes never left Marcus. When a tear slipped down my cheek, I saw the same building in his gray eyes.

"Since Kas and Marcus decided they didn't want to say their own vows, I'm going to do this my way. With a lot of love and a little bit of fun." Paz winked when I glanced his way and I knew I was in for it. "Kasper Wilder, do you promise to watch every one of Marcus's games and cheer him on? To go to as many as you can in person and let him kiss you in front of the cameras? Do you promise to worship his sweaty body and lick those tired muscles of his after a workout? To deal with his highs and lows, his victories and losses, and be there for him every step of the way, including when he invites his teammates over and they get drunk and rowdy as hell? And last but not least, do you promise to love, cherish, and take care of him for the rest of your days?"

I gently squeezed Marcus's hand. "I do."

"Marcus Warnes, do you promise to support Kasper in all his crazy business ventures, fly around the world with him when you're able to, and guide him where you can? To deal with his mood swings, especially the grumpy as hell ones, and know it's nothing personal but probably from something I did to piss him off?" Paz leaned in to whisper loudly to Marcus, "I do that a lot." Paz straightened again with a smile as Marcus laughed. "Do you promise to help him out of his suit at the end of a long day and help him work away his stress? To deal with his friends because let's face it, you're not the only one who has rowdy ones? We've all seen Evan in action."

"Damn right!" Evan yelled from behind me.

Paz didn't miss a beat. "And finally, do you promise to love, cherish, and take care of him for the rest of your days?"

Marcus smiled. "I do."

"All right, let's see those rings." Marcus and I both turned to collect them. "We're going to keep this part traditional because I like it. Repeat after me, with this ring, I thee wed."

I said the words and slipped the ring on Marcus's finger. It was identical to the one he bought me. We decided to have our wedding date and initials etched inside them.

Marcus repeated the words as well and slipped the ring on my finger.

Paz beamed. "You are now pronounced husband and husband. Kiss your man!"

Marcus and I both smiled with tears in our eyes and leaned in to kiss each other with a little bit of tongue and a whole lot of love. Cheers rang out around us.

When we broke apart, Paz exclaimed, "I present to you Mr. and Mr. Warnes-Wilder!"

We gave each other a quick peck on the lips and turned to face our families, friends, and our future.

***

Stay tuned for the next book in the Espen Emperors series, *Earned Run*. Star pitcher Ayden Thompson questions everything when he meets enigmatic Rome Kinley. Ayden isn't looking for a relationship, and to say Rome has trust issues is an understatement. When their paths cross, nothing will be as it once was.

Sign up for our mailing list and get an EXCLUSIVE BONUS SCENE of Marcus and Kasper
Newsletter Sign-Up: https://bit.ly/2WxxYTK

Want to hang out with us on Facebook? Join our Reader Group: Haven Hadley's Heroes

Other Books by Haven Hadley

Espen Emperors
Checked Swing
Base Hit
Catcher Interference
Earned Run
Foul Ball
Merry MVP

About the Authors

Haven Hadley is romance writing duo Rebecca Brooke and Michelle Dare. After being friends for years, they decided to venture together into the genre they both loved to read—M/M. Slow burn, sexy, angst-filled stories are their favorite. Both are wives and moms who love dogs, the beach, and baseball, even if they root for rival teams. With every Haven Hadley book, you'll get stories filled with emotion, romance, hot scenes, and a happily ever after.

https://havenhadleybooks.com/

Made in the USA
Las Vegas, NV
22 August 2023